# SPIRIT MACHINES

Book 1

GARRETT BROOK

# Spirit Machines

Copyright © 2026 Garrett Brook
All rights reserved.
First edition March 2026

ISBN-13: 9798249299156

No part of this book may be used or reproduced in any manner without written permission except in the case of brief quotations as part of critical articles and reviews.

No generative AI was used to write the manuscript text of this book. This book came from the human spirit.

Printed in the United States of America

# Spirit Machines

Book 1

# 1 – Marriage

*We are more than rocks falling into place,*
*Or erosions filling space*

*God, spirit, faith animates*
*This dead weight*

*These are the stakes*
*around which life winds and snakes*

*So, when all things break*
*Rise, stand up from death*
*And take what is left*

God loves you. And, within that all-encompassing love, He often most loves a specific portion of a person's life because *that* specific portion of a person's life is when they love Him best. Not that God's love changes, it doesn't. Rather, in His infinite, ever-present love, those that love Him best are most able to receive; strengthen the channel and bestow upon themselves the love He wants to give to you.

\*\*\*

"Cassandra, please, if not for yourself then think of your future children," Marie said.

Cassandra and Marie Albright were twins, eighteen years old, and constituted the ninth generation of Albrights in America, their ancestors first having arrived in the 1650s from religious persecution in Europe. Passing down the line the original Flemish name Albrecht emblazoned on their coat of arms in the French-style purple gold, three lamps of wisdom, a closed helm dexter, the Moor denoting the crusades, holding a lamp and arrow.

"There are so many other men out there. What about the boy that comes by the house? Dad just doesn't like him because he's Hispanic, but he's actually nice to you," Marie pleaded.

Each person has a purpose they are working toward within their life, similarly, purpose can be applied to all things – a lineage, an organization of people, a nation – unconsciously prompting them this way or that way, expressed as thoughts from the heart, yet never overriding one's personal choice.

Cassandra started to cry in response to Marie's words.

For Cassandra, as with many young people, in childhood and young adulthood the romantic affections of unabashed love toward the world, not yet tempered by time and wisdom, coupled with overabundant promptings of the heart and mind all reinforced her affection for her first love, Peter and his intelligent confidence. She made her choice.

In the following years, she pursued her goal of nursing the sick, having a family and a home. She pursued these dreams in the hope that once attained they would allay the angst, toil and torment in her mind; subdue the discordance in her heart and produce everlasting joy and comfort. Thus, in her twenty-second year, bestowed with all the rights and privileges of one trained in the nursing sciences from Rutgers University, she set about to practice in New Jersey, married Peter and gave birth to their first child.

***

Ten years passed, ultimating in three beautiful children, a large house, all the comforts of modernity, a stable career as a school nurse, and her husband owned his own architectural firm. All her goals had been achieved. The sun's eleven-year solar cycle, which had first started during her engagement to Peter and was once again hitting its chaotic zenith of sunspots, solar flares, coronal mass ejections and increased radiation manifested in her mind as an unknown agitation and confusion, welling up from the recesses of her subconscious. Cassandra lay awake in bed thinking, *Is this it? After attaining one's goals, where does one put their mind and soul? Is there something I overlooked? What else is there?* And in the free association of her half-conscious mind, she recounted specific events from the past ten years.

Her marriage to Peter had been strained from the outset as childhood fantasies played tricks on both of them. Peter himself realized he didn't want to be married after the birth of their second child. On hearing that, Cassandra's mind flashed the panic alarms: *single mother, single mother*. At that time, Cassandra interpreted it as the natural nuptial vicissitudes of life that accompany the challenges of achieving her goals – a sacrificial period of time that would pass – a period they would look back on fondly in old age as something that brought them closer. Thus the bond of fear and resignation became agreed upon and the resultant growing marriage dissonance found outlet in near-imperceptible manifestations within the family unit in things said, not said; done; not done and thoughts themselves all are perceived consciously and unconsciously, gain force, take root, manifest, spread and teach the mind of a child. Peter's negative proclivities such as sarcasm, crassness, coldness became more apparent as a balancing force to relieve his discomfort with marriage. He was not a violent man, but he was verbally abusive to the children through sarcasm, which he never used on Cassandra, and in her resigned acceptance, made her feel special.

    Now, at thirty-two years old, in the wisdom of time, she realized what she had traded for that consolation as she now saw those subtle negative forces coming to fruition with her children who used that same sarcastic and cold behavior on each other. Cassandra realized that despite Peter's vast intellect – there was one subject on which he could not talk: God. And that is what she overlooked. And a long-forgotten truth, once buried in the dirt, now grew – *Love the Lord your God with all your heart, mind, strength and soul. Pursue first the Kingdom of Heaven. But how do I get closer with God? How does one love and rely on God? I had faith, but what was I to do with it?*

    In the small hours of the night, she gave to God her years of disillusion, the anxieties of her soul, her confusion. God had waited all these years to reach out His arms, to hug her, to take on her troubles willingly onto Himself. She prayed to God for an answer to her marriage, as unbeknownst to her, the sun's magnetic field reversed, and a light that had fallen backwards out of her heart and downwards years ago now started to rise toward its ordained position in her heart. There was a palpable feeling of her heart lifting, confusion lifted, and she began to sob as she gleaned an iota of the complete and utter reliance of one's soul upon the Lord. The light now within the correct place in her heart she felt the sensation of a new heartbeat, a new path with God; and *that* was the start to God's favorite part.

    Cassandra never dreamt, but that night she had an odd dream of a farm and a grotesque floating cloud monster chasing her and other people. So, she hid behind wooden crates in the corner of a barn. As she was hiding, a terror rose in her that she would be found. Just as she had that feeling, she looked up to see the crazed face of this cloud monster staring down at her, and she awoke in an electrified startle.

    A few weeks later, during her daily morning phone call with her twin sister, Marie told her about an opportunity to work as a visiting nurse in the Somerset/New Brunswick area. Cassandra interviewed and was offered the position, but Peter voiced his consternation because the job was in a "rough" neighborhood. Yet, Cassandra, feeling this opportunity was a piece of that light that had risen back into her heart, quit her school nursing position and took the new job.

    Cassandra had worked at the new job for two weeks, when Peter asked "Have you gotten robbed yet? Oh, and how many teenage pregnancies have you seen?" He said in earshot of the children as the family prepared for the day in the kitchen. Typically, Peter reserved his snide comments for the children, which had made Cassandra feel special and protected over the years. Yet, as Cassandra started to express more independence and resolve, those comments slowly began to be directed at her.

"No," she humored him with a little chuckle, "And no teen pregnancies. All right I'm going to be late, have a good day," Cassandra kissed him, kissed all the children and left for work.

All her clients for the day were in one apartment building in New Brunswick, and after she parked, she walked toward the affordable housing building. As she walked, she looked up to the low morning sun falling directly on her face. It expressed a high degree of red/orange color that resonated with her auburn hair and fair complexion. She was temporarily blinded as her pupils constricted, the red acting on her photoreceptors one trillion times per second, and she had a vision of the apartment building. *It appeared as an old European monastery in the 1300s where once there were great enthusiasm and spiritual activity – yet now the aging monks and nuns, top-heavy in age, helpless and decrepit, withered away from their once grand aspiration of bringing about the Kingdom of Heaven on Earth.* She thought to herself, *how sad, they should've just had children to continue that aspiration.* The next moment the vision was gone, and she found herself staring at the sun, yet it didn't hurt her eyes. Befuddled, she then rubbed her eyes and continued toward the building.

The vision occupied her mind and intermittently superimposed itself throughout the day while caring for her patients, and she started to become anxious about growing older. Given her profession, Cassandra only saw the negative aspects of growing older: many of her patients did not enjoy life, many wished they were young. Many did not have anything they were productively working toward -- no goal of their spirit to manifest, thus the idling spirit seemed to want to leave prematurely. Senility often overtook them and they would say inappropriate things to her.

She had one younger patient, Arnold, who was a sweet blind man of forty years old requiring help with cleaning, medications, and shopping. Another man, Steven, also lived there, who refused to help Arnold with any of these daily tasks and resented Arnold for being handicapped. Yet, when Cassandra was around, Steven instantly became helpful, sat closely with her on the couch, grabbed at the same items as they were cleaning around the house for their hands to touch.

One day, while Cassandra and Arnold were sitting on the couch Arnold said, "Cassandra, when you're around, Steve is a different person."

"Hey, I help when she's not around, but yeah, maybe she *should* stay longer," Steven said as he came up behind her and started to give her a back massage, "That was a lot of cleaning we did today," he said.

"No, I'm okay, thank you though," Cassandra said.

"Sure was a lot of cleaning," Steven said as he continued to massage her. "Y'know Arnold doesn't see you, but I see that you need cheering up."

"Steven, you know I'm married," Cassandra said.

"Who could tell? Obviously, your husband doesn't see you either," Steven replied.

"Hey, Steve," Arnold said, "give *me* a massage if she doesn't want one."

Undeterred, Steven lifted the back of Cassandra's hair and began to massage her neck. He started to breathe more heavily. She attempted to lean forward, away from him. In doing so, Steven, with one quick motion, put his hand on her forehead, pressed her head back into his crotch and with the other hand grabbed her chest while saying, "Oh, I'm also blind, I'm just feeling around."

"Get off of me," Cassandra said as she raised her hands to push his hands away.

Arnold was legally blind. Yet at certain points in the day, when not fatigued, he had a semblance of visual acuity. As such, with the realization of Cassandra being in trouble, catecholamines saturated his nervous system, and he regained his sight. Arnold saw him well enough to squarely swing his cane toward Steven's face while Steven was pretending to be blind, breaking two of his teeth.

"Ah! You asshole, my fucking teeth," Steven said.

"That's what you get," Arnold said as the two wrestled for Arnold's cane. Cassandra ran out the door to the front desk security guard. They arrived to find, the years of pent-up resentment expressed in a moment of insanity; Steven had beaten Arnold until he became unresponsive and sent to the hospital.

After the incident, Cassandra went home and told her husband that night what had happened. Peter had an intense anger at the news and wanted to sue the home nursing company for putting her in that situation. "They should have known that was a potentially dangerous situation for you being with that other guy in the house. And we've gotta press charges against Steven also, so it doesn't happen to someone else."

"He just grabbed me, I'm fine. Arnold was the one hurt," Cassandra said.

"No, I was right about this whole thing," Peter said.

She could see what he was going toward, "I'm not going to stop working at this place. I'm fine, God was with me."

"Please, go back to working at the schools or take a break from working for a little while," Peter said.

Cassandra, now more cognizant of the impulses of her heart said, "I'm sorry, Pete. This did not happen to you, it happened to me and I am not going to do any of those things, we're not going to sue anyone, or press charges against anyone. Jesus never did any of those things."

Attempting to feel some measure of control, Peter said, "Fine. Would you just ask to be transferred from the whole building?"

"Yeah, they had already told me they would do that. The agency has been very accommodating, and they said I would have some time off from patient care and just answer phones during the day for a while."

Though Peter was getting his way, the way she said it irked him, as if his ideas and concerns were of no matter. He didn't like the feeling of being small and powerless in Cassandra's eyes.

Later that night she heard Peter yelling at their oldest child. It was odd because Peter often made withering remarks to the children, yet he had previously never yelled. So, she went into the hallway to see, and the berating was over by the time she arrived. Peter's anger with her was being transferred to the children, just as they had become sponges to the years of marriage stress.

Cassandra saw a change in the household, now prompted by Cassandra's desire to follow God. Peter's behavior was becoming more erratic as the balance of light and dark within their household had been upset. As Cassandra reached toward the light, attempting to be a light-bearer in their family, evil also became more brazen and blatant in its effort to rise up and nullify the good. Hoping to show Peter his own indiscretions, she began to sleep on the couch away from him. While alone in the still reflection of the night, she realized all these years she had been trying to change Peter, yet she herself was changed by him, and she apologized to God for marrying a man who did not have God in his heart.

In the intervening days, she met with the company's legal team. She always reassured them that she did not want to seek any legal actions whatsoever, she wanted to put the whole matter behind her, and she wanted to continue working. The whole ordeal culminated in a one-on-one meeting with the head of the company, typically a gruff, loud, yet congenial Italian man, who, now behind closed doors, took on a placid, poised and soft-spoken demeanor. He conveyed his indebtedness to her, and he asked what he could do for her.

"Just put me back to work," she said, and her humble and helpful attitude seemed to unexpectedly strike into his heart and move him. She could almost see the outline of his soul, now uplifted by this show of humility, breaking the self-imposed chains of preconceived notions. His eyes became brighter, and he took a moment to compose his thoughts.

"Thank you, and I appreciate your position," he said. "I'm going to put you on a light schedule, to ease you back into working. You'll be caring for a man I know personally." He stopped for a moment of reverie, staring off into space. "A man to whom all the world might one day become indebted. And, over the eons of time, that indebted world, understanding his sacrifice would turn to him to ask exactly what I've asked of you, 'what can we do for you,' to which he would give your same response," he said and then snapped back, "So, anyway, you have nothing to be afraid of. He recently had a motor vehicle accident and then had abdominal surgery complicated by sepsis and multiple compartment syndromes in his arms and legs, but he's stable. So, he's going to be fairly wrapped up, jaw wired shut from what I understand. Also, there's no patient chart for this one, just go there every other day and take care of him and then answer the phones on the off days."

She started the next day in Elizabeth, New Jersey. She parked and walked toward the small building of her new client, the morning sun low in the sky. She was now able to look at the sun without any pain or damage to her vision. Its radiations pulsated to the rhythm of her heart as she could feel the blood pulse within the orbits of her eyes and a vision came over her sight.

*She saw a Roman garrison in Syria on the far eastern border of the Roman empire, occupied by centurions. Though at that time of the day most of them had their armor off and worked in their tunics adding another row of palisades to the outer wall. There was some recent commotion to which they were responding with the extra fortifications. She could recognize the local Syrians who had their own unique dress and were employed as merchants and laborers around the garrison. Then, one of the centurions atop the garrison held up his hand to her direction. Cassandra looked down at herself wearing a Greek-style dress, her hair brownish red, and she raised her hand in response.*

The vision was gone, but her hand was still raised. The superintendent of the building waved back as he approached her from the house, stepping down off the porch.

"Ms. Albright?" he asked, as she snapped out of her daydream and saw a portly, balding man in his fifties, salt and pepper mustache of Hispanic descent.

"Oh, hi, yes," she said. "Sorry I was just making sure I was at the right place."

"Yes, I'm Leon or just Leo. I'm the super," he said, wanting to keep things moving. He saw her more as a checkbox on his list of things to do that day. "Please come this way if you would," and he motioned her to follow him. "Also, right off the bat, I know we're in a rough part of town, but you have nothing to be afraid of in this place. It's a good group of mostly older veterans such as myself, and that type has their own way to deal with outside influence that might hope to…intrude we'll say. But, they can be a bit surly at times," he said with a laugh.

She laughed, "Oh, that's okay, my father is a veteran as well. I know the type."

He gave her a quick tour. It was a large house that had been converted into a multi-person residence with three levels, communal bathrooms, communal kitchen, and a common area on the ground floor. Each resident had their own bedroom.

They walked up the stairs to end the tour on the third floor. She would be spending most of her time on this floor caring for Mr. Edwin Vega. As they ascended the stairs, a far window at the end of the hallway shined sunlight into Cassandra's face and she could feel the premonitory sensation of a vision coming on again. Yet she suppressed it by scrunching her face, clenching her toes in her shoes, stiffening her body, and taking a drink of cold water.

Leo saw the abnormal movement out of the corner of his eye as he spoke and asked, "Are you okay?"

"Yes, sorry I thought I might sneeze," she said.

"Yeah, the sun can be a little oppressive at the top of the third flight of steps. We don't have an elevator, so if you need those accommodations, then probably this would be the wrong assignment for you."

"No, I'm fine," she said.

"Okay, very good. Well, you'll be a welcomed face around this place," he said as he unlocked the door and stepped into Edwin's room to reveal a large man in a full body cast nearly too large for the twin-sized bed on which he lay. The room was nearly empty. It had a single wooden chair, a small monitor hanging on the wall, and a duffle-bag with clothes lying on the floor.

"Ed, It's Leo. Ms. Cassandra is the nurse here to assist you while you recover, he said. Yet there was no answer from the large man lying motionless in his bed.

"How did he…?" she said under her breath.

Leo noticed Cassandra's reticence, yet he wanted to get on with his day, "He's a good guy, please let me know if you need anything. Here is my number, don't hesitate to call. So, I'll leave you to it and just send me a text in an hour or two to make sure everything is going okay." Leo then left them and bounded down the hallway to the next item on his checklist.

Cassandra stepped in and put a door stop in the door.

"It's just a little hot in here," she said and introduced herself, "Hi Mr. Vega. I'm Cassandra, I'll be your nurse for the next month or so. Can I get you anything?" A faint echo was produced in the empty room.

He was lying on his back. An uneasy silence filled the room. He didn't say anything or attempt any communication. His eyes followed her around the room as if she was holding him against his will.

"I'm just going to do a visual inspection of your bandages." His whole body and face were wrapped in bandages except his left arm was free lying at his side, which had multiple cuts and bruises.

"Okay, please let me know if you are uncomfortable, and the bandages look okay," she said. "Are you able to speak?"

He did not answer. His eyes were the only things that gave any hint of cognizance as they moved to follow her hands and her eyes. He appeared to be paralyzed.

There was a single wooden chair in the corner, which she pulled next to his bed. Her boss had spoken highly of Edwin. She figured this latest accident had resulted in a cervical fracture, traumatic brain injury and resultant cognitive impairment, disallowing any meaningful communication. So, she sat silently in the chair, awaiting some instruction. Edwin's blue eyes stared at her from behind the bandages. Then he swallowed, looked up at the ceiling and closed his eyes.

There was no motion in the room except for his melodic breathing as he rested. He let out a large sigh and the air wafted from his large breath, flowed through the air and rolled over and around Cassandra's head like a large warm hand lying on her forehead, blessing her, creating a slight turbulence of air at the back of her hair and then continuing around the room. A faint tendril of her hair dangling in front of her eyes became perturbed. She hadn't been sleeping well since she started spending nights on the couch. In the silence, the premonitory feeling on the stairs which she had suppressed now rose up in her again more forcefully and she fell asleep – *Rest, the little death.*

*Cassandra was looking down over a continent that vaguely resembled the North American continent, yet a large sea had formed from the Great Lakes to the Gulf of Mexico flooding parts of the Midwest and nearly split the*

United States in half. She was looking at the land from the vantage point of a personal hovering device high in the sky. After taking in the geography, she dropped down into a beautiful futuristic New York City. She hovered above a crowd, many of them had a grayish complexion. They were getting ready to move, they had a sense of urgency about them. They lowered themselves, and a man from the crowd stepped onto the craft with her. Cassandra had the feeling that he was her great grandchild many times over. He wanted to show her something, so he held out one hand, palm flat and upward, and with the other hand took his brain out of his head and placed it on the flattened hand. It looked slightly different from the typical brain shape which she was familiar with in nursing school, and he became aware of her confusion. So, he held up his brain so she could see the profile of the inner workings of his brain. The man pointed out the corpus callosum, caudate, but also other midline structures she didn't recognize. She moved to see it more closely. There were faint wisps of movement happening within the brain – which is what he wanted to show her. Faint blue wisps of light would progressively well up within numerous scattered portions of the brain, become more vivid and more pronounced; like slow puffs of blue smoke floating upward in the shape of a little blue jellyfish and then each one progressively faded out in unison as they moved upward. As those faded out, other blue wisps would become visible in the gaps. And those blue jellyfish would swell upward and then fade out in synchrony, like a chorus of responding voices, back and forth, one set of wisps, then the other, completing the cycle.

He then turned the brain so she could see the whole brain head on. It didn't look like a normal brain. It was more rounded. The man, noticing her thoughts, conveyed to her that her observation was exactly what he wanted to *show her – the falx was nearly missing as those dural veins became decentralized and the convoluted gyri and sulci gray matter took the place of the main dural tents which previously fixed the brain to the skull. The frontal and parietal lobes were larger, the optic nerves were larger, and the occipital lobe was naturally increased.*

*A different man from the crowd did not understand how those people were able to take out their brains. Cassandra's grandchild explained it to the other man just as he did for her. But the other man had a confused look and said, "I guess so,"* and the dream ended. She gently awoke to notice her head had nearly slumped over to rest on Edwin's bed beside him. She lifted her head to check on him. He was already awake and met her gaze. She performed another inspection of the dressings and saw that blood had seeped through one of the bandages around his left leg.

"Oh, let me change that for you," she said and reached over to begin undoing the bandage. As she reached over, Edwin's left hand slowly disappeared under the edge of rumpled sheets. They looked at each other, aware of each other's motions.

"I'm not going to hurt you," she said, but soon became preoccupied when she lifted the bandage to expose the leg to see multiple jagged cuts, deep puncture wounds and hematomas underneath the dressing. Globs of blood-saturated bandages that had been packed into the wounds then fell away, bringing with them pieces of skin and deep tissue that had dried and adhered to the bandages. The deep gashes easily reopened and dark red blood poured out as if from a wine bottle to which she quickly replaced the bandages and held pressure to it.

"Oh my," she said. "What happened to you? These are *not* fasciotomy incisions for compartment syndrome. How did you get these? From the car accident?" When the leg was redressed, she called Leo and said that Edwin needed to go to the hospital.

"Are you sure? He just came from the hospital," Leo said.

"I'm afraid he might go into shock from blood loss."

"Okay, okay, just hold on, I'm coming up, can you wait outside the room?" Leo said.

Cassandra waited outside the room with the door open, periodically checking on Edwin. She heard Leo's loud footsteps trudging up the stairs. When he arrived, Cassandra went over what happened and ended it by saying, "And, these are not fasciotomy wounds, did someone do something to him? He needs to go to the hospital."

"Ah, okay, okay," Leo said, trying to calm the situation. "Let me go speak with him, please stay out here."

"What do you mean, isn't he," she said, not knowing how to put it delicately. "Isn't he nonverbal, paralyzed and cognitively impaired? He hasn't said one thing, tried to communicate, or even performed one action while I've been in there," Cassandra said.

"Just one second," he said, and slipped into the room and closed the door behind him.

Cassandra put her ear to the door and heard Leo say, "Do you want to go to the hospital...No? Okay. Are you cognitively impaired...No? Okay, then don't scare her like that," Leo said as he chuckled and he walked back toward the door. Cassandra acted as if she had been waiting patiently the whole time.

"Ms. Albright, I appreciate all the concern, Edwin appreciates the concern, but the bleeding has now stopped, and he said he doesn't want to go. You've done a fantastic job, and I am glad you called me. I know this is strange and irregular, and for that I'm sorry, but it is his choice."

"Okay, I think there is some miscommunication. I am under the impression that this man is nonverbal, paralyzed, cognitively impaired, currently losing profuse amounts of blood as we speak and has sustained injuries inconsistent with what I was told. You seem to be implying that none of those things are true."

Leo chuckled, "Okay, okay, Ms. Albright. Here let me show you."

They reentered the room, and Leo again asked him if he wanted to go to the hospital. Edwin turned his left palm flat and upward as if to present something.

"Oh, he wants a pad to write," Leo said, and gave him his phone on which Edwin typed, "No."

"Well, I can't leave him like this," she said.

"Ah, okay, well, check the wound and if it's still profusely bleeding then you can take him," Leo said.

She unwrapped the bloody bandages to reveal that all the bleeding had stopped. She turned to both of them in amazement and said, "It's a miracle, how…"

"Ah, okay. Well, your shift has just about ended, I think that's enough for today. You're doing a great job. You're a great nurse, and you're correct to want to bring him to the hospital, but it is just Edwin's choice, and he can be a bit particular at times, let me tell you." Leo helped her quickly redress the wound, then led her out of the room as Edwin never broke eye contact with her.

# 2 – Redd the Chemist

*You want development of the spirit?*
*both hold the Earth, and let it go*
*But being earthly it is hard to know*
*how to put a finger on a soul*

All over the world, the most devout and eccentric chemists, microbiologists and tissue pathologists secretly pride themselves on the extreme degree to which pungent and malodorous chemical scents stifle their labs and waft like an extending miasma of swamp gas down into the corridors of their academic buildings. As if it is a representation of their commitment to their profession to sacrifice their health for their work. None had embodied this prototypical character more perfectly than Dr. Redd Minor, who had the most profound logic and imagination, but was bereft of sanity much of the time. His sharp intellect, ambition and undying energy was all undone by his prickly, abnormal behavior and disregard for the people who shared his workspace. Thus, an inevitable pattern plagued his professional life whereby a laundry list of inventions, discoveries and revelations awarded him an academic position with an advanced lab for a few years, which was then taken away just before achieving tenure. No one actually wanted him to work at their institution – they only wanted him to *have worked* there to claim the prestige of associating themselves with his success and thus convincing other potential students to come to that university. And so it went with every new position he held, an unspoken agreement; four years of work, denial of tenure, and then laid off to start the four-year cycle again elsewhere. However, that cycle was interrupted on the fifth iteration.

It started out normally; smiles, excitement from the staff, eager collaborators with the faculty, a host of doctoral candidates and graduate students working in his lab. And it continued normally; complaints of the smell by everyone within a half-mile radius, complaints of insubordination, complaints from students learning nothing in his courses. He also had a large romantic appetite. He could set his watch by all these events. What had changed during this cycle was that he sued the medical center, the medical school attached to the university and the insurance provider for incompetence. In his suit he wrote: *The idiots are attempting to reattach severed fingers on children, the idiots are chopping off good limbs when not necessary, standard of care is more like standard of crap.* Redd's most impassioned work was in regeneration, particularly the pockets of electrified and magnetic stores and channels set up within the body used to signal regrowth. He could very nearly regrow and heal anything anywhere and thus did not understand why his research was not more widely accepted and became offended when the hospital did not follow his advice.

He cited all his own work in the suit, yet the laws governing the present state of healthcare were largely dictated by the very hospital systems and insurance agencies that he was attacking, and therefore the suit was summarily thrown out; he was fired, and soon had the stark realization that there was not another eager university offer letter on which to fall back. He no longer had access to advanced equipment, regulated reagents, funding, a small army of lab technicians, graduate researchers and volunteers. So, the dream fell away and he sat in his chair at home, finishing the few manuscripts he had pending, and then allowed his mind to wander.

Without the daily tasks of his scientific endeavors to keep his attention focused and occupied, his intellect was like a circuit without a load, without a resistor, and the near instantaneous movement of electrons ran full bore from negative to positive terminal, burning via friction the minute rivulets and tendrils within his mind which acted as the very structures to harbor and channel these energies, and the brain became enraged, enthralled, fired, unmetered, unleashed, chaotic, with a small injection of resentment toward the established order.

When lightning storms would hit, he would become excited into a frenzied mania walking the halls, wandering the streets to feel the electricity – which he called water. In the evenings, every person he passed in the apartment building he attempted, with a simple handshake and a look in his eye, to change the very internal electrical and magnetic circuitry of that person. The next day, when the sun was shining he was possessed again of complete reason and judgement, and he would sit quietly by the entrance to the apartment building greeting everyone, handing out fruit, and document any subtle changes he observed in the people he touched the night before – their posture, mannerism, emotional state, "How did you sleep?"

Many strange habits and strange publications were produced during this six-month period, when he was visited by a man who introduced himself as Mark. They shook hands and Mark began to explain that he was part of a large collection of other scientists, thinkers, artists, engineers who worked on a secluded island, free and supported to follow their passions in innovation, art, industry, love and wisdom.

"You will have more unencumbered time pursuing your own projects than any university can offer you. We only ask a few things; You do not publish outside of the island; that you donate part of the earnings from your ideas and inventions to the community to help sustain it and allow others to benefit the way you will have; and that you act as a subject matter expert from time to time when we are consulted by institutions outside of the island. You see we are attempting to set up a kind of hierarchy, a new order, with our community at the head, and particularly difficult questions get kicked up progressive levels of the hierarchy – easy questions being answered at lower rungs and the most unanswerable questions being given to us – the top. We hope. You see there are other groups that also compete for that place if we fail to answer such questions. But, given the level of expertise on the island we usually can answer them. We charge them a fee for this and we also, slowly, shape the world into this more efficient and better organization. You will have access to more advanced equipment, and we do assign assistants as well. If you want to give lectures, you may, but it is not mandatory. We encourage collaboration, but again, it is not mandatory. Think it over, and if you would like to know more than call this number," Mark said and handed him a card.

Redd's mind worked with a small lag – he remembered everything that was said, though he kept it stored in the background to his active thoughts, to look at it a few moments after it was said. So, when the man outstretched his hand with the card for him to take, Redd did not accept it at first as he was still attempting to ascertain if his handshake had caused any acute changes throughout their conversation. *Possibly,* Redd thought, but he would need more time to assess. So, he tried to stall. "Would you like to come up to my apartment to discuss this further?" Redd said, looking at the man from different angles.

"I am just here to deliver this offer," Mark said, his hand still outstretched. Redd, without touching the card, leaned forward and very closely visually inspected underneath the card, to the sides, on top of the card and then looked up at Mark. Having satisfied his curiosity, Redd leaned back in his chair and half lifted his arm and motioned with a nod of his head and pointing with his finger for Mark to place the card on the far table holding the flowers near the entrance of the apartment building. Without a word, Mark spun, walked five paces to the other side of the foyer, placed the card on the table and warned Redd to be careful and not to let it fall into the wrong hands, and then Mark left.

As Redd sat there, he thought Mark's words sounded vaguely like a threat and he became even more suspicious of the card – not wanting to even look at it directly or take a breath near the card. However, as Redd was pondering what to do with the card, other apartment residents were circulating in the foyer and Redd fumbled around with his tablet to continue to record observations of their electrical impressions. People seemed to be walking through the proximity of the card without harm. He asked an older lady to please hand him the card, which she happily did with an ungloved hand. Redd didn't want himself potentially hurt by this card, so he untucked his shirt, put his hand into the loosened shirt flap that dangled by his waist and crimped the edge of the card with his fingernails protected by the shirt. The woman made an exasperated and confused face at this seemingly unnecessary action – she walked off perplexed and slightly offended. Redd made his way back to his apartment – washed it in polar and nonpolar solvents, started to write the number "+688 3141592" on a different piece of paper and then abruptly stopped.

"Oh, that's funny," he said to himself, "Pi – hmm, some sort of circular significance to this organization – though he called it a hierarchy which is probably shaped as more of a triangle – I will suggest a different number to him," he said, placing the card in a small clear plastic bag. He ran various experiments on the card, microscopy, spectroscopy, electric and magnetic properties, acid base tests. Yet all signs pointed to a generic card purchased from a large business card printing service. Exhausting his options, he then sat in his chair staring at the card in between long meandering peregrinations in his mind.

"Well, if they wanted to kill me, the card could do it, or what the card leads to could do it. Or the alternative – this is real." One of these things is true. But he was well versed in the scientific world, and the supposition was implausible that all the greatest minds in the world just up and left their universities or research labs. There were some who abruptly stopped publishing – that happens a lot, it could be them, but no one had ever disappeared – so what pool of innovative scientists are they drawing from to populate this secret island? And there is apparently more than one? Also, most smart people are able to do well for themselves in regular society, and likely would have no incentive to run off to a secret magical island – especially if they would have to share their earnings and were not allowed to publish. To publish your ideas and make money off those ideas is the goal of every artist, scientist and innovator.

As Redd's mind once again took flight in contemplating this situation, a paper was slid under the door of his apartment.

"What is this now? What kind of clandestine international contraption am I getting caught up in?" he said to himself and cautiously approached the paper on the ground.

"Oh, phew," he said, he was relieved to read that it said, "Eviction Notice" for "persistent unlawful behavior". "But what did I do that was unlawful?" He suspected it was a part of this organization's plan to coerce him onto the island. So, he stormed into the apartment manager's office for an explanation, and Redd was shown the volumes of complaints from apartment residents – most revolving around picking up dead animals and bringing them back to his apartment. He had also helped a few pets in the building who had various ailments, but with attempting to help, sometimes he could not, and his experimental efforts were blamed for the death of a few pets.

"I have a friend that comes to the apartment sometimes," Redd said to the apartment manager, and described Mark's appearance, "had he talked to you at all?"

"No, I don't know who that is. Why?" the apartment manager asked in a matter-of-fact tone.

Not knowing the true answer, Redd studied the paralinguistic features of the man's response – it sounded genuine enough. So, Redd quickly thumbed through the volumes of complaints, reading random portions to check their validity: *June 10: Redd poisoned my dog, then said the death was my fault for letting him get so fat.* It seemed the manager had a genuine case against Redd.

"So, this was serendipity?" Redd said.

"Seren-," the manager said confused, "No, this is the opposite, this was a number of events compiled judiciously over a year, and you harassing people in the foyer is what made me pull the trigger – it's hurting my ability to sell other apartments and the smell from your apartment is repugnant," the manager said.

"No, not you. I was talking to myself," Redd said and walked off. As he turned into the hallway, he saw the older woman from the foyer who was standing down the hall hoping to eaves drop. They locked eyes with each other and in a scowl, he walked off. He returned two minutes later, "Sorry, I'll be out by the end of the week," he said, in a calm collected tone.

And so, at approximately the same time Cassandra married Peter, solar activity at its zenith, Redd followed Mark to the secretive scientific utopian island.

✞✞✞

After three years on the island, Redd had a wife and his interest in regeneration dove-tailed into human cloning. One evening, after finishing pathologic analysis of a series of neonates, a colleague from engineering, Bill Reiter, walked in with his head down deep in his own thoughts, and without introduction Bill said, "Redd, I would like to continue our discussion from two weeks ago," he said as he picked his head up. "Oh, sorry, were you in the middle of something interesting?"

"No," Redd said, without missing a beat, "machines will never have rights."

"What? Oh," Bill said, shocked that Redd knew exactly where they had ended their conversation, "No, I think they will."

"You already said that two weeks ago, this is where we stopped last time. Okay, I'll reiterate what I also said two weeks ago – how could they?"

"Okay, it is because, in the infinite future of humanity, can't you imagine a future in which technology reaches a state that sufficiently develops robots enough to warrant having rights?" Bill asked.

Redd said, "If I thought that, then I would be working on robots and not the living," Redd looked down at the deceased babies at his work bench, "I mean *formerly* living specimens. First, when we said 'rights', it was not the rights that a piece of property may have, such as one cannot destroy property of someone or things like that – we know what we are arguing – the rights recognizing a living being."

"Sure," Bill said.

"Okay, back to your infinite humanity point, you're very hopeful for humanity's infinite future. But anyway, robots do not have a soul, so how could they have rights? They may only ascend to the level of an animal's rights, perhaps," Redd said.

"I think this is where we got confused last time. I'm an atheist, I don't believe in a soul. But, hypothetically, if that's what you need in order to potentially justify robots having rights then I guess we can continue there. So, if humans continue to survive, surely, we will reach that level of creating something other than another human which could house a soul," Bill said.

"So, Bill, you want to create life? My advice is to start a family," Redd said.

"Very funny, but no, seriously," Bill said.

"Hypothetically, if you were a soul, would you want to be housed in something made by a human or would you rather be a person? And another thing, a system cannot analyze itself, therefore, if we are a soul, then, inherently, we cannot understand it. That's a law of nature. So, as long as we are human, then we cannot make something else human. Therefore, even in the infinite future of *humanity*, we cannot bestow humanity to another," Redd said.

"But your argument supports my argument – if you say that you are a soul, then you are not a body, we're not trying to *make* a soul, we're trying to make a body," Bill said.

"Fair point, but wouldn't we have to understand the soul at least somewhat in order to develop that body-soul interface? We don't understand the soul at all, how are we going to give it to something inanimate?" Redd said.

"Okay, well let me ask, how do you know *you* have a soul? Or what is the evidence of a soul – that you may judge if something has a soul or not?" Bill said.

"As I just said we can't really analyze ourselves and also, I've never *not* had a soul. Therefore, I can't really answer your question, so I don't know, I just know. I mean how can you feel you're the same as the rocks and the animals."

"Well, you've never *not* had a finger, but you can describe a finger. And, I agree, I'm not the same as rocks and animals, but it's not because of the soul. Yeah, so tell me two things – what is the soul? And, you don't think rocks or animals have a soul?" Bill said.

"Well, perhaps they have something – but whatever they have, we have something that they do not."

"So, they might have something like a prototype soul?"

"Maybe we're saying the same thing, but I would phrase it most like the building blocks, or the animals have elementary particles of what our soul/spirit gathers up and makes an identity out of."

"But there is absolutely no evidence of that, what are you talking about, Redd?" Bill said, "I'm beginning to think you are just disagreeing with me to disagree with me."

"You're a smart guy, Bill, why would I try to 'just disagree' with you?" Redd said.

"Okay, then what is the soul?" Bill said, "You did not answer that."

"It is the vehicle of the spirit after death."

"What is the spirit?"

"That portion of God."

"That portion of God…what?"

"Sorry, I mean just that, a portion of God."

"Oh, I see, but what is the evidence of the soul while you're alive, here on Earth? Where do you get your beliefs?"

"It is the autonomic nervous system and the subconscious which comes out in the dreaming life."

"I really have no idea what you're saying, and it feels like you're just making things up. Also, I thought you said that the nervous system wasn't the primary seat of the soul last we spoke? And so after death our autonomic nervous system lives on? Constantly living in that state of subconsciousness."

Bill was becoming frustrated, with each supposition of common ground upon which to extend an olive branch, with each strange answer Redd gave to Bill, the argument seemed to reveal a greater distance between them until their whole lives, both scientists sitting six feet from each other, seemed two completely different viewpoints. How could the two of them even converse when their thoughts were so different? Bill became more frustrated with Redd's outlandish ideas as the argument continued.

"I know, yes, I did make it up – it's called thinking and logic and pontificating. But I concede, I still have some points to figure out in that department. But why do you get so mad about it? And, yeah it would be, in a way, our subconscious that lives on."

"Logic? How is your belief built on logic? Where is the logic? And how can you be so confident if you don't even know what you believe?"

"Well, did you invent the equations and laws for quantum theory? No, you looked it up and read other people's thoughts on the matter and came to your own decision – yet you did not make them. I read other's thoughts and consider them likewise. However, you believe these things because the general community believes them. If the general community did not believe them, then you would not also. I am able to believe unpopular things." Redd said

"But the greater scientific community believes it because it is true, proven."

"But spiritual matters are more difficult to agree upon," Redd said.

"Next thing you'll tell me is that you don't believe in gravity," Bill said.

"I believe in gravity," Redd said, "But see, that's it, we can't really explain gravity, but I feel gravity, I feel God, the spirit, intuition."

"You're impossible, Redd, and probably a little crazy," Bill laughed. "Well, let's pick this back up in another two weeks."

They both cooled down, saw that it was getting late, cleaned up the area and thanked each other for the company. As they parted ways Bill said that he would be transitioning into regular life taking an academic position in Princeton, New Jersey.

"I just wanted to give you a heads up," Bill said, "I will be back and forth from the island the next year as I wrap up and hand off my various projects."

"Very well," Redd said, analyzing Bill's eyes as Redd had once studied the eyes of those in his apartment building, "I've enjoyed our conversations,"

It was 2:00 a.m. when Redd left the research facility and his mind came alive at night as he walked home. Bill was a smart, conscientious man and the impossibility of bestowing robots with souls tantalized Redd's mind. It was the ultimate challenge for himself, for this time period, and for all of humanity's existence – he could be listed as the foremost luminary in the annals of human history if he were successful.

As Redd walked through the night air, he heard the mild gyroscopic whir of the cisterns producing water vapor, drones scattering in the night air to stabilize clouds over the island, the reciprocal chugging ocean water back into the cistern for processing; all to produce the rain falling on his head.

Redd's lab was the island's cloning center, he often thought of the spiritual implications of cloning, yet he never thought to use it as a tool to potentially analyze the soul. Cloning somewhat refuted his own argument against the future rights of machines, because clones were somewhat human made, yet they were granted the same rights as any other person. They seemingly had the same evidence of a soul as any other person, even though the specifics of the evidence were hard to detail.

The soul doesn't reside in an arm or a leg because only a functioning brain is needed for consciousness. It is not, strictly speaking, a right hemisphere of a brain or a left hemisphere. Rather, one hemisphere of a brain is the smallest receptacle which can house a soul.

Injuries to children often proved that a body-soul connection can adapt to half a brain, depending on a number of factors including the injury, the soul, the body, the amount of damage and the age of the body at the time of damage. If an adult loses a hemisphere, then they are completely changed and the soul would have difficulty expressing itself in the new body structure. It is as if the soul-body interface becomes "set" and less able to adapt after adolescence or adulthood. It was as if electrical circuitry of the brain produced a magnetic field which then, like an electromagnet, attracted and developed the soul. So, all a brain had to do was maintain the correct circuitry to attract the soul. Then, that soul would exert some reciprocating force either on the brain or on the mind.

Redd thought to himself, *I've already indirectly created a soul cyborg by creating an artificial womb to gestate a human fetus. If I could just, by grade, somehow inch closer to the body to replace the natural with the artificial then I could understand the soul, how it behaved, its nature.* Dissections and cadaver studies would be wholly insufficient as a dead body lacks that actuating principle of the soul. Therefore, the interface of the soul-body connection might be studied by prospecting through lysis or inactivation of small segments of a person's living nervous system, to see which portions of the soul they mainly retain – similar to the early Penfield experiments. There are only certain ways in which the human body can act and be acted upon: anatomically, mechanically, physiologically, chemically, electrically, gravitationally, magnetically and those fundamental nuclear forces. Are spirit and soul a different force? Or is it subject to those same forces?

If we are to consider the mind as part of the soul, then hypnotism and the placebo-effect must, in part, be some evidence of the soul as there is no change in the body system other than a belief. The mind and thoughts would therefore be some manifestation of the soul. But, the mind, while creative, is limited in that it can only imagine things of which it is familiar and therefore reliant upon the body. But, if the hypnotism/placebo effect is greater in children than in adults, imagination/thoughts are greater in children, then the soul is greater in children. The soul, presumably, gets a sense of itself through its time on Earth. To allow it to individualize itself through decisions. Yet the soul-body connection is less "set" in a child.

Redd took a moment to rest his thoughts. The bowery promenade was lit with elegant streetlamps amid the lush, hybridized trees swaying in the wind. Large grand cathedrals to science set off the main boulevard were inspired by and hybridized various periods and cultures of Earth, further combined with advanced architecture only found on the Island. Everything seemed to be reaching a unity on the island, a grand culmination of all the nations of Earth – the buildings, the people, the plants and animals all combined the best aspects of other varieties and something new was starting to emerge which Redd couldn't put his finger on. As if the very principles of evolution and progress could dream. Even the geology of the island was a combination of continental shelf and volcanic crust. It seemed only fitting that this soul cyborg be the crown jewel of hybridization that this island would produce.

    As he walked, an automated transport vessel pulled up to ask for his destination. Redd didn't answer as he was lost in thought, and the small personal transport slowly stalked him as he walked by, "Destination?" it said one last time and then stopped just before reaching the intersecting road. Redd stopped also, turned to the personal transport and as it opened its doors and lit up its interior lights, it said, "Destination, sir?" Redd threw all of his things into the car – "Twenty-one Utopia, please, take those things, I will walk." Redd said and the vessel closed, reciting his instructions back to him, its interior lights dimmed and the car shuttled off, leaving Redd alone to walk freely down the road in the rain.

    Yet why would a soul *want* to inhabit a robot or cyborg? It must offer a better experience than the one a regular body could provide. One of Redd's beliefs was that souls reincarnate upon the Earth as a testing ground, like a school or class to learn patience, love, justice, balance and all the principles found at the foundations of the universe which, once learned, would allow that soul to move onto greater positions in the universe, utilizing patience and love just as we utilize oxygen and gravity here on Earth. And so, a soul has a personality before it re-enters the Earth as a neonate. Similarly, science had summarily refuted the "tabula rasa" argument of children and found that general personality and disposition traits were passed genetically just as physical features. Therefore, the pre-incarnated soul and the gestating fetus had that in common – they both contained pre-formed characteristics prior to life on Earth.

Presumably a finite number of souls are reincarnating on the Earth, a finite number having moved on as well. Perhaps there are new souls which would therefore have no preconceived tendencies and would therefore be a better "pilot" for the soul cyborg.

A soul associates with the body of the neonate based on proclivities and propensities of the soul aligning with the inherent tendencies of that body, and the mutual affinities conjoin in the human-soul compact. So, if he made the most beautiful, smartest, physically fit clones in the world (which had been his work on the island) then most likely he beaconed the most beautiful, caring, deserving, humble, spiritual souls back into the world. Yet, if they were procuring such magnificent souls, then those amazing souls would become concentrated on the island, and that finite number of magnificent souls would be less stocked with enlightened souls to incarnate outside the island and therefore less able to make the world at large a better place.

This dawning project would likely take up the rest of his life, and it would extend past his life. So, he had to explore and describe the components of the soul's interaction with the physical body so that others could carry on his work after him. Even if he were wrong it would act as a starting point.

At that moment, he reached his house; the car he sent home was sitting at the front door, under an awning, its vessel doors open, lights on, waiting for its contents to be emptied. He crawled in, took his things, walked into the house and greeted his wife, Emily, who was still awake with some of her girlfriends.

Emily was herself a clone, as were many of the companions for the scientists on the island, whether male or female. The allure of a beautiful spouse to the brilliant scientific men and women was one of the many ways in which scientists were attracted to this scientific utopia. They had been together three years, and she embodied the warmth, affability and innocence which he himself lacked. The next generation of island dwellers were just hitting their teen years, yet, for unknown reasons he and Emily had been unsuccessful in having their own children – *perhaps it was something in his or her soul*. Unfortunately, she unduly developed a complex over this issue as she put the brunt of the blame on herself, despite no clear evidence that she was infertile.

As Redd walked in, she said, "Hi honey, the girls are over, did you get caught in the rain?"

"Hello, my dear," he said, with a big smile "The rain got caught in me." He laughed, but no one else did, "But…um, I hope your evening is going beautifully! Honey, can I talk to you for a second?"

"Yes of course, what is it?" Emily said as she stood up from the couch, "One second ladies."

"Oh, it's late," one woman said, "We really should go."

"No, no, please stay," Redd said. "It will only be a moment, pardon the interruption." Emily followed him into the next room.

When they were alone, Redd turned and said, "You are so beautiful," looking deeply into her eyes, and couldn't help but kiss her.

"Aw, thank you my sweet man. You just brought me in here to tell me that?" She laughed.

"No, no, I should have said that in front of everyone else," Redd laughed. "No, I brought you in here because I want you to help me with an experiment!"

"Oh," she was surprised by that answer, "Okay, I love your ideas, what can I help with?"

She was always so loving to him, and Redd thought to himself;

*I could exist*
*Solely in the eyes of this little miss*
*But what I love*
*I must be suspicious of*

And, despite his deep belief in spirituality, Redd had the tendency to treat people as an experiment, as organic tissue, as things to bring his own ideas to life.

"No, better not," Redd said, wanting to avoid what would surely become a difficult situation.

"No, it's okay, I want to help!" Emily said.

"Okay fine, I'm going to create a soul cyborg!" Redd said.

"Oh!" She said, trying to share his excitement. "What does that mean?"

"I am going to document the presence of a soul and hopefully use that knowledge to create an artificial domicile for the soul, just as bodies are the soul's current residence."

"Oh, wow, you think souls will go for that?" she said, laughing again.

"Certainly not at first in the rudimentary phase," Redd said. "But with time and progress, then yes, I do! And Bill believes it, too!"

"Okay, that sounds amazing!" she said. "What do you need from me?"

"I would like to clone you twenty-four times," he said.

"Wow! That's a lot of me running around," she said.

"And two of them, if you are up for it…two of them I would like you to carry them to term naturally," Redd said.

"Oh, what are you saying? I'm going to be a mother?" Emily said, her eyes welling up with tears.

"If you'd like!" he said.

"Let me just tell the girls that I'm going to be helping you for the rest of the night," she said.

When she came back he said, "I chose you because I know you so intimately that I would be able to discern minor fluctuations in the personality of the clones and thereby possibly grasp at the threads of a soul and those differences in expression in personality would allow for some observations into the operator behind those differences – the soul. Or, if there was even a soul there or not. Twenty-two will be from your tissue, gestated artificially in the lab, while the last two would be a natural gestation and birth – twins. The twins would be created by autologous cloning by taking your bone marrow cells, dedifferentiating them into totipotent cells to form your own autologous zygote and planting that into the uterine wall and then from there developing into a normal fetus."

She joked through the happy tears and said, "Sounds like I'm going to be my own mother."

"According to the Earth, yes. According to the universe, I hope no," Redd joked.

## 3 – Edwin

*Hold back*
*See how they react*
*They excitedly whip, rise, fall and run*
*With elation, depression*
*And anxious fun*

Cassandra was scheduled to see Edwin every other day, and she was nervous about returning because it felt as if a whole unseen world of cause and effect was taking place without her having much cognizant awareness of it.

Despite her bewilderment she persevered, and on her next visit she walked into Edwin's room carrying two bags of IV fluid in case he started to lose excess blood.

"Hi, Edwin, do you understand me?" He motioned with a thumbs up but continued to silently stare. "Okay, I apologize, I thought you were mentally injured from this accident when I first met you. You gave me quite a scare the other day, so I brought some IV fluids to help, is it okay if I give them to you?" Edwin gave no indication or hand-gesture. "Okay, well, we will have them on hand if the occasion arises," she said, and momentarily put them on the bed as she went to bring over the wooden chair.

As she turned her back to get the chair, she saw with a flash out of the corner of her eye. Edwin's left hand moved from under the rumpled sheets to reveal a pair of scissors he concealed and plunged them into both IV bags with such force that he punctured the mattress. Cassandra, startled, jumped back with a gasp as the fluid soaked into the bed and onto the floor. He then put the scissors up to his mouth, stuck them in, as if he were a dentist wiggling a tooth free. There was an audible snap, as the scissors cut through a small wire, and he repeated this five times as Cassandra watched in disbelief. Edwin then threw the scissors on the floor and wrapped his left hand around his jaw and said softly, "poi…son."

She would have run out of the room for self-preservation if he weren't in a body cast. She was instantly reminded of a man in the hospital who was equally paranoid as a result of sepsis from a urinary tract infection. "I am not trying to poison you; those were to help you."

Edwin was uncomfortable with talking and took great effort, "No…you…" he gestured with his hands to convey up and over, "Suhm-mhm…else."

"I took those straight from the nursing agency this morning, no one else would have had time to replace them."

He reached under the covers with his left hand and pulled out a twenty-dollar bill, crumpled it up a little and threw it to her. "Cu…ban…Mam…bo," he said. He then held up a tremulous left hand, pointed with two fingers to himself, then her, then he overlapped the two fingers and pointed skyward.

She stepped out of the room and found Leo to explain what happened, "I think he might be in sepsis," she said. "He's acting very paranoid, and he has every reason to have an infection. I'm afraid he might injure himself. He just cut the wires keeping his jaw immobilized."

"Ah, okay, well he must have been in sepsis for the past two years because he's always been extremely paranoid. He refused to see the other nurse that was supposed to come on the days you weren't here. It honestly drives me up a wall sometimes. Before he was injured I never even saw the guy leave. He does leave, but not when I'm around. Even before this whole incident, he wanted metal to line the attic floor – he paid most of it, but still, it's expensive! Anyway, sorry, I'm rambling. He wants two Cuban sandwiches from Mambo down the road, one for each of you. I don't know about the other hand motions."

"He's been living here for two years, and he only has a duffle bag of clothes?" Cassandra asked.

"Yeah, all right. He's harmless. He won't even kill the stink bugs that come into the room." Leo then stepped away and Cassandra, still flustered, took out her phone and found "Mambo Down the Road" and ordered two Cubans. While she was on her phone, she asked it to interpret Edwin's hand positions if he were using American Sign Language, which her phone said that he was signing the sentence, "We are going up."

She then went to pick up the food, thankful for a brief reprieve from Edwin. After she returned, Edwin said, "Sorry…scare you," then he pointed to the bed, held up his wallet and said, "nothing else."

She pulled up a chair next to him, cut up the Cuban into small pieces and cautiously handed it to Edwin as he happily used his free hand to help himself chew.

"News?" he said.

"Oh, sure," she moved the chair away from the bed and turned on a news program on the wall monitor while they ate. She noticed her leg bouncing up and down. Typically, she was embarrassed by her own inherent anxiousness, but now she felt it served a purpose as she didn't want to risk falling asleep again.

The segment showed a beautiful young woman in a white dress reminiscent of a Greek toga, yet a modern cut. "I'm forty-five. I had an opioid addiction for almost twenty years – usually no one has an opioid addiction for twenty years, if you know what I mean. But, for fifteen of those years I've tried quitting over and over again – nothing worked. I came to Heis one year ago. He did different mental exercises and some other things, but he also taught me how to control myself and be patient. He told me steps I needed to take to allow the soul to fill in what I had been using drugs to fill in. He taught me how to get outside of my own head and find happiness in other's happiness. That was one thing he was definitely good at – appreciating others. Some might consider his tactics as abusive or persecutory, but they worked!" She then took a moment to look down at her dress, pinched the edges of it and slightly flicked it to create a slight ripple in the fabric to allow the dress to fall neatly and squarely over her body as she composed herself.

She continued, "It is funny, I've been clean for one year, and in a way the difficulty of the situation has not changed. Although symptoms were most violent early on, and Heis' approach, as I implied, could seem heavy-handed to an outsider looking in – but, it was early on that I was most enthusiastic and desperate to start sobriety – and those great tumultuous waves of addiction were nullified by a great leader with Heis and a great enthusiasm with myself. But, now as the drama and excitement of early enthusiastic sobriety has died down, and now sets in the awareness of those first causes which initially brought me to the doorstep of chemical abuse, I have to remain vigilant, not get bored with sobriety, and not allow myself to slip back into old habits," she said as she looked down, turning her palm upward revealing an empty open hand and linear white scars tracking up the underside of her forearms, disappearing into her upper arm and armpit. While looking down, her mind revisited those old times, as if those memories and those previous conditions were a small memento on a shelf from a trip abroad that she could pick up and examine. She briefly became entranced in that thought, and she slowly glided her hand along the scarred ripples in her arm – and then she stopped herself. Stopped the slow glide of her hand up her arm, and as she looked up again, she quickly rubbed her hand up and down her arm a few times, audibly creating a little friction, almost expecting the scars to vanish like rubbing a stain.

"But of course I couldn't imagine going back to those first days now. I looked like a ghost, a ghoul, a zombie, but worst of all, people thought I looked sixty-five when I was thirty-five!" She and the reporter laughed. "So, yeah, Heis really helped me. He told me to take his seminar, and now I'm fully recovered from the disease – I no longer think about getting high *all* the time," there was a pause, "…Just some of the time." The woman and reporter giggled together again. "Joking about it is healthy," she said. Then, she became silent. The smile faded and she turned her face downward.

The reporter said, "Well, you look great, I love this dress – very chic, and I'm glad to see you're doing so well."

As the interview continued, Heis began speaking over the reporter's footage presented on the screen, like a voice-over commentary, "Yeah, see that's Julia, it pains me to say that she died of an overdose later that year." Then the camera cut back to Heis, wearing a curving metallic helmet shaped like an infinity symbol lying on his head. "I think she really wanted to get better, but I didn't help her, even in the year that she was sober. I can now say that it was all her doing and anything I provided was purely placebo. Because she put her faith in me, which I told her not to do, I told her to put her faith in God, ask him to help both of us – and so, it was that inability to connect with God in herself that, I think started her down the destructive path years ago, and then impeded her progress toward recovery when I was working with her. Because well…I hate to say it…well, no, I won't say it, but just to say that she was kind of putting me in that role where she should have been putting God."

The reporter, Veronica Stensi jumped into the interview, "Okay, well, first of all, what are you wearing on your head?"

Heis said, "I'll answer that much more fully later, but I know you want to talk about this earlier footage first, so please I don't want it to distract you."

The reporter said, "Okay, we are getting right into something I wanted to bring up. You are often blamed for this woman's death."

"I think that is a little strong, don't you? I mean people die of overdoses every day, and you don't blame the doctors or the opioid manufacturers. Why are you blaming me?"

"I am not blaming you, I am saying that – by your own admission you did not help her, and it was while she was going through your program that she and others had not received any real help and therefore continued to spiral into a fit of self-destruction."

"Wait wait wait, let's just get this straight. You *are* implicating me as being responsible – just be honest about it. Don't shy away from it. And also, I tried to help her. You're not making sense; you put the onus of fault on those that try to help? Don't you think that is backward reasoning? Aren't you making her a victim? I mean she is an adult; I tried to help her. Are you going to blame her parents for bringing her into the world? Are you going to blame God, because she wasn't able to connect with Him? Well, actually I might blame her family a little bit, I think they enabled her to go ahead with her addiction when she first started using. But I really don't know why you are blaming me."

Veronica said, "Well, again, I'm not blaming you, but rather allowing you to address one side of the story – that's how journalism works. And don't you think that it is a little juvenile that you don't take responsibility for your own health practices? As if you're asking us not to judge your actions and your results."

"Okay, well, I didn't know anyone blamed me until you brought it up, and anyway, I'm trying to take responsibility for it. I said I didn't help her. I am acknowledging my ineffectiveness. What you are saying is in hindsight. I tried to do my best at the moment. You're not showing all those people I helped," Heis said.

"Well, it also seems like you are talking about her death so flatly, as if you had no part in it," Veronica said.

"Again, why are you blaming me? Why not blame her illness? It is as if you think I caused the illness?" Heis said.

"Well, she probably saw you rather than going to a real doctor like a psychiatrist," Veronica said.

"She came to me *because* those people were not helping her," Heis said.

"And you took her money, sold her something that you admit does not work, and now she is dead," Veronica said.

Heis said, "I did what I thought was best, as a *practice* – which is exactly what those psychiatrists tried to do, who also took her money and also did not help. So, if it's on me, then it is on them too. But do you know what the difference is? I don't practice that way anymore – I learned. Those psychiatrists blamed *her* for not responding to treatment and still continue to treat patients that same way and justify their actions based on popular opinion and 'standard of care.'"

Veronica said, "I'm saying you shouldn't be practicing healing people when you're not a doctor. Who knows what this new treatment is that you're using now. How can we trust you when you admit this past way did not work?"

"I can help people if I want to. What's wrong with that? And I think it is particularly for that reason that you *should* trust my methods. Because I am able to admit my faults and try to explore new ways of treatment. For instance, when medicine is monetarily driven, unfortunately both the physician and patient become the victim in this complex and are often automated to write this or that medication and not even put a hand on the person. Healing is not as easy as just swallowing a pill, and you know who always puts things in their mouth to solve problems? Infants, so let's grow up and abandon this oral fixation. What I want is to exploit that kernel of perpetual self-improvement that is latent in everyone – allow *that* to heal them – so they can heal themselves –" He stopped abruptly, as if he had said too much.

"Why did you stop?"

"No, nothing, I'm just saying that; as time went, I collected more long-term results – that is when I was able to see what led to better lasting results – what I termed Soul development." Heis became quiet after that. He stopped talking and Veronica cut back to the old footage which was cut in mid interview.

"-oped, and there was a great white light as usual, yet the migraine was not there." The old segment was coming to an end as the reporter wrapped up, "with so many lives changed, this new approach seems very promising."

Veronica came back into the segment, "Your practice was called very promising – what do you think of that interview looking back on it?"

"I would have agreed, it did seem promising and still does as it has evolved. It all just goes back to God and figuring out how to decrease that barrier between Him and yourself which is the root of all healing. And I was always cautious in my promises. Other people gave me praise, I always gave it to God, because when you accept praise, then you allow the potential to accept negativity as well. I wanted to remain on my own course. I was my own best critic. And, you know, confidence in your healer is *part* of the healing process; even if that healer is completely wrong, the patient's own confidence in the practice influences the outcome. So, I try to humbly facilitate an air of confidence among those who seek my help, as a way to help *them,* not as a way to inflate my own ego."

"But your techniques lead to so much confusion, loss of property and at times – loss of life."

"I didn't want anyone to put complete faith in me, rather in God. I always said that. I tried to help those people. If the person put their faith in God, and there was still that loss of knowledge, property, life, then that is between them and God. Death is not the worst thing to happen to a person, because you just arrive back at your abode in Heaven – the worst thing is loss of faith in yourself, in God, in others and the negativity that accumulates and buries you under that; like the spiritual zombies."

"Here is a healer that says death is not the worst thing – it's like a plumber saying that a leak is not the worst thing."

"You think a leak is the worst thing? A leak isn't the worst thing," Heis said.

"But you hire a plumber to help you with your leaks, right?"

"Yes, that is generally correct, but you shouldn't fear death, everyone dies. The goal of life is not to only avoid death – some people's whole life is made worthwhile by dying for their friends. Life and health are greater than death."

"Mr. Heis, you are being naive if you think you don't have some responsibility for what happened. People called you a cult leader. Many people did what you told them to do. Do you take any responsibility?" She did not let him answer and he held his tongue as she said, "–And, when we come back, we'll explore his answer, why did he then disappear for five years? And how does he claim to know such deep secrets about the mysteries of the soul?"

Cassandra asked Edwin, "Do you want to keep watching this?"

"God…hears…you," Edwin said, as if he was holding water in his mouth, and he made a big sweeping gesture with his left arm, "Cass…Angel."

Cassandra paused the news segment.

"What are you saying?" she asked, excited yet mystified by his comments. Yet he didn't answer. *Does this man ever say anything normal?* She thought to herself. She dropped the issue and resumed the news segment.

The segment opened back up on a monologue from the host, with lots of different camera angles zooming in on her in dramatic fashion.

"Hello, and good evening. Welcome back to Armory News, and thank you for continuing to join me for this, as you'll see, very interesting report. The existence of a soul, and an afterlife in general have been the topic of heated debate over millennia, but today I'll be speaking with a man who claims to have first-hand evidence of the existence of a soul and get this – he wants to patent it! He said he has developed technology to help you experience what he has experienced – which is undebatable evidence and utilization of one's soul."

Heis quickly interjected and said, "Yes, and no longer do you need to spend a lifetime secluded in a mountain side to develop your soul. With this spiritual technology, that process can be facilitated in a fraction of the time. Busy mothers, fathers, students, anyone can try this."

"So, you're the man who will end the age-old debate of 'is there a soul?'"

"Well, it was never a debate for me, and I assume it was never a debate for a lot of people with faith. And probably the people who have the most faith will be the ones who get the most out of this device – but of course it is for everyone, and I encourage everyone to use it," he said.

"Well, before we tackle that subject, let's go further back, because you're an interesting person. Let's go to the town you grew up in – Red Bank, New Jersey."

The news segment cut to a pre-recorded interview with Veronica and Heis walking on the beach near his childhood home.

"So, yeah this is where I was raised by my mother and step-father – who were both great people. My biological father was a prominent scientist who I haven't seen for ten years. Red Bank itself was actually started as a bit of a social experiment based on the philosophy of Charles Fourier – who, in my opinion, could do as much for the human race as Jesus. Of course, he was not as enlightened as Jesus, but Jesus' presence on the Earth was short lived – and Jesus himself said he had more to tell us. Charles Fourier promoted that same social and moral cohesion similar to Jesus, and he continued elaborating and trying to achieve that Heaven on Earth of which Jesus spoke."

"Interesting, I've also lived in Jersey most of my life. I had never heard that," Veronica said.

"As a kid growing up here, I felt engaged with the world; felt I had a grand purpose because in my daydreams I would save people or even die for them. But I was never able to develop an early practicable passion or skill that could live up to that beautiful feeling. I was too impatient to mold a skill into that feeling. I was always a little envious of those kids who knew what they wanted to do and were driven to achieve their goals. I admired that they were up and doing things, and I also admired what I perceived as their deeper contentment, confidence and faith, which was underlying and driving that passion of theirs. I was also excited *for* them to see what they accomplished. I didn't excel nor struggle at anything because I was kind of interested in everything, and it was a kind of flat, lukewarm existence. Things just never seemed to break my way, and I was easily discouraged and often scared of the judgment of others. That was why I was envious because those people who had passion and a dream – things seemed to work out for them via some invisible hand. So, I felt them advancing and moving on when I was not."

"And, so, you had a very circuitous path. You first went into the self-help space as a therapist," Veronica said.

"Yeah, after high school I didn't know what I was looking for but I knew it wasn't in front of me. I didn't have many options. The only skill I had was that I was a good listener and I was good with people. So, it became that *listening* was the only thing I could offer people. But, I had no formal training to call myself a psychiatrist or psychologist, so I just said I was a life coach, and offered to listen. Here is a funny story that shows how God guides our lives: I decided not to charge the first couple people as I was still trying to figure things out. Yet, no one wanted it. Because in my first ad giving it away for free, two women contacted me – but never manifested into anything and one guy offered me a job to paint his house. I could have easily stopped right there – I did not get a good response for an ad that cost me money which offered a free service – so how does one humble themselves even further than that? I wasn't sure how to make things more enticing. But, I guess it was my time to do something, because that quiet voice got mad at me any time I would have flown away so easily because of early disappointments.

"Anyway, I took out another ad online for *listening therapy* – which I was not aware at the time was an actual specific type of therapy that required training – which I was not offering – I was just offering to listen to people. Even still, at that time, even with that little voice guiding me, most people calling me were not looking for what I had to offer, they wanted that other listening therapy. Yet, that mistake is why I received any calls at all, and about 5 percent of people were like 'Okay, why not it's free' and eventually, you get one patient, then they tell someone, and so on. And after two years I was able to do this 75 percent of the time and charge a reasonable price so that I could take care of both myself and the person seeking help. And, I realized all my endeavors could have been made possible at an earlier time in my life if I had just learned to listen to myself, as I listen to others, and be patient and allow time and God to work their magic. Another funny thing was that a common type of person to use my services were those same people who were driven at a young age, pursuing a passion, type A personalities, early bloomers – those same people I looked up to when I was younger, now felt they had not experienced a childhood, or they distinguished themselves too early and were handed too much responsibility early in life; or they didn't know how to continue to handle that prompting impulse that spurred them onward when they were younger and now felt burnt out. But, I suppose an alternate theory would be that those driven type-A personalities were the most successful and therefore they were the only ones that could afford to spend money on a life coach, and therefore they were no more messed up than anyone else, yet it was a bias in disposable income. I don't know!

"Anyway, I can't really say I did much for them myself, which was good because after an afternoon with each one of these smart, driven people, I quickly found out I was not in a position to give them advice. Nevertheless, the business thrived! Half the time they were giving me advice on how to grow a small business! I felt a bit like I wasn't doing anything, so I was confused as to why it was thriving, and these people were just looking for a friend, a confidante, a moral guide and sounding board to talk to outside the normal hustle and bustle of their daily lives. Things were happening in such a different way than I expected. But, let me tell you the secret to a successful business as a life coach and probably just as a friend too, is to just care, and act on that despite your own anxieties. If you just care about them, and talk openly to them like a normal person, eye to eye, then the inherent warmth bleeds through from you to them and that warmth is often what is lacking in their life.

"For me, since I was a good listener, I would listen in an engaged way and without interrupting. Speak to them in their own vocabulary. Often, I didn't even need to arrive at a solution, the therapy was just them talking to me. They didn't want advice, but rather someone to share the emotional or mental load! But if something novel popped into my head while regurgitating and summarizing their thoughts, then of course I would share it. That was usually the only time I said much. Seeing how these people, who I envied growing up, thought through problems – it helped me realize *how* they were able to be ambitious. They were all smart, but in addition they would make a decision – right or wrong, they made a decision – and regardless of if it was right or wrong the result was the same – they would understand why that result was produced and keep moving forward. And, yes, each one relied on varying quantities of concrete facts and inward guidance to arrive at some new creative conclusion or solution. See, when I was younger, I was looking at them, and trying to emulate what they had, which was my mistake because I was overlooking the things inside of me and disregarding my own impulses. In overlooking my own self, that is why things didn't work out for me, because in me emulating them, they had already filled that position and that position already had that thing work out for it – God did not need another one of those people. God did not need to repeat himself. God, by his own beneficence was waiting for me to be myself. There is a whole world inside of each of us. You, everyone, is a piece of the truth – a different piece of truth trying to gain both new understanding and new expression of itself. Pieces of truth fit together because they all come from one in the same place – God. Therefore, it is natural that they complement each other rather than become one another. So, that is the reason other people's personality, when expressed by you, seems like a mask – you're trying to express *their* truth. That is kind of where the whole belief came from that I could just be a facilitator to a person's own development – Have them answer their own questions. This was the crown jewel of knowledge that I developed from my life coach endeavor and signaled to me to move on. It wasn't until I followed my own internal voice that things started to work for me – which was this first life coach endeavor!"

"You say this is where you learned to appreciate the soul as guiding a person. Yet, what I'm hearing is someone who could be potentially acting as a charlatan and putting on the ruse of helping people, when really you offer nothing," Veronica said.

"Interesting point, I hadn't seen it that way, but I do understand what you are saying – first people falling for this listening therapy, which I said I wasn't really doing much, and then again with the addiction treatment where I said I didn't help. Yeah, that's a good point, but it just gets to a truth of mental and psychiatric issues – it often goes back to the person – even antidepressants, running does more for you than antidepressants, so they aren't a magic bullet. At best they just blunt your emotions, so you don't feel one thing or the other so that you are not depressed or happy – which is okay as a short-term solution, but not a long-term one. What matters is changing your mind, the fulcrum of the soul."

The news segment cut back to Veronica talking over general footage of the town, "For the next two days I interviewed him while walking in the woods, in his home, kicking a soccer ball around, or at a friend's barbecue. In his effort to develop the ways in which people could help themselves. This led him toward the health of the soul – the root of all disease and health, the essence of homeopathy, and the mystery of every age – now revealed itself to him. Check our longer supplemental report for the full five-hour program because it was too long to include here. We will stop there and continue an even more exciting interview next week." And the news segment ended.

Cassandra and Edwin looked at each other, eyebrows raised. "Interesting, but they didn't even get to the good part and they just stopped it," Cassandra mused. "Well, maybe we can watch the next segment when I come next time."

# 4 – Experiments

*The decisions and burdens were great*
*Not knowing if they were mistakes*
*And it was tempting to be done*
*With both anger and love*

As Cassandra and Edwin were watching the interview in Elizabeth, New Jersey, Bill was returning to the Island for his last visit before fully transitioning to normal life. During his yearly visits to the island, Bill had heard by word of mouth many of the troubling developments surrounding Redd's family, isolating himself in his basement lab, not taking visitors. Now, during his last visit to the Island he wanted to visit Redd to check on his well-being before permanently continuing his life in the U.S.

    The small transport vehicle shuttled Bill down the road to Redd's house located on a low prominence in an isolated portion of coastal jungle. The house had been transformed into a large array of sun-tracking heliostatic mirrors reflecting sunlight to a central receiver above the house. The central receiver then funneled the sunlight into a large hole in the middle of the house, looking as if the center of the house had collapsed inward. Bill cautiously walked up to the front door, his face was scanned, and the door opened automatically into the empty entrance room.

He had been here once before for a party that Emily had given for Redd's birthday.

Bill walked through the entrance room calling for Redd and then stepped into the kitchen and living room and was nearly blinded by an immense solar funnel channeling a dense beam of concentrated sunlight between two large lenses from the top of the house, down through the living room and into the basement. The center of the house had been cut away and lined with plexiglass to accommodate this intense beam that would have burned or desiccated anything within a ten-foot radius. Skirting around the perimeter of the living room, Bill went to the cellar door to further investigate, and found it was locked. He then knocked on it and yelled for Redd.

Redd was in his basement, deep in thought as the knock came through the door. "Bill?!" Redd said, disgruntled as if he'd just been woken from a nap.

"Yeah," he shouted through the door. "May I come down?"

The door opened and the stench of death and decay wafted up and out of the cellar in a plume, strangling Bill's nostrils – he tried to breathe through his mouth. As Bill stepped down the stairs, he saw the basement was dug out down into the Earth some fifty feet and splayed out into a large circular room one hundred feet in diameter. Various geodes and other geological formations jutted out from the continental shelf with wires attached as if they were lab equipment. The concentrated sunlight was diffused throughout the underground cave by a series of crystal Fresnel lenses forming a large chandelier that poured down light onto a lush forest amid the huge rock formations. The sides of the cavern were a series of gently sloping terraced walls around the periphery. A metal walkway attached to the rock circled around the cavern and became nestled in the dense jungle terraces. Birds, reptiles, small mammals fritted about and brought music to the underground atmosphere. As he walked down and the lab came into view, the beauty of the scene was negated by the grisly and morbid scene contained at the heart of the basement. He saw twenty corpses lined up on tables with various organs and appendages and unidentifiable tissue and bones strewn about the tables and floor, haphazardly thrown into waste bins, or sitting in small jars for later use. Dead animal bodies lay next to the corpses and had a myriad of wires like creeping vines connected to those dead bodies.

    Redd, seeing Bill, tiredly put everything down and pushed his chair away from the work bench. Bill didn't recognize Redd as he seemed to have aged twenty years in the past seven. Redd now had a large white and red beard, appeared ragged and worn out, thin and emaciated. As Redd stood up to greet Bill, Redd's heart instantly welled up with fraternal affection, and he staggered toward Bill who was standing at the base of the steps. Bill was frightened by the abrupt oncoming motion of this strange-looking man, and Redd, with his last ounce of energy and strength hoisted and hurled himself upon Bill, wrapped his arms around him, falling upon his neck and giving him his weight, attempting to somehow replenish his soul with the love of their friendship. Bill stabilized himself against Redd's weight and embraced him.

    Redd, almost in a sob, and still embracing Bill, said, "You were right, Bill. Despite yourself you were right! I focused on the soul. I know you don't believe in the soul, but that's what I focused on. What if I could prove it existed? For you, my friend. What if I could prove it to you? If I could prove it, would you believe it?" Redd said, picking up where they had left off from their conversation seven years ago.

"It's good to see you too, Redd. What have you been working on down here?" Bill asked.

Redd released Bill and stood on his own. "Our conversation that day was very informative to me. Thank you, Bill, for your friendship. So, I thought to myself, is the brain the connection of the soul to the body? The soul pervades the whole body, but which areas of the brain are most responsible for connecting the soul with the body.

"My wife and I agreed to approach it from two angles. One, I had started with biological material, i.e. sixteen of the twenty-four child clones were assigned different portions of the brain to be emphasized during gestation and development. The other eight had near-identical normal brains. Only later on did I start stripping away areas of the brain to see the effect, and two, I started with artificial material and progressively added biological tissue i.e. a nervous system, visceral organs.

"Is the soul an emergent property of biologic tissue, or is biologic tissue merely the receptacle to a soul which had already existed? Or, could both be true? As limited-perspective beings we cannot assume these two ideas are mutually exclusive. Or, is there a third unknown option?

"I mostly focused on the nervous system. The brain is a miracle that I was attempting to explain, the least understood system as housing that aspect of humanity which we least understand.

"As the clones grew with all their varied nervous tissue organizations, I had to have some way of assessing the soul. At that time, I was very careful not to harm them, and I devoutly nurtured them as a way to most fully develop their innate proclivities. I had no device to measure the soul directly at that time. Therefore, to indirectly quantify the soul and by extension measure my experimental progress, I developed three parameters to quantify how likely it is that a soul is present in a body, or how *much* soul was present in a body. I did not know if a soul was an absolute unit, or if there were degrees and quantities of a soul. I defined what it meant to have a soul – or at least the spectrum of physical parameters upon which the manifestations of a soul can be graded. These parameters are learning/memory, improvisation, and novel ideas.

"Yes, yes, the implications are immense, that is why I did not want to publish it – even on the Island. If you would like to publish it you may, it is up to you, I think we would agree on that as much. The ramifications would reshape our understanding of what disease is and how we view disease such as dementia and autism, just to name a few – but all would be impacted. But, let the masses debate the validity, these definitions were intermediaries more for myself, in lieu of something better, rather than to directly impact other's beliefs. But, an interesting offshoot of this I felt was the term "advancement" – meaning, did subsequent generations advance existing understanding from previous generations? Advancement being a derivative of the three aforementioned parameters, it summarized what most distinctly separated humans from animals. Which obviously I was unable to measure in my cohort, but it would also suggest that the "soul power" of the human race is growing because we are advancing at an exponential rate compared with previous generations. Animals, from generation to generation, do not advance, again let the masses debate the validity, I do not care, that is what I am going with.

"This soul definition would at most only stay within our close scientific community on the island or underground where it would not be sensationalized or emotionalized, but rather studied dispassionately with cold calculation as well as understood with a kind of intuitive sense. Truth is not political here, I'm sorry, you know already, that is why I like you."

Bill interrupted, "Redd, where are your twenty-four children?"

"Two are over there," Redd said, pointing to the play area with two children napping on a couch.

"Where are the rest?" Bill said.

"Oh, yes, right. The others are gone. This is all that's left. Oh wait, no, come over here," Redd said, leading Bill to a metal closet, opening it to reveal three jars side by side on a shelf. One jar contained the head of a six-year-old child, she looked into Bill's eyes, opened her mouth in exasperation as if to scream. Yet, she could not speak. She had no lungs. Her neck was mounted to a polished wooden fixture at the bottom of the jar as if it were a trophy. Then the mouth closed, the exasperated expression turned to a look of placated resignation and stared off again – the light in her eyes now gone. Numerous tubes went in through the bottom of the jar, and the rest of the closet was filled with machinery to keep her and the other two alive. The next jar was just the same although this child did not move, its eye lids remained half open, mouth slack, eyes static and pointed in different directions. The third was a long clear tube containing a brain and spinal cord turned upside down, wires attached to all the cranial nerves and spinal nerves.

"And I know what you're thinking, Bill, yes, they do have souls – can you believe that? Everything is stripped away except the brain and still, the soul is housed. I found out that if a brain is totally disconnected from all sensations, then it goes insane within a matter of six hours. So, I connected the nerves of sensation with electric and magnetic stimuli, and I can see that the brain is acting in a novel and organized manner in response to these sensations and its electrical activity is not flat. And, when there is no stimuli, the opposite is true, the activity is chaotic, thereby supporting my insanity conclusion. See, in death the EEG is flat, death is the flat plain, and it's definitely not flat.

"Before the others were sacrificed, I noted their personalities, it was all well documented. They were all well delineated, they all had souls – I could see the impact that those different souls had on the same DNA. Obviously, they all had the same DNA and environment, so any changes must be due to the changes I made in the brain. The eight controls/placebo clones had their own personalities which was also used to study the differences in their souls. So, I could see those riverbeds of the soul – where it moved, *how* it moved. I could go over all the experiments perhaps later; they are all documented. Y'know I really think that electricity is the motive principle of the universe – I mean that the arborization that electricity expresses as it moves through a medium is recapitulated on a slower time scale in the mineral veins of the earth, plants, animals, humans, the brain, stars, the universe! So, I knew what to look for when looking for those riverbeds of the soul."

"Redd, this is beyond insane," Bill said, "You killed them?"

"*You* say killed?" Redd said, as if he had just won an argument, "My wife and I raised them as loved children, but it was all part of the experiment, that was the plan. She didn't want to go through with the plan, so who is to blame? She tried to stop me, but she had already agreed. I'm now realizing that I don't think she ever had agreed, in her heart, to the plan. She only said so to appease me."

"Redd, I'm completely disgusted and appalled, how could you bring yourself to do that? I know we have very few laws on the Island, but what about your heart? They were children!" Bill said.

"They were clones of my wife, as far as the Earth was concerned, they were the same person – wouldn't you agree? But, these last two are my crown jewels of all this research – one has a larger corpus callosum, the other a larger pineal – you see it's the midline structures, where two halves become one. Those predominately house connection to the soul," Redd said.

"How could you do this?" Bill repeated.

"They were sacrificed. It hurt me, just as it is hurting you now. Do you understand the sacrifice I made, weep for the living, not the dead. If they had a soul, then they are away on Jupiter or Neptune receiving greater instruction and will be back at some point. If they did not have a soul, then it would be no different than slaughtering an animal. Do all humans have souls? We shall see," Redd said.

"Redd, this is too much, the council will decide on this. I am going to tell them about all this," Bill said.

"Do as you wish," Redd said.

"You just said the children had souls and, since your goal was to produce evidence of the soul interacting with the body, then you were operating on the assumption that those children had souls. And, therefore committed a crime against sentient beings."

"But, Bill, aren't you curious about my other results and what I found?"

"Redd, first, we first have to settle upon how you got there. I must say, I am very worried about you. The community is worried about you. You've isolated yourself to an extreme extent."

"Honestly, I think you and the community are jealous. But, sorry, I mean, I know, but isolation wasn't the original plan or intention, nor is it my current intention. I want to share this *with* the community at some point. That is why I had kind of been using a visit from you as a natural stop gap to bring this to the community. I didn't know when you were going to visit, but I certainly had a lot to keep me occupied while I waited. It seemed only fitting given our discussion started all this; and here you are after seven years and acting as the very thing I had predicted you would act as – that impetus to share this with the greater community by telling the council. How amazing God is – you see Bill!"

"But why didn't you just invite me over?"

Redd looked at Bill with a deep, bloody thought behind his eyes. Redd was disheveled, gaunt, he looked homeless when he used to be so handsome and lively.

"I spent it all, Bill. The spirit has been spent," Redd said, his eyes and voice quivering as he lifted his thin and weak arm to show Bill the extent of his privation. "Three years of isolation. Seven years of desperation, pushing myself past my limits, all sacrificial offerings on the altar of progress and validation. I was alone purely in my mind in vast stretches of uninterrupted thought. I traveled in my mind. I barely spoke two words each day. I thank God for such an amazing opportunity I was granted, and I didn't want to squander it and it honed my focus and creativity,"

Redd said. "Do you know what it is like to have continual revelation after revelation enveloping your mind like successively larger and larger ocean waves crashing down on you, trying to teach you by pummeling you into the sand. I didn't want to miss a moment, so I let myself be pummeled, unprotected, receptive, night and day. You just want to sleep, but you can't. And it was as beautiful as it was terrifying – the thoughts I have been presented with from the heavenly bodies, the understanding I've gained. At such times, one is not in control of their mind, but rather on an exciting ride, and the two hemispheres of my brain nearly tore my mind apart in ecstasy – and I couldn't bear another moment."

Bill said, "I think the prolonged mental strain and hyper fixation on this goal and belief has slowly, insidiously expended and deranged your mental faculties. You wouldn't have done this seven years ago. You were more reasonable then."

Without acknowledgement Redd said, "The phosphorus holds a deeper purpose and I saw the brain as a series of spinal cords composed of local groups of nervous reflexes and regions pulsating within those groups with magnetic upwelling surges from ventral to dorsal which would dissipate, and the dissipation would nearly coincide with the upwelling of another group – one after the other. Each force within the body was composed of all forces – electrochemicomagnetophysioanatomiconuclearmechanical . But where was there room for the soul when so minutely tracing each impulse, tracing it back in time, almost to the very moment of conception? It was as though I could see the soul when I stood back, but then the very act of reaching for it pushed it deeper, just out of my reach. The multitude of these upwelling chaotic motions were captured on the MEGs, EEGs, fMRI, tractography, and on a new device I invented."

Redd then brought out a device from the base of his work bench. It was the size of a backpack, black, shaped like a mountain, as if hewn from the surrounding rock, it appeared dense and heavy as Redd had to lean back as he brought it over to the lab bench and set it down with a dense metallic thud.

"Feel it, completely solid, no moving parts, no weld marks – the engineering itself I am proud of, not to even speak of its capabilities. It does not run on batteries, rather it generates energy from the magnetic field and electric field of the earth and from those perturbations I can pick up on some interesting signals. There are internal workings within it, however it cannot be accessed by opening it, rather you must use this pair of magnetic gloves and a special pair of glasses to see into the device and activate it.

"The quantum encephalogram, aka The MacDougall. You see, when someone dies, I can measure a loss or a perturbation between 10-50 picovolts and just a few femtotesla occur between the central nervous system and the autonomic nervous system, which are higher in children. The device also uses neutrinos from the sun measured before and after they pass through the person and based on the difference, we can further isolate that very faint electrical and magnetic signal. I don't know if this is the best place to measure such an occurrence, I had only a limited supply of subjects and sometimes it doesn't happen, but it's fairly reliable. Therefore, I believe the soul is interacting with this device and the device is also interacting with the soul – remember that," Redd said, expecting praise and applause.

"But that is nothing new, as you said, the EEG and MEG become flat with death," Bill said, momentarily forgetting about the horrors around him.

"Ah, there you are Bill, now you have joined me here. Yes, as you said, Bill." Redd perked up, his vitality restored, almost jubilant, as he reached his hand over to place it on Bill's shoulder and smiled deeply at him, "Good, Bill. Yes, we already have the EEG to tell us when the soul has departed after a person has died in their brain, yet their body is kept alive with various machines, hormones and medications for organ donation, that is all known. Therefore, consciousness is tied to the brain because in that situation of artificially keeping the person 'alive' for harvesting organs, then only the brain is not working – their heart still beats, their kidneys still purify the blood, the intestines still exhibit rhythmic contractions. In that time there is no consciousness and the EEG is flat. They still have functioning organs, they still have functioning reflexes that arc through the spinal cord as deep tendon reflexes, but cranial nerve reflexes that arc through the brain are not retained. So, it must be purely the brain for consciousness – we already know all that.

"The brain is the portal through which the soul comes to associate with the body, while the nerves are channels by which the soul drapes and pervades every cell of our body. The very active portions of the soul are split between the central nervous system being the consciousness and the autonomic nervous system as the subconscious. The reason the soul has been so hard to categorize within the body is because we only study dead bodies in anatomic dissections. But, I've been able to get around that here on the Island. So, that *consciousness* is in the brain, but the soul is more than consciousness. The soul is also represented throughout the body, in the autonomic nervous system as well and through the peripheral nervous system the soul interacts with even the stones of the body – the bone I mean; and the bone therefore is part of the eternal soul.

"But the added revelation with this device is that I can see the electric and magnetic frequency of what I term the *soul*. Because it's different for every person I've studied, about fifty subjects in total, there is a signature, almost as if I can see the very room in the many mansions of God's house that we will occupy. You see, the burst suppression pattern on EEG indicates the soul is about to depart, and the quantum EEG would show a slow decrement in voltage and magnetomotive force. The EEG would consistently become flat about twenty-four hours after the quantum EEG would hit zero – so I have verification there. That is mostly my justification for calling this the soul frequency.

"It is useful to understand how I isolated this frequency. I built a deep hole in the bedrock of this island – as you see. I characterized the electric heartbeat of the surrounding mineral deposits, of the Earth and the atmosphere, and the sun, even more distant celestial bodies. Yet, electricity produced by decomposition cannot substitute that living electricity of the soul – they're different types of electricity. I hypothesize that this signal only emerges when run in context of those surrounding frequencies as if it's like a call and a reply – the Earth-Sun complex echoing against the spirit/soul. Hypothetically if that same soul were put in a different universe, or even a different solar system with different local frequencies then that same soul would reverberate differently, meaning it would manifest differently under whatever the presiding frequencies and laws were present in that locality. That is part of the reason why it looks like a big piece of Earth rock and the implications of which are endless!

"One implication I might speculate, that the soul maintains that frequency in response to our Earth-Sun complex regardless of the body! But I have no place to put my electrodes and dipoles just yet to prove such a hypothesis. Also, I figure some form of this device could help maintain the soul-body connection to help people live longer or heal or just generally keep the body healthy. I already started building a device to inject that same current and magnetism back into the body based on that body's specific quantum frequency to facilitate the body's own healing mechanisms – but again it's a different type of electricity that I use to produce that frequency – it's like a cast.

"From there the implication might be that we are able to prompt a newly departed soul back into the gross matter from which it departed to live again. It would be simple enough to add this to the regimen of medical interventions used to keep someone's body alive for organ donation – I just haven't done it yet. I was actually saving those twins to do that experiment because they have the same DNA, so I don't know if I would be able to do a soul transplant.

Bill said, "That is all very amazing and interesting and Earth-shattering, but I still don't understand why you waited for me? Why didn't you share this device with the community before today?"

"Because, even our little community suffers from being human," he said, becoming indignant. He was emotionally labile and now rushed into a frenzied pressured speech once again.

"They would not understand until it was finally proven as a foregone conclusion. People are people because they are not angels nor animals nor computers. The atheists, among them praising science for its empirical reasoning, have no imagination for such a thing as a soul and would therefore reject the study of something that does not exist to them. You fall into this category, Bill, but there is a light in your thoughts despite yourself, which you don't see yourself because – as we said, a system cannot analyze itself, and I don't think you're as much an atheist as you think – you think you know God and reject your conception – but you're wrong, you oxymorons of atheism.

"Then, the general spiritual community at large – they are too often scared that their beliefs are not real, or too certain of themselves that they need no further education on spiritual matters, or too often ascribe an amorphous divinity to an effect to which a real definitive and empirical cause and effect should be understood. Therefore, a frank inquiry into something as fundamental as the soul would threaten their superficial hopes and dreams – because they are scared, they are wrong and not able to prove it or totally disinterested in the matter – just like the atheists. But the tide of the universe, including that tide which washes our planet in love and wisdom, is rising. When I was very young, I thought God did everything, and for science to then explain away natural phenomena, it felt as though God was losing the battle and retreating into the as-yet-unexplained phenomenon and it was only a matter of time until science explained God out of everything – a juvenile belief I admit.

"Do you know the story of Duncan MacDougall, the guy who claimed he weighed the soul? He was laughed at, berated, discredited. The church denounced his experiments because the church falls into that blind faith category. Faith need not and should not be blind – Faith is your call to which God responds. And, not one person tried to recreate his experiment. Why? That was his mistake, he brought his experiment to his community too early, and he defeated his own purpose. I know better. Better to wait."

"Redd, what about your wife?" Bill asked.

"Please don't ask stupid questions, Bill, really," Redd said, "I thought we were getting somewhere. I'm sorry, she left, there was no debate. I did not fight to keep her here. I understood, I kept at work. I have nearly forgotten her completely. You see this is the only thing I have left, even before they left, even if I was out in the community – there was no escaping this for me, only through, that's why I had to sacrifice the children. I so easily let them go; I am somewhat afraid of my own capabilities. I know what I look like. I know this is not the most morally pristine way, but I can't let go when I am so close."

Bill turned his head down in despair and said, "...Redd...please...Emily didn't leave, she killed herself. I was told by the administrators of the Island. Redd, think of your own soul. Aren't you afraid of what is becoming of your own soul by these decisions you are making? You are not possessed, you have your own will, you did not have to do those things. If there is a soul, then in trying to find it, you've degraded and nearly lost your own."

"Compassion...it was not one of the soul criteria..." Redd said trailing off, "Oh my...Bill..." Redd became quiet, pale and sickly looking, "I've been secretly hoping for this moment, another revelation, the last one I can face. I am glad you are here," Redd said and the thin, unkempt man then fainted into Bill's arms. He was unconscious for a moment as Bill held him.

"Redd, you've obviously invested and sacrificed a lot," Bill said.

"Yes, what of it?" Redd said defiantly, and pushed Bill away and stood on his own, wanting no consolation.

"Does the admin know about this, is it registered, I mean?" Bill asked.

"Bill, you don't stop asking stupid questions, do you? When do we register studies, okay? When we want help."

"And, you don't need help?"

"No, the admin suffers from the same lack of imagination as outside admins do. So, no, they would only hurt the project."

"Redd, you have uncared for children in the corner. I think you need help."

"I had help! And then she killed herself – Help just slows me down and weighs me down! They want more than they give me! No one is as strong as me! So, no thank you. Even you, Bill."

"Even me?" Bill asked.

"You're too weak to see this experiment to its conclusion," Redd said, "Only I could have done it, and now you get the easy part."

"Oh, you're saying why you are not asking for my help?"

"Stupid Bill," Redd said.

"You know, I am going to report this simply because of your kids. If it were just you in here I couldn't care less, but those kids need care. Redd, what you did here is grounds for expulsion from the Island. And then you won't have any more access to your research," Bill stated.

Redd went back to work, paying little attention to Bill, "Okay," Redd replied.

"If I report it, then this would likely halt your work as you would be mixed up in investigation and, as I said, likely forced to leave," Bill said.

"Yes," Redd replied, still diligently working at his bench.

"Redd, you killed your children and that is all you have to say for yourself?"

"Technically, they were not my children, as they were clones of my wife – but yes, I understand your meaning," Redd said.

"So, I am saying that it is not ethical what you have done, you should pay the price for this issue. What if everyone were to kill children for experimentation?"

"It would not be right. It would not be a world that I would want to live in. But, as fate would have it, you are the only one who knows about this issue, everyone else is, well, deceased," Redd said. "I'm not telling you what to do. You can go to the authorities, or not, that is your decision. I planned for that decision; whichever you choose."

"So, I can go to the council and tell them everything, you don't mind?" Bill asked.

"That is what I planned for. Everyone is free here. You are exercising your freedom to do what is right. So, in what way would I mind?"

"Redd, I see you care about your own life about just as much as you cared about the lives of those little children," Bill said.

"Bill, don't you see how hard I am working to achieve something that will help everyone? Especially you! To prove a soul," Redd said.

"Don't blame me or anyone else for killing those children, I didn't ask for that," Bill said, "The world will be changed by each person helping just one other person, and the whole lot of salvation does not fall on to your shoulders, Redd. There is a wave that you set in motion the moment you committed that crime that will, in time, bounce back and nullify the very goal you are trying to achieve, and if you had just tried to find a way around it, asked God for help, a new way would have been opened to you."

"Well, look who's turned spiritual all the sudden – how convenient. But, I've always been spiritual. So, I say, let that fall on my head, because truth is truth, and it cannot be hidden for all time. The soul is true, and I will prove it. Once that happens, then my work will be done, and I will be okay with the karma that comes from my decisions. Perhaps in the next life, I will unwillingly lose my children despite all my intelligence, or I will be sacrificed in the name of truth, or if I am successful then I will come back as a spiritual cyborg clone and then be killed for experimentation purposes – those would be karmically fitting, but I'm not God, it's up to Him, I'm not telling Him what to do. I know what I did was wrong, but I didn't see a way around it. And, it seemed a measure of my commitment to overcome it."

"Okay, well then, I will go to the authorities, *and* I will take away the children. I don't want them to be with you another moment," Bill said.

"Goodbye, Bill, and thank you," Redd said and he continued his work.

Bill went to gather up the children from the far corner of the lab. The most beautiful children, exactly like their mother. They had been quietly watching Bill the entire time, fascinated with the unknown man.

"Hi children, what are your names?"

"Ava and Beatrice," Ava said, introducing them both.

"Would it be okay if you come with me while we let your dad work?"

Without a word the small children looked at each other and started to cry in unison.

"The birds?" Beatrice said, through tears.

"There are lots more birds outside, can I show you?"

The children looked to Redd, who, without a word, flung his arm up into the air.

"That means go away," Ava said. Bill took Ava's hand, and Ava took Beatrice's hand and allowed Bill to lead them away. Beatrice continued to cry as they walked up the metal steps that circled the large, stepped walls of the crater-shaped basement jungle. Bill's heavy footsteps on the metal walkway startled a colorful jungle bird from the underbrush near the walkway and it flew up toward the intense beam of light at the apex of the dome, past the chandelier, and became incinerated as it flew into the plexiglass encasement of the beam. Plummeting into the foliage. Bill then picked up Beatrice who had started crying more uncontrollably from the sight. He hurried them out the door as Redd continued to work at his lab, unfazed.

Bill returned the next day alone. The door remained open for him, which he took as a good sign that Redd still wanted him around, even after taking the children. "Okay, Redd, how can I help?"

"You didn't tell the council?" Redd asked.

"I did tell them."

"And…"

"And, I don't know," Bill said. "I told them. I have no idea what they will do with the situation. I hope they come and arrest you, but after speaking with them I think they are more inclined to finance your work and develop it."

"And, they told you to come help me?" Redd asked.

"No, I decided I will help you as a friend while we wait for the authorities to arrest you," Bill said.

Redd seemed to gain some semblance of his sanity and humanity back after seeing Bill come back voluntarily and care about him and his research.

"Okay, good," Redd put his hand on Bill's shoulder in solidarity. "And you can continue this work after I am arrested. I didn't mean that about you being weak. It was actually your thought that inspired all of this. You can even say it was all your idea, as it kind of was. In fact, I want you to do that if I should be arrested and taken away," Redd said.

"Well, I don't quite know if I want or deserve that title, so one step at a time, my friend. I partly blame myself; I should have visited, it was pressing upon my mind to visit. This would not have happened if I were here, we would have developed a way around it," Bill said.

"See, that's what I'm talking about, Bill, that's our two souls talking in the upper atmosphere of existence," Redd said.

"Okay, Redd, first of all, we need to deal with those three remaining children in the cabinet. If we can help them in some way, we will do that. If we cannot help them improve their quality of life, then we will have to find some alternative solution. I would not want to live like that. I've started a family off the island, that has made me more sensitive to these things and changed my beliefs somewhat. I'm a Buddhist now."

"Very good, I'm happy for you. I agree to your terms," Redd said and discussed a more detailed account of the experiments over last seven years.

———

As they were concluding their long discussion, Redd said, "...And so, after the clones ran out, and I didn't need the small army of nannies to care for them, then I used many of the derelicts of society who had given their body over to science and were shipped here," Redd said, "I've toyed around with replacing organic parts with artificial instruments with variable and unreliable outcomes.

"My long-term goal is still the spirit cyborg. Because, y'know, Bill, you were right about robots potentially having souls – well you didn't say souls, you said 'rights', but I interpreted that as having a 'soul', but anyway, I've revised my stance. After trying to coerce a soul into the robot frame, I think robots may have rights now. I have a working model on the theory of soul-cyborgs down in my basement, yet I only get indistinct flickering and muscle twitching. And now I am confused because I feel my experiments are correct, yet I am not having much success. I think that a soul might need time to be able to handle the controls of materiality – more time than I am able to give it.

"Oh, also, I've played around with a device that mimics the electrical pattern in utero which I was hoping to use as a possible carrier frequency as another way to entice the soul back into a body. Then, maximizing the efficiency of that life-giving electricity and putting that into portable packs around the waist of the specimen, running it through the navel – the cord of life. You see, Bill, there is an organizing principle to consciousness – meaning entropy is all around us of course, but the opposite force is consciousness and where it is then lesser forces will fall in line in order to best express that consciousness. That's why I defined the expression of a soul as such. Y'see, in a way the soul doesn't care about impediments, only expression – therefore it finds a way around impediment to express its full force in a beautiful, inspiring and vivifying way. But these things in the basement are walking around mindlessly, doing things mindlessly, it's all just echoes bouncing around preestablished circuits in the brain – they're not attempting to express anything. If I can just make the soul-cyborg advanced enough that its abilities could express the proclivities of a soul, then that would be my final work. Yet, I feel I am at an impasse in a way and just need a little inspiration to get me over this hump."

# 5 – New Worlds

*We wanted to tie-dye our hearts*
*but all they had was glow-in-the-dark*
*Heaven turned us inside out*
*making shadow puppets of our doubts.*
*We ruffled our own feathers, hands and fur*
*Letting us joke about who we were*

Cassandra regretted taking Edwin's assignment, *why can't I have a normal patient? Now I have to watch myself when I am there alone? And what is he going to do when he can actually move around?* She told herself that if anything else happened she would again ask for a reassignment – she still had some built up rapport with the boss upon which she could capitalize.

She was in a sallow mood when she walked into Edwin's room to see him, body and face still bandaged, lying in the exact spot she left him two days earlier.

"Hi Cassandra," he said in a deep, soft voice. He was proud and excited to show her he had his voice back, "Cassandra, I'm sorry for the other day and for scaring you, of all people." He then rolled all the way to one side of the bed, patted the sheets to show her that he had nothing else hidden in his bed."

"Wow, your voice," she said, "Your voice healed quickly, and that's okay about the other day. You seem to be moving better as well. Are you on a steroid taper or something?"

"No, no there would be no point to steroids. There's no inflammation or infection, and it would impede the healing process."

"Oh," she said, "are you…do you work in healthcare?"

"Yes, I work all day every day in the hospital…but as a custodian!" he said as if delivering a punch line. "Yeah, at the hospital here in town."

"It seems like you know a lot about medicine," she said.

"Well, you pick up more than trash while working there," he laughed. "And I always like to do my own research – especially the brain. The brain and the ocean are the last two frontiers left on Earth. The brain is our vehicle into the future. Humans two thousand years ago had more of a division between the hemispheres of the brain. It is possible if we get together, and do things right that it would only take a few thousand years to fully utilize the space within the head, but then again it may take longer around the same time the star Vega comes into position as the north star, which would be less good."

"Oh…uh," Cassandra was at a loss for words, "That's very interesting. Wow, I just had a dream exactly like that."

"Maybe you'll be a part of it," he said.

"What? What do you mean?"

"You're a special person," he said and didn't explain further.

In the silence, Cassandra took the opportunity to check his left leg bandage – the same one that was hemorrhaging last time. When she unwrapped it, it was nearly all healed with bright red scabbing, clean edges without the slightest evidence of infection.

"This was the leg I checked last time, right?"

"No, it's the left," he said, joking again. "But, yes, that's the one."

"What, how is this possible? How did it heal so quickly?" she asked.

"I had a good nurse," he continued to laugh. "One time a doctor wanted to study me, for a different reason, but he was equally impressed as you are."

"Oh, wow, I can see why. What was the reason?"

"I kept stopping my heart," he said and burst out laughing. "Well, not stopping, because where does the first heartbeat even come from? But, rather I slowed it so much, effectively stopping it. Then he calls a code, and everyone rushes in, and I am sitting there pleasantly unaware, 'oh what, I'm just on my phone,' my heart is beating normally. And, everyone rushing into the room had big, shocked eyes just as you had. They were ready to defibrillate me. When they realized I was totally fine, they all looked at that experienced doctor as if he was a resident and then when everyone left, I hate to say this, but I did it again," he said, laughing even harder now. "Do you want to see?"

"Oh, well why were you having your heart checked in the first place?" she asked.

"They thought I had a heart attack. Then, that doctor wanted me to come back because he realized I was messing with him and he wanted to study me. But, I'm not a fan of being a patient in hospitals and clinics. So, I didn't go back."

"Wow, I didn't know that was possible."

"Everything is possible with Father, you'll see. But there's also a lot of evil in the world, which makes things…less possible," he said, trailing off in thoughts. At that moment, Leo walked in with two Cuban sandwiches, leaned in the doorway just enough to quickly hand them to Cassandra, and then left without a word.

"But, not here, all things are possible here," Edwin said, "Thanks, Leo! Oh, let's catch that interesting interview this week that you liked," Edwin said.

"Yeah, let's put it on as we eat."

\*\*\*

Back in the studio with Heis and Veronica sitting at a table, Veronica continued, "So, that segment was your humble beginnings, but now, as the mustard seed grows from your faith in your purpose, you have achieved what some might say is impossible to achieve."

"Wow," Heis said, "That is really a beautiful statement. Yes, and just so I can get up to speed in my own mind so I don't skip anything I am going to talk this through – Yes, that helper/listening period gave me a greater appreciation for the depths of a person's internal life, their soul, but also their ability to tap into that recess and help themselves. I inherently had a great interest in understanding our soul and spiritual sides – which are different mind you. I felt that, one, it is possible to empirically study the soul; and two, as a human civilization, it was time. And, I cannot go into the specifics of my journey developing this device, but I felt the hand of God on my shoulder, guiding me, just as I had when I started the listening therapy – almost telling me what the next step was to be. Once again, I would love to discuss the specifics, but by keeping things secret I can raise money, with money to help disseminate this technology better."

And that is when the interview took on a different tone. He stopped talking with the reporter and started talking into the camera – directly to the audience.

He said, "I have built a machine that can facilitate the soul's interaction with the body. A sort of spirit technology or spirit tech. At first it was to help those on their death bed. You see, when they put on the device it either hastened their recovery or hastened their departure. I performed a listening session with them, and those souls that seemed to genuinely want to stay then the device seemed to give an 'extra nudge' to – what I was the interface between soul/body to rebuild those spiritual centers and help continue to house the soul. On the other hand, if I performed a listening session and the soul seemed to want to leave, then the device seemed to facilitate the opposite, and those centers would wither."

"So, you facilitated their death? That doesn't seem right," Veronica said.

"You do not work in palliative care," Heis said as his once soft and gentle voice became deep, resounding and strong. His demeanor itself changed. "You would not understand the statement that, sometimes, in some situations expediting the natural death process is an appropriate goal. You think the goal is always 'healing', but it is not. Most people are okay with death but are afraid of the dying process. But anyway, that's just how it started. It is something completely different now. I kept going further. I've opened up a whole new world that is natural, spiritual and scientific. But, here is the catch. As with any innovation, it will come at a cost.

"I am trying to get my story out there because the government is trying to unlawfully force me to either sell them my newest spirit tech or reveal how it is I am doing this. My apartment has been raided a few times, but I think they are so baffled by the product that they do not know how to go about analyzing it, and therefore have stopped raiding it because the repeatedly stolen property gets them no closer to the answer. And, I think they want me to continue this research in the hope that one of these devices they *will* be able to understand. But, also, they are frustrated and turning to brute force to get me to comply."

She tried to interject, "Can we back up a little bit – this isn't what was discussed in our pre-interview," but he would not stop to answer her questions. She did not know what his intentions were at this point because he very nearly did not pay any attention to her and hijacked the dialogue. In her ear the producer told her, "Let him go, he is interesting."

Heis continued, "Well, I am frustrated too. I've been patient my whole life, so I'm allowed a little peevishness now. Did you know the government can track you in your own home? Because that is what they told me, and they were intending it as a threat. They are trying to cow me and, for that matter us as a nation, into submission because we don't have the technology that they have and they use that against me and you, the general public. They are not democratic in their distribution of technology despite the fact that it is *you*, the taxpayer who pays for this technology that they use against you. It's all about control. They do not trust us, as Winston Churchill said, 'The best argument against Democracy is a five-minute conversation with the average voter.' Why would a leader such as Churchill say that about his own people? Because he doesn't trust them. But, God trusts you and therefore I trust you. I am trying to give you this spirit tech before they take it from me and before it becomes just another technology that they have and we do not have. They don't want us to be as free as this spirit tech would allow. They want us to need them, and they do that by keeping technology and that keeps us powerless. So, now I am trying to empower you. Now I appeal through this fourth estate to the people to help support me in my quest to keep the government from unlawfully seizing my intellectual property and keeping our spirits free. They want to take your spirit! The government never once offered to pay me a fair price for this device, nor would I believe them even if they did. Did you know the government uses psychics? I did some consulting work for them in that capacity with the aid of my tech, and they have yet to pay me because they said it would 'look bad hiring a psychic'. I'm not a psychic. It is precisely my not being psychic, I've shown you I was just an average person, and by using my spirit tech to produce a psychic phenomenon that drew their attention in the first place – so, anyone can achieve what I, through God, have achieved. People, while still alive, would now get to visit, enjoy and contribute to that place they would go to after death, while still alive on this Earth. That's the new world I discovered, and you can, too. And, I am trying to sell to the public this device so that they can enjoy that superior and refined sphere where one feels the presence of the Lord more closely."

Veronica tried to interject again, but was now cut off before getting any words out.

"Of course, you think to yourself – *'why does he charge money if he is so passionate and good-natured?'* Because it costs money to produce these devices and also, going back to the fact that my services were not wanted if I didn't charge money as I said earlier. Furthermore, it's not like the indulgences of the old Catholic Church where one could pay the church to enjoy yourself. This is a new world and the laws of the universe themselves are set up for our enjoyment, even this sphere. The Earth wants to provide for our every need if we would only listen. But, do you want the government to regulate a heavenly sphere like they regulate the Earth? In the next sphere, there is no religion but one religion, God, nature, the principles of nature that also encompass the spirit – the spirit has a more palpable presence in that other sphere. Is that something you would want the government to control? It is that same government which threatened me, a man trying to work, innovate, advance and explore. But, if these devices are kept with me, then all would get to go where they would in life and death – it would be no big secret. You would only have to buy one ticket for this device. Do you want the government controlling your departure from Earth? Your departure from the Earth takes your whole life. There are many strata or radii within the spiritual cosmos – which is just another name for the more refined parts of the regular everyday universe. There is no difference between the natural and supernatural in the universe – it is all just nature. Your spirit and your soul are physical things. Just like air and water running through our hands are both physical things. The Bible says to not fear that which can destroy the body but not the spirit – which is why I don't fear the government, which is why they want my inventions, because I do not fear them and they largely operate on fear, because people themselves largely operate on fear, and therefore remain in need of the government. What if we just did those things ourselves that the government is supposed to provide? We would not need them. That begets the necessity of the ticket price, and yes, a little of those proceeds does allow me to have a nice life. I am being honest about it, but who knows maybe I shouldn't, I don't know myself, maybe tomorrow I will make them free. But the purchase price entices you to 'buy in' to the commitment and allows the most committed to purchase the device before those who are not as committed. At this time, it would be a waste to give those not committed because their lack of results would work against my effort. We need bold, intrepid and desperate truth seekers to pave the way. They raise the tide for those that are weaker. Once those pioneers establish this new activity, then it becomes more popular and commonplace, and the reticent masses come out from behind their walls and this new activity takes hold of the imagination of the world. For instance, when new and truthful advice is given to a society it is difficult to perform that piece of advice, like doctors washing their hands, but as more people do that thing, then it becomes hard *not* to do it, and hand-washing has now become one of the most basic and essential routines of a physician. Which is why I want the most committed people first – to set up that tendency."

"The Bib–" The reporter started to say, but then was interrupted.

"No, the Bible says only to fear that which can destroy both body and soul. Which is what the government would then become if they got this technology. And as you learn more about what I have accomplished, please do not throw around the words prophet, false prophet, or Jesus. I am none of those things, prophecies do not apply to this situation – I am a spiritual scientist, and this is where science is taking us. Some people already see God and goodness in everything; this step makes that a little easier. Think about how happy you would be if tomorrow morning you woke up feeling God's presence and feeling closer to God, and you were closer to that thing that you so desired today – God and closeness with God is better than your dreams because they are your living dreams. And this device can get you to that appreciation. So, now you don't need to worry about that part in the Bible warning of people calling themselves prophets, because I am not. And no, I am not somehow socially engineering the situation by inserting the word prophet into the conversation, and by falsely denying it, somehow constructing the situation for it to land back on top of my head. I am telling you all this to get ahead of it as we speak."

Heis and Veronica locked eyes as she held up a finger to insert a thought, yet Heis continued on, saying, "You may say, 'it sounds like you just want to supplant the government's tutelage in this new adventure with my own supervision, and how would I guarantee I am more responsible than the government? Good question," Heis said, as if he were talking to himself, "Well, didn't you hear me? I gave you my whole back story, you decide. And, I just said the government lies and coerces people – I, I literally just told that story, didn't I? What do you think?"

He seemed both confused and frustrated. The reporter began to say something but was cut off by Heis, again. "Some aspects of government are necessary. For instance, in America, you pay taxes to allow yourself freedom, liberty and justice. But, I am saying that those good-intentioned taxes are now being used for the opposite purposes. In that same sense, I am trying to bring that model, in a smaller, yet more impactful and distributed sense, to this new place. Meaning, every person will, in a way, play a part in their government – but not in the way you are now thinking, not each holding an office, but rather the people will embody the government in their daily lives and the people and the government will be one unified body under God and in line with natural law. There are unwritten laws that people uphold, and if someone does not uphold them, then that begets a reaction from society. In that same sense, in the new world, people will dust off their apathy and apply their principles and morals in an active way; naturally, joyfully, every day. In such a world where citizens are empowered, then there is little need for the old type of government because people will act upon the inclinations of their heart. It is not anarchy, it is trust. Just as things happened in an unexpected way for me in my listening therapy story, so too does the Lord who speaks to us from within the temple of ourselves move us in unexpected ways that are unique to each individual. And we must trust people are maintaining and acting upon the impulses of their heart and what will be good for one person will be good for all. And, as people are more aware of their sense of His presence – better things will be produced. We are going toward a land that does not use money in today's sense – however to act as a transition point the monetary tax to enter this new place is a one-time fee to purchase the device. By paying this fee, you allow yourself unimaginable liberty, freedom, justice, wisdom and LOVE, the love waiting for you out there and in here," he said, motioning to his heart "is unimaginable – and of course it is here too," he said, motioning to the room, "it is everywhere, but just a little more palpable over there, which produces revolutionary changes. The taxes are not supposed to be oppressive, but rather uplifting, because work and contribution are held to be a fundamental human necessity in love and natural law. Further, the intention of the tax is to further contribute to building a better universe. Those who are not interested in such a place or such a device – then it is not for you if you do not want it. Rather, I am speaking to those people who feel what I am saying is true, and are on the fence and are either confused about how, or if, to move forward. I say to those people, FORWARD!"

Veronica was becoming angry she was getting her voice bulldozed by Heis. Her mouth hadn't even opened to speak before he started again.

"You are going to say, 'Well we all have different morals we live by, everyone is different.' To that point, one quick aside about freedom, now that I have your ear. Freedom allows both good and evil to prosper – there is no getting around that. I believe that to be an immutable law in the universe – freedom is God, God is the light, the light shines on all, and try to see *some* things in a new light. Anyway, just understand what you are getting yourself into as we move forward. If you uniformly restrict freedom as a way to restrict the bad, then you will also restrict the good, there is no getting around that. So, rather than trying to eradicate the Earth of germs, rather, simply practice a healthy lifestyle yourself and you will largely remain healthy and protected from those germs, even though they line the Earth. Each soul is inherently good or 'in line with nature'. Similarly, we must teach and show that goodness is the better way for each individual and for the whole of humanity. Goodness cannot be outsourced to an external entity such as the government. And, that is why every person will uphold a portion of those unwritten rules which a collection of people may live by, and you will look after your neighbor and he after you and that nucleus of affection will protect you. The more you love, the more you can use your will, the more you practice wisdom the more you're protected.

"So, if goodness and evil exist in step with one another as I have said, then what is the benefit of freedom, or how do we progress society if we have both those who do good and those who undo good?" And in a solemn tone he added "Allow God the increase. Allow for movement, with wisdom as the natural moderator. You will gravitate toward those who are more congenial to you, and movement will take place as you progress and associate with others and the natural association will set up the radiata through which we will move. Radiating around what? The Lord – the perfect benefactor of all goodness! Right now, we are all tied to a space, a property, a lawn, an apartment and probably we like some of our neighbors and do not like some of our neighbors. But, if you were able to get up and move without much effort to bring along those you want to associate with and they want to associate with you then your life would burst forth with creativity, peace, perfection and others would also and the reverberation of each person living out their passions and thoughts will reinforce others to do the same. A cloud has all the propensity to form rain, but it is one little nucleus of salt that can transform the entire disparate cloud into mobilized water droplets to bless our Earth. I am trying to be the salt, yet try to avoid becoming salty about it.

"In the past, people have called my inventions high-priced junk. But, y'know, I started hearing that a few days after each invention hit the market – or just after someone had bought a device. Meaning that you have to give it time – it will take longer than a few days. My spirit tech are nothing on their own, they require the prime movement of spirit and soul to act upon them, and within their metallic architecture and machinations they focus forces of creation and harness love and annihilation innate within all of us.

"I've heard many people say, 'why doesn't the device work for me?' And that is because you have not learned how to use it. I admit it is not as easy to use as plugging in a computer – but even computers would be impossible to use if it was your first time using it. These devices are still new to you – and it is certainly owing to my own shortcomings as an engineer that it is not easier to use. But nevertheless, it works for me and I'm confident it will work for you if you have patience. I will try to make it more user-friendly, but in the meantime please work with what we have. So, when you use this device, do not cause doubt in your mind by expecting results too early and therefore saying that the device is defective. But rather, assume the device is functional, pretend you're already there, and resign yourself to patient practice.

"People also say, 'can you show me how to use it?' But, the thing is, I used to put others' devices on my head, and yeah, in 99.9% of cases it's working just fine. But, I stopped doing that because, without going into the mechanisms behind the quantum lattice, nuclear – Ahh blah blah – forget you heard that or else I can't patent it someday. Suffice to say that the subtle yet powerful energy of immensity with which this device operates – it conforms to you, your biospiritual signature and for me to put on your device would do us both an injustice. And, that is where patience comes in, you and the device need time to adjust to one another. Also, the reason I cannot more explicitly show you how to use the device goes back to the fact that it is sort of a freedom device – everyone needs to understand how to use it in their own way. Everyone's mind produces the effect differently. It is like that old adage – there are many paths to the same peak – my specific path was facilitated by the device; your specific path will be facilitated by the device – it is the same in that sense – but our two paths are different. Maybe you are most spiritually alive after a run, in the morning, after talking with your sister, at the end of the day. Maybe you like incense, or you have to focus on when you were a child, or imagine yourself on your death bed knocking on Heaven's door – everyone's path is different.

"Do you understand that this is a type of enlightenment, and a type of evolution in thought that I am offering? The road to get there will be hard. More trials must be done. It is a journey wrought with triumphs, shameful misconduct and disappointment. The hermits, monks, bodhisattva, sadhakas all devote their lives to reaching an inner mental state that is similar to the place I am speaking of – and this device makes that journey easier – but it will still take a concerted effort and time commitment. So, then your next question is – How then did I get to using it and making it work? By using my imagination, I felt that this other world was out there, and it would be so close to going there, and I pretended the prototype devices were working, I tried to stay patient, and then after a while, the device coupled with my imagination, confidence and patience in arriving at this new place started to become a reality. At first I didn't know if it was real or a figment of my imagination – but then I realized it was both! And, that is how God works – it is a co-creation between you two. And no, the body, at least at this point, doesn't go somewhere else, it is your consciousness, your mind, which does the work. How do I know it is the device that is working, and not just my meditation and imagination or whatever? Because I learn knowledge, true facts, while at this other place, which I would not otherwise have been able to know. With those new facts, I can apply them to this current world we are in right now – and being a part of that other world has also made this world better for me as well. It's a win-win situation. Furthermore, I can't really do those things without the device.

"So, yes, as you've heard on this very program, I've been accused of being a charlatan. When you ask why doesn't the device work for me? You have not learned how to use it! And so, I tell you – quell your passions, subdue your frustrations, because if you don't, you won't be able to sense the tide coming in or going out if there is a storm raging inside you. You say that you have done that – yet it still does not work. Well friend, ask yourself what it is you hope to accomplish with this device? Do you *need* to be there? Or, is your mental state okay with where you are now? Were the religiously persecuted okay with staying where they were, or did they *need* America? Thus, I assure you, if you follow those instructions, it will work – God will help you."

Veronica had so many questions, but mostly she was becoming livid with Heis' behavior. She had built up a nice relationship with him over the few days she interviewed him. He was charming and sweet and they shared chemistry. Yet, she was infuriated by him right now.

"You ask, 'what can the device do anyway?' What do the shores of America offer to immigrants – they offer opportunity for growth in a realm more free than that which they previously resided in. Become a spiritual Yankee now with me – train your thoughts. Be one with God's purpose!

"I understand this may baffle people, but our modern society is no different than what I speak about. You can't see electricity, but take away electricity from our society – take electricity away from all the computers, phones, television – and those things are then useless. Yet – *with* electricity, comes all the blessings of the modern world – we all live better than kings lived hundreds of years ago. Those people in the Middle Ages would look upon us and think they were in Heaven. Do *you* think we are in Heaven? But, see, it would be Heaven to them! What is Heaven to us but some perpetually better future society? Anyway, we don't really see electricity – even lightning – the epitome of electricity – is not really what electricity looks like, but rather what happens when it creates friction, it creates light. Pure electricity is invisible to our eyes, with modernity as its byproduct – just as the energy for the spirit tech. Our modern society manipulates electricity as my spirit tech manipulates spirit or soul energy." Heis paused,

"Oh, I know what you are thinking, electricity has lightning, computers can run code, cell phones can communicate, but, what is the evidence of the soul or spirit? And I am telling you right now, here, what I am doing, this is the lightning, this is the communication. I am reading our reporter's thoughts – what I have been answering when I say, 'I know what you're thinking' – those were her questions in her head that I did not let her ask! I have been answering her questions throughout this interview without her knowing, and *attempting* not to let her interject a question, so that I may prove to her and through her testimony then prove to you, that this is real. Or, at least just prove to one person – her – that this is real." He paused again, and took off his helmet as he noticed her become uncomfortable. "My apologies, Veronica, but I hope you, if no one else, believes me." The reporter's face blushed, her eyes became wide, and she said to take a short break as they brought in another guest.

When the program returned, there was another man sitting with Heis and the reporter at the news table. He introduced himself as Dr. Brandenberg, and after a few introductions, it became clear that he was brought in to challenge Heis' claims.

Being a straightforward man, Dr. Brandenburg quickly entered into his argument, "Mr. Heis, it sounds like you would like to become that very same thing you abhor in this world, for the next world. You say you have found a new, undiscovered place for people to go; however you've shown no evidence, no one else besides you has gone there. You say that your past devices or techniques were not helpful – and I think that may be the only point we agree on. How is it you are certain that these devices *are* helpful

– if no other people are able to use them. It could be in one year you are back here with an update just as you are now, looking over old footage and casually brushing off your errors. Or, perhaps all of this is just a figment of your imagination, and you are really going nowhere. We have no evidence to support that you have read the reporter's mind except for her blushing face. Now, I've bought one of your devices for study and my colleagues at various national electrical engineering organizations have found no appreciable evidence that this device in any way manipulates electrical currents or magnetic fields, aside from its general metallic properties. You bring religion into the conversation, and antichrist, as if anyone would think so highly of your inventions – and that is the type of megalomania which is classic of people suffering from mental illness – when the only thing you and the antichrist have in common is that you both are probably incorrect in your understanding. You could read my mind right now if you wanted to, so do that."

"First off, I will do as you request," He is said, "But first, I must make one thing clear: You use the fact against me that I acknowledge my errors. You cherry pick examples of how I did not help others and the very few times in which a person was hurt – possibly as a result of my actions. But, I've helped countless people, you didn't interview any of those people. Also, who doesn't make errors? How does one even know *if* they are making errors if they are unable to stand back from themselves. Doctors are great people in their hearts – eager to help others – but the current state of healthcare often harms. It does what you accuse me of – offers a red herring solution when really the healing can be done by other means. And it is not due to anything they have consciously done, but rather in subscribing to a closed-minded system of health which often makes the physical, mental, spiritual state of the person worse. And, please don't misunderstand – modern medicine is a blessing and a boon to the human race, and I cannot wait to see how surgery and pharmacology develop in the future. But the way we practice medicine in this current era will not resemble how we practice medicine in the future. Healthcare itself is the third largest cause of injury to a person! And, it is because we acknowledge our errors and from there change, develop, grow. How do you think we were able to leave behind bloodletting and leeches? So, things are improving. Now then, back to your request; you want me to prove to you my spirit tech works by reading your mind?" Heis said.

Brandenburg replied. "Yes, go ahead, you have my permission, this could all be settled right now."

"Very well," Heis said as he put his infinity-shaped helmet back on his head. "And, begin to focus on one thing only."

"Okay," Brandenburg said and sat back comfortably in his chair, relaxed.

"Focus on one thing please," Heis said.

"I am focusing on one thought as you asked."

Heis closed his eyes and sat silently as if in meditation. Heis tried to go deeper and relax into an alpha rhythm. He pictured his brain waves slowing down. He pictured himself being receptive to Dr. Brandenburg's thoughts. Brief flashes of colors, emotions emerged in the

blackness behind his eyes. He saw Dr. Brandenburg not as
a person, but a series of intentions laid over a central
radiating light, like a projector displaying a film reel,
projecting onto a wall the thoughts that occupied his
conscious awareness. The mental sphere of Brandenburg's
conscious awareness was like a snow globe in which Heis
tried to look into. Yet, the projected image of his thoughts
were obscured. Heis took a few more deep breaths and let
out a loud sigh as he slumped deeper and deeper into his
chair at the table, putting aside his own anxious nerves and
slight agitation to calm down and gain a little more clarity.
It was as if the two were too far away and the distance itself
obscured any further detail of Brandenburg's thought. In
moving closer to him through sympathy, Heis was able to
only see the general filter of intention which essentially
amounted to the word, *Bullshit*. Again, Heis tried to
understand those things that were giving a poor connection.
Dr. Brandenburg was not an open or gregarious person,
which slightly added ambiguity. Heis tried to resolve those
impressions by becoming nearly catatonic in his physical
body. Brandenburg was a true atheist, which again
obscured his thoughts by decreasing the amount of light
that was filtered, like a very faint projection. Heis saw
small threads dangling from the atheistic thought – Dr.
Brandenburg was brought on the show as a debater because
of the well-established, powerful and widely-known
skepticism and incredulity. Heis saw that Dr.
Brandenburg's emphasis on empiricism took on a life of its
own by providing him with success, flattery, and acclaim.
Thus, the weight of his intention was taken off of the spirit
and placed on that skepticism and empiricism. That choice
in skepticism and its material fortunes then bounced back
to exert a regimenting pressure on his soul to produce

atheism. He saw that Dr. Brandenburg did not start out as an atheist, but rather an ardent supporter of truth. Heis became confused why Dr. Brandenburg continually and consistently reinforced and promoted such atheistic choices over years. It made it difficult for Heis to sympathize and connect with him, which prevented him from getting closer.

After five minutes, Heis awoke and said, "You are a difficult man to read, Dr. Brandenburg. At least part of this ability is from your end, and I didn't feel that you believed or you didn't want to make that connection with me."

"I thought you might say that," said Brandenburg.

"Well, here is what I saw. You are an atheist; you have made a career of being skeptical and promoting purely empiric knowledge. Which you are good at, but empiric data while helpful can be a snag to the intuitive voice of your soul – which is the more powerful force of the two. Anyway, as much as I could see you were thinking the word, pardon my French, *Bullshit*," Heis said.

Dr. Brandenburg gave Heis a smug smirk and said, "No, Heis, I was imaging the scene outside my office which I've looked at for the past ten years and I'm sure I could conjure a clear image in my head of it: The green lawn, the trees in fall, red orange and yellow, the leaves on the ground and the students trotting the paved walkways."

"Oh, that's a very nice scene, but I wouldn't put too much emphasis on just one session. I could show you how to be more receptive to make my job easier. We could try a few more times until we get it – it should only take another;

I don't know four sessions or so. Would you be interested in that?"

Brandenburg was taken aback by the proposal, "That was not the game we were playing. I gave you an opportunity today. I am a very busy man. I cannot commit to that."

"Oh, so that's it? You said you wanted me to read your mind. You don't want that anymore?" Heis said.

"I don't think you *can* read my mind."

"Oh, well I didn't know it was a game," Heis said at a loss for words. Brandenburg shrugged his shoulders and remained silent. "All right, well you didn't tell me all the rules. But, I'd like to be proactive and say that maybe we can achieve the correct conclusion in a different way. May I try again with someone else?" Heis asked.

"Sure, but I get to pick the person."

"So many rules. I thought games were supposed to be enjoyable. Okay, but pick at least three random people for me to choose from. The quality of the impressions is dependent upon a few physical traits of a person, the disposition of the person, and the strength or capacity of those things."

"Well, I think you're a fraud," Brandenburg said, "and you demonstrated that when you weren't able to read my mind, and I'm confident that you will not be able to read other's minds as well. So, I will play your game so that you do not have anywhere to hide your failures once this all fails."

"I wouldn't call it a game, but please go ahead," Heis said. He felt himself flustered with the impulse of antagonism toward Dr. Brandenburg who had no idea, in his excellence of worldly wisdom and material mindedness, that he had lost and belittled exactly that power which Heis had clung to for the past many years – the spirit. Heis didn't realize how far most people were from their own spirit. He felt sorry for them because he felt himself as very spiritual, yet even he was still grasping, clawing, making his way in the dark in attempting to understand the spiritual side of things. Heis, who understood in some small way that the spirit and the spiritual laws guiding the universe seemed at times completely counter-intuitive and in direct opposition to all other laws, and in that way, Heis could at times get turned around in his reasoning in how to frame his heart. So, to an atheist, spiritual matters would be all the more bewildering.

In the suppression of ego to allow God's voice to come through during this combative time, it became hard for Heis to recognize which of the multiple voices coming into his mind was stemming from God. Thoughts flashed out of antagonism, panic, fear, love, courage, confidence – *no, no, no – those are all me,* he thought – none of those, *God, God, God, it needs to be – God, I need you.* And he started saying the Lord's prayer when Dr. Brandenburg interjected, "Do you agree to this compromise?"

But, Heis did not hear exactly what was said to him, "I'm sorry, what? And, I appreciate you giving me another chance. It will be worthwhile – God willing."

"Very well," Brandenburg said. "So, I will now pick three random people from within this room, and you will choose one, two, three of them perhaps to read their minds, though personally I believe you will choose none of them, because I think I am now able to read *your* mind, Heis," Brandenburg smiled, pleased at his own joke.

"Very well," Heis said. He scanned the audience and the staff. There were people here and in the back rooms that he felt were better to participate, yet, the choice was not his. The name Cassandra came to his mind.

"I will now call them down to the set," Brandenburg said, as he looked around the room. He looked into the audience first, "Ma'am, the blonde-haired woman next to the gray-haired man…Yes, you. Is it okay if I call you down here for this experiment?"

*He had a nice way of talking to other people,* Heis thought, and some of Heis' animosity toward the man dissipated in his appreciation. The woman agreed, shuffled past the other audience members, made her way down to the news set, introduced herself as Brenda, visiting from Indiana with her family. Then, in the same way, he called down a man visiting from China.

"And…let's see, for the last person," Dr. Brandenburg said as his eyes scanned the staff. "You," he said pointing into the camera. Each person at home watching had an immediate visceral reaction that the finger pointing into the camera was meant for them and that they were the third person to have their mind read. As Heis sat patiently, he felt the upswelling tide in the hearts and minds of the thousands of people watching the program across the country. He quickly noted the phenomenon and then furrowed his brow and dispassionately pushed it aside.

Cassandra also, watching from Edwin's room, felt her heart sink believing she had been selected to become part of this. That communal mass thought then produced its natural consequence of confusion and bewilderment as each person came to the same conclusion – each viewer, watching the same broadcast could not possibly be the third person.

Brandenburg himself seemed to have picked up on this confusion as he quickly corrected himself, "Oh, no, sorry," Brandenburg said. "You, as in the cameraman, would you join us?" And, with the realization that Brandenburg was talking to the cameraman behind the camera, each person's lifted heart was then let back down to its original position and Heis smiled as that upwelling tide, briefly tumultuous, then receded back into the sea. The cameraman looked to the set director for permission, who gave him the thumbs up. The cameraman took off his headphones, dismounted from the large camera and wore a quizzical and amused look on his face as he walked to the stage and found himself on the other side of the camera.

"Sir," Dr. Brandenburg said, as the cameraman took a seat alongside the other participants, "What is your name and where are you from?"

"Patrick Flaherty," he said. "Originally from Boston but moved down to New York last summer for this job, which has been great."

"I have no doubt. Thank you for joining us," Brandenburg said, and then turned to Heis, "Okay, these are my three picks. They have all agreed, and all seem excited and willing to participate. With whom would you like to work?"

Heis spoke and said, "First, I attempt, in all ways, to be a servant to the spirit – the spirit given from God, the spirit housed within the temple of the body, the spirit which shares a connection with each and every person – if willing…" He paused to gather his thoughts and composure, "which of you is willing?"

They all, in their own peculiar idiosyncratic ways demonstrated their willingness. The man from China eagerly shook his head in agreement without saying a word. The woman from Indiana bashfully raised her hand. And the cameraman, after observing the others, gestured with eye contact and a firm head nod.

Brandenburg, sitting comfortably intrigued, looked at the scene while thumbing his beard, as if quietly watching a chess match.

"Each of you is willing, and therefore, I say so am I. God, if it is your will, allow me," Heis said, attempting to show his humility to God in front of everyone's eyes. He tried the same technique he had tried on Dr. Brandenburg, relaxing into the alpha frequency, hoping for a more congenial connection. Yet, everyone felt far away and they were even more obscured than Brandenburg's thoughts. *Why?* At Heis' current state of development, spiritual law was often paradoxical, and thus as he tried to dig deeper into his own mind and prompt a connection with one of these three people, then impressions from everyone, all over, watching the program from around the world, from in the audience, all inundated his mind like a thousand slideshows all quickly flipping through images, emotions, desires, questions, scents attempting to express themselves in his mind just as vividly as in the minds producing those thoughts and sensations. Each time he tried to pick one, to hone in upon one, he was rebuffed and the increased effort of reaching for it made it slip away all the more quickly. It was like a crowd was yelling at him – his mind became overwhelmed. Anxiety and panic started to overtake him, and he felt like he was going to accidentally ejaculate from all the sensations coming through him, and he quickly took off his headset. The images receded from his mind. He relaxed and secretively felt his pants underneath the helmet to double check nothing had happened.

"Please give me a minute," Heis said, as he stood up from the desk. He didn't want everyone to see that he was crying, so he kept his head bowed, and pardoned himself. It was clear that he was visibly shaken and the three participants now had misgivings about being party to this activity.

Veronica said, "You have five, we will return in a little bit."

He walked away from the set and tried to casually conceal his streaming tears as he looked at the ground, avoiding eye contact, while he walked through the hallway to the bathroom and found an empty stall to sit down and reconnect himself with God and his own soul. "I'm sorry, Father," he said, as hot tears ran down his face more profusely, "I did it, I'm sorry I brought things to a head and tried to reveal your face according to me. I don't know what to do. I'm sorry I tried to force the issue on my time, on my confidence and not with patience. I was not strong enough, I misstepped. I tried to parade you around as if I controlled access to you. Father, help me, please, I don't know what to do, tell me what you want me to do." He wanted to sleep, he wanted to just go to sleep right now and wake up when everyone had left, forget about this ill-conceived plan of his to reveal to the world the existence of a soul.

Typically, he had an inflow of inspiration which naturally came to him when he was humble and genuine, yet, that inspiration, that miracle in the mind telling him what to do – it was not there. He couldn't get to that far-off place he spoke of, where he wanted to lead everyone else. He felt abandoned, deserted. He was supposed to be a leader and innovator. This was the moment to convert everyone to his cause, yet he was letting God down. What was he to do aside from take his own advice and move forward – *don't give up*, a quiet little voice seemed to say to him. That was it, he recognized the little angel voices anywhere, that was the connection he sought.

Encouraged, he stepped out of the bathroom, still distraught, weak and tremulous from the high state of emotions. Regaining his composure, he walked onto the news set just as the reporter was reintroducing the segment.

"Just in time, what a coincidence," Veronica said. "Would you like to continue?"

Heis stood in front of the participants, where moments ago he nearly lost his mind. Heis said nothing and everyone stared at him in anticipation.

Dr. Brandenburg broke the silence, "So?"

"What I expected to happen, is not happening," Heis said, "but please let's keep going."

Veronica said, "Okay, great! Now what we have all been waiting for, the grand finale!"

"I was connecting with too many minds during that last attempt," Heis said, "So, I'm going to whisper something into your ears and think of that for a minute when I say 'go', then think of anything else after that minute."

Heis again put on the headset. The participants received their secret word, and it did help him filter out all the other noise, yet he couldn't accurately see their thoughts. And, after five minutes of deep focus, the images altogether slipped away from his mind and he was standing in an inert black room of his mind, his energy spent.

Heis smiled and let out a reasonable chuckle, "I'm sorry, I can't read any of these people's minds right now, and I'm not going to guess. Before you picked anyone, I did have a strong impression of the name Cassandra – but no one here is named Cassandra, so I blame you Dr. Brandenburg for not reading my mind, as you said you could, and picking someone named Cassandra," Heis said with a laugh. "Or, maybe you really can read my mind, and you intentionally chose not to pick Cassandra," Heis said again.

"Funny," Dr. Brandenburg said flatly.

"I know this wasn't part of the deal," Veronica said, "but is there a Cassandra here?" The reporter asked the room, and after 30 seconds of silence, no one came forward.

"That's okay," Heis said, "I so wanted to be the one to show the world its own soul, to show each individual person their own soul, to give them proof of it, and in a way, I still think I can. However, in this instance, for whatever reason the conditions weren't quite right to do that. Maybe they'll never be right, and each person has to find their connection with God, through their soul, on their own. Maybe it is not for me to subvert or usurp that personal journey in the way I was attempting to do here – by external means. Or, maybe something beautiful was supposed to happen here today and now. Perhaps evil, in its myriad forms, stopped from happening. But, it's okay. Thank you," And, the three participants returned to their original positions.

With this acknowledgement of his own shortcoming, addressing it head on, it took some of the sting out of this incident and relieved him of his own mental burden and embarrassment. Not wanting to dawdle, Heis once again started his enlivened speech, albeit it to a less enthusiastic audience. "You see, in America, the liberties of freedom allow both good and evil to flourish in each other's presence. Yet, we have on our currency, 'In God we trust' and, ask yourself, would you rather live anywhere else? Look at the triumph that can take place by trusting and gambling on freedom. It is not a gamble. This spirit tech generates even more freedom. And, it is your decision whether to use this spiritual technology for good or evil. My spirit tech is nothing on its own, they are tools – as any technology. They require the prime movement of spirit and soul to act upon them, and in their arrangement further focus or manipulate those forces. Like electricity with our modern society,"

As he spoke, he could tell the audience was not as captivated by his orations, by his stories and monologues, by his new knowledge that he used to attempt to break through to people to see how beautiful their lives could be. He wasn't sure how much longer they would allow him to speak – the once thunderous awe that filled the room and pushed aside any force that attempted to stop him, was now quieting, and he felt he was now loitering and pacing a disenchanted atmosphere. *Don't stop*, he thought to himself, *perhaps this is not for them, but recorded for the unborn future generations of America, perhaps Cassandra was yet unborn, and she will hear him call to her in the future.* So, he began talking to the future generations.

"Cassandra," he said, and Cassandra's eye perked up, "A society of high technology as we are ushering in right now is greatly dividing society into those that can manipulate high technology and those that cannot. The divide is not developing between the rich and the poor, but rather the intelligent and the less intelligent. Technology is similar to the fractional distillation of crude oil. The intelligent, the ambitious, the innovative rise highest, move the most in distillation, to become gasoline, the driver, while the least able to utilize technology move least in distillation, and become asphalt and driven upon. It is not that anyone is so low that they cannot contribute to society and to the human race – of course everyone has a purpose – but rather we must guard against this divide and remain united because we all have a great purpose. This is not a new phenomenon – I am saying that this phenomenon is exponentially increasing as technology is exponentially increasing. Anyone who says that the divide is not there, or it is because of lack of resources, really doesn't know much and is probably one of those asphalt people of society. To blame it on a lack of resources is really only a minor argument, and all the more reason to allow greater movement in society. We all long to be around like-minded people. What do we do when a child is more intelligent than most of his class, we move him to a smarter class – the same with a child who struggles in class, move them to a different class. It is not an insult or a compliment, but nature. I want to do the same thing for all of society, and this technology will, in small steps, allow that same consideration we give to children. As alchemy gave way to chemistry and astrology to astronomy, phrenology to neuroscience, I want the same thing for religion to give way to spirituality. Yes, it will cause a further divide, but paradoxically also enjoyed by everyone – meaning the divisions will be self-chosen. So, this is my long-winded way of saying that because I can manipulate this new technology and you cannot, there now establishes that divide, similar to that divide created by higher technology now existing within America. Because I can manipulate this spirit technology, I could therefore be your king and take that position above you by force and take it away from all those billionaires and world leaders. In a way I am greater, or rather, wield greater power than they, than you. But, just as Father wants to hand you the keys to the kingdom, I also want to have brothers and sisters here with me. I don't want to be a king. I want to be your helper, your friend."

As Heis took a moment to think and take a drink of water, Brandenburg quickly made a comment, "I'm sorry, are you really still talking so fervently about the certainty of your own power and yet you've barely acknowledged that you said you could read my mind, the mind of three other people, and you weren't able to? I don't think we need another thirty-minute dissertation on every random thing you think about. I'm not worried about you becoming a king."

Heis put down the glass of water, "There are some things I want to say to your children. And, I acknowledged my shortcomings, what do you want me to do, flagellate myself? Or, stop innovating and condemn myself to the depths of Hell?"

Veronica interjected, "No, no, it's okay. Please go on."

So, Heis endured the mounting skepticism he sensed in the audience and abroad. Some people got up to leave the audience, some turned off the broadcast on their monitors. Heis continued, "The rocks, the moss, animals, everything has some degree of those things I now study and manipulate, and more primitive cultures, in their ignorance to ascribe everything to a supernatural source, were more apt to pick up on this, but the presence, behavior and direction of this substance into a craftable, palpable force always took patience, and results were seemingly inconsistent – as I've just shown – not only from person to person, but even by the same person. But, even still, I'm surprised it has taken so long to develop this technology. It's almost as if modern society is making the exact opposite error that the ancients made. One group errs by ascribing to all things the supernatural, while we err equally by denying it. What I am saying is that in the meekness of the ancient human race – logic, reason, innovation were the difficult path to study and while faith and the mindfulness of the intercession of spiritual phenomena were more effortless, and now, as technology is advancing at an increasing rate, and we all live better than kings – the roles have reversed and the empirical evidence taking precedence and comforting us while the spiritual now beguiles and frustrates us. The freedom of the spiritual and its downward flow from the mountains of God does not follow the riverbeds, but rather its motion remains with God, and its presence and culmination into a craftable, palpable substance, for me at least, as you could see moments ago, are not determined by man, but by God. The spirit's results – the products of the spirit, descending from beyond infinity are, to me, uninterpretable at times, and stressful, and I want to just watch TV rather than listen to and act upon impulses from the inner environment. With me, and as I presume with others, spiritual study, acting paradoxically, could not be grabbed with only rigor and intelligence, but bequeathed in patience and humility. But I have captured it, in most cases at least.

"All force in the universe is a different expression of one force. This force is much finer than electricity and magnetism and we only discovered those three hundred years ago. This force almost defies control and, by my own misunderstandings and short-comings, seems to act in opposition to all other laws and it's almost like a paradoxical behavior because you must operate according to the promptings of your own soul rather than material promptings of Earth, to look past all other forces to harness, or rather be harnessed by, that will of the Father God, rather than your own in order to harness it. You see, it is even hard to explain. But, as you grow in wisdom you see that your own promptings ARE the promptings of God and the voice in you – once subdued in patience, slowly becomes the voice of God – and you are not you anymore but more and more Him and you can't say I anymore, but He/I and Him/me. And, based on the poor response that I've seen people get from this device, and I also sometimes get, it seems like as a people we don't understand that paradox fully. That is the same thing I am trying to tell you about freedom. The spirit may not be caged. You have to let others act according to their own internal sense. The more heavily you try to direct them the harder they resist. It is a spiritual principle that acts paradoxically. That freedom is this technology, this fluid, this light. It, in a way, offers understanding and appreciation of those freeing forces. One would have to come to terms with those *unsavory* aspects of their personality that impel them in a certain direction.

"So, in those old days, people would pick up on this force, and then understand it incorrectly and become frustrated with the dedicated study of this subject to the point of doubting whether or not something was even there – or it takes a vast quantity of discipline to harness it that only a few have been able to do so in a consistent way. But I have nearly understood it, and it is a new world of understanding promising to both overturn and stabilize everything! But, I can't do it alone. The rocks, the plants, animals and the earth are continually refining crude force – like crude oil, into a refined force for us, people, to harness. The Earth wants to be abundant and give to us all our needs so that we too may go through that refining process along with the Earth and sing heavenly songs. There is always something new in development. The physical, mental, emotional, spiritual aspects of life are continually refined in all directions. I can't tell you, I can't describe to you," Heis tried to speak quickly to finish the sentence as his voice quivered and he became choked up attempting to relay, through evocative intonations the beauty of the universe as seen through the spiritual lens. He took a moment to compose himself.

Dr. Brandenburg interjected, "Okay, I have no idea what you are talking about, I'm sorry I have tried to be respectful and patient, but I was brought on this news segment for a specific purpose. I feel I have accomplished that purpose – so I don't know what we are still talking about anymore. So, in order to put the final nail in this coffin, and then I can leave, so you can continue your rant without my interrupting you, I will ask one more question." Brandenburg turned from Heis to the reporter, "Miss Stensi, do you think he read your mind? As he claimed just before."

Her eyebrows raised at the unexpected question, "Oh," she said, pausing a moment to reflect, "I would say yes, I do. Or, rather, let me say that when he was talking earlier, before he said he was reading my mind, and when he was talking quickly and not allowing me to get a word in – I was thinking those exact questions as he answered them, and I even noted to myself in the moment how great he was at anticipating my questions and filling in areas he did not fully explain."

"Okay, well that is still not proof. So, therefore, the final nail in the coffin will be…Heis, please read her mind right now."

Heis did not immediately answer, as he reflected on the request, "Isn't that funny? Once again, the freedom, the power, the creativity of the spirit of God, has my head spinning every which way when really, I just need to trust in Him. So, I would say that you already have her answer, and therefore you have your answer, and therefore my answer is 'not at this time' and, things as they are, is the way they will stand for this recording. I don't want to keep you, Dr. Brandenburg. That is all for now," Heis stood up, thanked everyone for being here with him, thanked the audience and the staff and said, "Same time next week? I didn't get into half of the things I wanted to."

"You didn't?" The reporter said, baffled, "But you talked for an hour."

"I did? It felt like a minute," Heis said, and walked out the door, leaving Brandenburg and the reporter alone.

"Well, that was certainly an unexpected twist at the end there, giving us all a lot to think about, and we will certainly be inviting Mr. Heis back next week to continue his interesting thoughts – and if you'd like to join us Dr. Brandenburg you will certainly be welcomed back also," the reporter said.

"I won't be here next week, I think I have to get a few root canals that day," Brandenburg said as the program faded out.

As the program ended, Edwin turned to Cassandra and said, "That man, Heis. He is very smart and idealistic, but he's going about this whole thing in a very naive manner. Everyone, in finding their purpose and pursuing their purpose, holds the whole fate of the world in their hands – You, him, your own children. For him, in relentlessly pursuing his purpose combined with his own high degree of spiritual and intellectual prowess has become a juggernaut on Earth. Yet, he is unbalanced. Although he gives off an easy and affable air, he is also mentally strained and attempting…" Edwin trailed off, and gestured as if holding something and attempting to balance some great weight and then dropping it. "Every man falters. That persistent mental strain can distort reality, at which point the mental powers invert and become unreasonable, at which point evil appears to help carry the load, and in a way subvert the magnificent ends, the blooming flowers of his life and use them to their ends. He needs a woman like you, so when he falters you keep him on the right path, but there are no other women like you," Edwin stared off again,

*"There are deeper laws*
*Than effects and cause*

"Every man needs a woman like you, the whole world needs women like you, and you could heal the whole world. But, even if you were cloned, it wouldn't be you. So, therefore he needs you, that's why he mentioned you by name. New York is tough, but you should get down there next week. That's it for today."

Cassandra was taken aback by his words, *was he telling me to get together with Heis?* She wanted to ask more questions, but he seemed very tired and was drifting off to sleep, so she said goodbye for the day.

\*\*\*

The next day Marie and Cassandra talked on the phone early in the morning before the start of the day. They spoke about Edwin, Peter, and the interview and agreed to see the next showing of Armory News in person. Cassandra also needed help interpreting these dreams and visions she had been having. After explaining the dreams, Marie read from a book on dream interpretation, "While in waking life our environment generates thoughts and ideas, yet in dreams it's reversed. Ideas generate the environment, objects, events. So, I guess it's saying what idea might you associate with something in the dream. Um, okay next part: Equally important are a few other things. First ask yourself a few questions: What were your feelings during the dream – was it generally positive, negative? Were you worried, happy, confused, calm?"

"Well the first dream of the cloud I was scared, worried, panicking, maybe slightly confused and overwhelmed at first," Cassandra said, "Then with this last dream I was very curious and interested in what was being shown to me, but also a little shocked by how he was showing it to me like when he took his brain out of his skull."

Marie continued reading, "Okay, not only are the events and feelings of the dream important, but the thoughts you had to yourself during the dream."

"Okay," Cassie said, thinking to herself, "Well with the first one I was thinking I had to hide and then when I was hiding I was thinking, *he's going to find me.*"

"Next," Marie said, "Pretend everything you see in the dream is an extension of yourself. Okay, I think they mean, all those different people and events, they actually represent something about yourself – rather than the literal person/item/event being shown to you. Like, if you see Mom, she was a gentle person, so in the dream that might represent your gentler side, or if you see me maybe it is your beautiful side," Marie said with a laugh.

"Marie, we are twins!" Cassandra said.

"Oh, well, lucky for you," Marie said, and the two continued chatting before starting their day.

# 6 – Heis

*I'm not the best at anything*
*But I'm up for any challenge*
*Really not too much skill*
*I rely more on faith and will*

*Everyday'll be a little hard*
*Everyday'll get a little hot*
*I'm not*
*Afraid to start*

Heis had fasted for a few days leading into the interview to help get his mind into an appropriate degree of humility as he was presenting his ideas to the public. But he was conflicted about his behavior during the interview and felt he may have been too harsh at times.

It's difficult to translate spiritual concepts into words and convey that to others as the myriad of peculiarities and ostensibly conflicting conclusions and details are often used in the same breath to describe such spiritual concepts. At his level of development, the infinite and finite were difficult to reconcile, and he saw himself still as someone that was mired in the mud and quicksand of the finite world attempting to stretch out his hand toward the infinite spirit and comprehend the spiritual sphere. Yet, only groping and clasping in the dark with the tips of his fingers little twigs and branches not sturdy enough to pull him out of the mud themselves but, if he were just patient, and not grab the little tendrils too forcefully then he could use those small fragile spiritual truths to lower down the sturdier branches of spiritual enlightenment and, with a muddy, torn, tremulous hand, take hold of those sturdier branches to pull himself up from the mire and walk among the infinite forest of spiritual laws.

Jesus did it; perfectly translating the infinite into the simple finite sentences to extend to everyone sturdy branches to pull themselves out of the mud that are both practical and infinite. The words he said were branches, and the simple act of attempting to emulate his demeanor, not the instructive words per se, to emphasize acts rather than facts, was itself a branch one could hold on to.

He felt the spirit welling up inside of himself and wanted to take the opportunity to visit the outer world and capitalize on this humble energy as a way to trek deeper into that territory.

He put on his helmet and hopped into a sensory deprivation tank that was injected with slightly more oxygen; 23 percent compared to the normal atmospheric 21 percent. He built the capsule himself to look like a small space capsule – but it was still essentially just a bathtub. He laid back into the water of saline solution that mimicked the amniotic fluid of the womb, warmed by a heating module to keep it at 98.6 degrees with a small amount of white noise slowly cycling through the chromatic scale to filter out the outside world. He relaxed into the bath, his head held out of the water with a small pillow that was kept cooler with the feet slightly warmer, and he slowly faded away from today and into the next world through a transition of a vast featureless gray sea as far as he could see. He started in an area of very dark gray that mimicked the darkness of the sensory deprivation tank, and he followed a light to lighter and lighter gray areas. There was formless movement present in those darker strata, which he could not discern if it was alive or not or what it looked like. Years ago, when he first started these excursions, he could have spent time exploring those places, but the impulses of his heart told him to rise higher; that he was not yet at his stratum. Up through the layers until, akin to the visual aura of a migrainous striking white light filled his mental vision and then slowly receded and he was now in a place similar to Earth – with grass, trees, buildings – but it was radiant, invigorating, brimming with sensations. He had about an hour before the bath alarm would sound. An hour was no time at all when he could simply spend the whole time looking at a fallen branch or the bark of a tree, connecting with it, understanding and appreciating how there were whole worlds existing within. But his heart compelled him to move on to some unknown destination in mind.

There were people there, going about their business similar to the regular world, but to describe it as the same hustle and bustle of life on Earth would do it a disservice.

He noticed a shimmering building in the distance that radiated and pulsed in the same rhythm of the pulse he felt in his face. He could almost hear someone talking to him and he took a moment to consider what he was hearing with his spiritual ears. It was a deep voice, there was the cadence of language, it seemed to be some kind of explanation in casual conversation, yet he discerned no words and understood nothing. He stopped someone on the street to ask them a question.

Communication in that sphere was telepathic and faster. And, with a flash, the particulars of the background information that led Heis to this moment was conveyed to the man, who in a slightly concerned tone signaled for his child to walk on with her mother and that he would catch up with them. The man on the street bowed his head in deep reverence and impressed upon Heis that he should attempt to resolve that unknown voice he was hearing, or rather, that is what he would do. Now, the reason for the interaction satisfied, their two attentions drifted from one another, but with a quick last word Heis asked where he was.

"The sixth sphere of star Thuban" the impression came back. And the man smiled and walked on.

Heis moved through the town attempting to clarify the words he heard, walking in one direction and then the other, cognizant of his time limit. Then, he saw the top of a beautiful building which acted as the civic center for the town with a large steeple at the top. The bell of the tower rang and seemed to resonate in his heart and the subtle vibrations conveyed to his sight made the building appear to shimmer and reflect more of the sunlight.

"That must be the place," he said to himself, and walked toward the civic center.

He soon arrived and walked up the stone steps, looking up to see the bell tower that rang earlier sitting atop a large, highly detailed, baroque stone building that had a lower simple and sleek brutalist glass edifice on the bottom five stories. The whole building was shaped like a cathedral in that it had two large stone towers flanking the main high-rise.

He went in, guided by his intuition, walking up to the top floor with a single room. His anticipation mounting and almost now running in excitement toward his destination. Heis opened the door and stepped into the room. A large man, thick and tall, with thick white hair and white beard, appearing to be in his early sixties yet very spry and youthful demeanor stood up as if expecting Heis. He looked exactly how he imagined God would look. Heis became startled by the imposing image of the man and reflexively asked, "Who are you?"

"God," he said.

Heis fell to his face to worship and bow down before God. His face became pale, he became tremulous, all the years of torment, doubt, lack of faith, surviving on little comfort all in the name of drawing others to this place he now stands in the presence of God.

"What is the purpose of your visit here?" God asked. Heis was still in a bowed position supplicated on the floor, his mind still disoriented. He didn't know whether to look up, stand up, or begin speaking while his forehead was still touching the floor.

"Yes?" God prompted again.

"You know my heart, Father. What is it that I do?" Heis said through that near instant communication.

"I know your heart, but as a way for you to better comprehend things in your own mind, please express your questions to me."

"Well, I want to help people with their own faith and bring them, willingly closer to you, if I can just get them over this little hill of doubt and frustration that everyone in the world seems to run into. And even though it is a small hill, because people don't know where this little hill crests – they think the hill is a mountain. I'm trying everything, for years I've developed different approaches, and so now my latest approach – this device that goes on the head, again it's the same recalcitrant skepticism, doubt and unwillingness with which all my other approaches have been met."

God spoke, His voice clear in Heis' mind. "All will become one in the end – like globules of oil floating in water – combined, so will your soul go back to me, its original home. You are a piece of me, analyzing itself, and in a sense that is how the universe was created when I made all spirits when the material universe was also created. As the universe ages, entropy takes its course, and in the great eons to come when stars are undone and all mass and energy is evenly distributed and homogenized will be the same time all globules will have returned to me."

Heis was not sure if God had heard him correctly, as he was not sure how this all answered his question.

God continued, "People must make up their own minds. But, your device could have a positive effect on the souls of Earth and possibly, eventually, greater than Earth and thereby make this long arc of the universe more enjoyable to souls. So, I say to you, there is a time for every season – to be forceful and a time to be receptive. You have thus far been docile, unassuming and receptive. Yet now, there was a change in your heart that allows me to say things to you. So, let me show you something."

God put into Heis' mind the imagery of a race of protohuman spirits who were given everything, and they did not thrive because they did not know how to do things for themselves. They also turned into ugly creatures and took advantage of other lower life forms to do everything for them.

"You see, I also took your same approach with these first protospirits, and it did them no good. So, you have been encouraged to be more forceful with people. There is an inflexion point beyond which, if your effort is not manifested more fully in the lives of people, then the people of Earth may become like those protohumans. Now it is time to reap, the wheat is ripe, and the time is approaching when the fruit will rot. The souls don't know which way to go, they don't feel my love, it would be better if they were to use your device. You have your orders yet keep this conversation to yourself."

The large bell from the tower rang and Heis instantly awoke in the sensory deprivation tank to the sound of his alarm.

# 7 – Father

*With every doubt*
*I think about*
*The signs from above*
*Push toward love*

The next time Cassandra visited Edwin, Edwin was a different man, as if Cassandra had passed some unknown test that validated who she was. He was elated to see her, yet she was still ill at ease toward him. He already had the Cuban sandwiches ready to go and handed one to her.

To Edwin, the Cuban became a merry routine for them and seemed to take on a life of its own. Edwin asked, "So, so what's your Cuban – like what would you be happy doing with your life if you could only afford one Cuban sandwich a day, regardless of what you were doing?"

"Edwin, what was all that about me poisoning you the other day?" she asked.

"Oh," he said with a mouthful. "I thought you were going to kill me," he said.

"Kill you? Why?"

"Not you," he said, doing the same over-the-hand gesture. "Someone over you or using you. But that is only half of it."

"And so, on our first visit, did you think I was going to harm you when I went to undo your leg bandage for the first time?" she asked.

"Yes, I did."

"And, then you reached under the blanket where you were hiding the scissors, which you eventually used to puncture the IV bags on the second visit," she said.

"Ah, you see more than you show! Yes, I did."

"So, if you thought I was going to harm you, then why did you refuse to see the other nurse and allow me to see you," she asked.

"Because of who you are," he said. "You are caring, loving, kind, beautiful; but it's more than that. You're smart, resolute, creative, talented, faithful; but it's more than that. You are…" he paused.

"I am?" she asked.

"God's first angel," he said.

"What do you mean?"

"The best angel," he said.

"Edwin, I am not an angel."

"Don't be so negative. You are the first angel. The world has not yet been told how souls are created. But, I know. I know you were created first. The best."

"I think you are very knowledgeable, Edwin. But, how could I be? I have bad thoughts. My sister Marie would be the first, she doesn't have bad thoughts," she said.

"Everyone has bad thoughts, but God needs someone with grit, a little edge, in order to give them the necessary tools to accomplish great heavenly works," Edwin said.

Cassandra didn't answer. *Why am I playing along with this? This was it,* Cassandra thought. *I said if one more thing happened then I would ask for a transfer and this was it.*

"Cassandra, I love you," he said. Cassandra instantly thought, *Oh, no, not again. Another patient hitting on me. Can't you see the wedding ring? This was definitely the final straw.* She just had to get through today, make sure he was okay, and then she wouldn't have to see him again.

"Oh, okay, thank you, I love you too." She tried to minimize and move past the comment.

"No, I'm *in* love with you," he said.

Cassandra thought to herself a moment; *can't you see I'm married with three kids; they need a father.* She said, "I'm flattered, but you don't even know me."

"I know you. In Heaven, we are already married in a way, whether that happens on Earth is up to you, Father and circumstance, and look, here we are! Father has done his part. I saw you when you were eighteen years old before you closed yourself off to God, then I saw you again at thirty-two when you opened yourself back up. God found you again and therefore I did too. That's why I didn't want the other nurse. Finally, we had one more chance, this chance, Thank God and circumstance, and now it's your choice, you see, it's always been your choice – that's why I tried to say, 'God hears you'. Don't you believe God hears you?"

"I do, but…" She struggled to find the words, "I didn't think it was like that. I'm not anything special."

"Nobody is special, all are instruments of God."

"But, then, so why me?"

"Because you're the first angel! Your lineage going back to David. Hopes and dreams of ancestors imprinted on DNA, all down the line. Things are coming to a head, now is the time for some to be chosen." He made a curvilinear motion with his hand. "The next ten years will decide if the world is going to end or not. Your youngest son, he sees objects as blue sometimes, this is his alien side. Tell him not to be afraid of it and to develop it. It could turn into something very special for him one day," he said.

"How could you know that?" Cassandra asked because her son had just told her yesterday that he saw random items as being blue out of the corner of his eye and then when he turned to look at them, they turned back to their normal color.

As she was preoccupied by her thoughts a large glob of oil had dripped onto her new pants.

"Oh no," she said as she started to dab the oil spot with a napkin. Edwin flattened his hand and moved his wrist in a small brief sweeping motion. When Cassandra looked down and pulled the napkin away, the oil spot was gone.

"How did you…did you do that?" Cassandra asked.

Edwin was frustrated by the question and shook his head. Then his demeanor changed. He stood up from his bed now with full use of his entire body. He stood up without saying a word. There was a change in his deportment. He took on a regal, majestic, self-possessed, and humble air as if the bandages were his kingly robe – his pale skin gathering up all the sunlight filling the room and perfectly reflecting it as the morning sun pulsated into her eyes prompting her into a faint hallucination. Edwin did not look like himself, previously his hair was combed back and thinning, but now he had a full head of wavy black hair combed back in the Spanish style.

"Edwin?" she paused, "Are you Edwin?"

"I AM," he said.

"I am who?" she asked.

"I *AM*" the voice spoke in a deep resounding tone, "I would like you to call me Father."

Cassandra instantly went to her knees, bursting into tears. She couldn't believe it was true. Father God was standing in front of her.

"Please stand," he said and Cassandra, still in tears, stood to face him. He said, "The name God does not have as intimate a feeling as the name Father. You are my child, my daughter, my first angel, and the world contains all my children."

Cassandra asked if she could hug him, to which he responded by reaching out his arms toward her. She remembered, it was the same feeling of her heart lifting that night she gave all of her troubles to him and trusted him. Her knees felt weak and she leaned on him more heavily. Her arms shaking, her tears poured out, christened and saturated his bandages.

After they hugged, Father told her all about her life. He saw her in her early career when she blamed herself for being too slow to call a rapid response for a man who had a pulmonary embolism while in the hospital. That had always weighed on her mind, and she was forgiven. "It's just that evil is in the world," he said. He told her about a stray dog in her neighborhood which she was always nice to. He told her about Edwin approaching her when she was eighteen. Which brought Father back to the present quandary and her helping to save the world.

"What can I do?" she asked.

"The union of Cassandra and Edwin would do it," Father said.

"But what about Peter?" she asked and she instantly remembered her prayers to God when she decided to bring God back into her life, apologizing for marrying a man who did not have God in his heart.

"It is your choice, it has always been your choice," Father said. "You would need to be divorced from Peter." And there was a long pause. "Do you want to continue?" Father asked.

"Yes," she said, and Edwin lowered himself back into bed.

After that five-minute conversation, she was ecstatic. She couldn't imagine she had just spoken with God – or rather Father. She had to change her vocabulary. She had to tell Marie. She had to tell everyone. Cassandra, her heart aflutter, hugged Edwin. Edwin, groaning as he lowered himself back onto the bed, hadn't remembered any of the conversation that had just taken place.

"Was Father just here?" he asked. Cassandra only nodded her head because she was still in tears and couldn't speak. Edwin said, "You see, I kind of get visions like you, but mine are a little different."

***

Everything was different after that. She didn't know how to contain herself. She wanted to love the world as God loved her. God's love permeated deep into her unconscious mind and the nervous psychomotor agitation of her leg bouncing up and down as she sat was gone, and in a way, she was both excited yet calmed. She didn't want to leave, but they both agreed it was okay and they would have plenty of time together in the future.

Cassandra felt in her heart that in saying "yes" to Father, she took one step closer to Him and as such, was brought one step closer into the throne room of the Lord. While on her drive home, she had to pull over, her heart and stomach were overwhelmed from a spiritual ecstasy and her thoughts became flooded. During these past ten years she thought she was waiting for Father, but Father was really waiting for her. He was working for her as he works for everyone, even when she did not see Him doing it. Father will do His part, yet you have a part to play. It is a relationship. God wants us to be bold, and she now felt herself being strengthened and emboldened.

She returned to her house, charged with the overflowing love she felt from Father. She wanted to share with everyone as a way for them to all feel closer to Father and wipe away the cobwebs of negativity accumulated from time spent on Earth. She did not yet want to tell them about what had happened and what was happening, but she wanted to *show* them and give them that same feeling of comfort and excitement.

That evening she expressed that desire simply in a bright happy demeanor, talking openly about Father, sitting with her children as they played video games, stroking their hair; they ordered out to celebrate Wednesday. The food tasted better, their company was joyous, they all played board games and seemed to let down their own pensiveness and merrily laughed and did what came to their minds. Peter seemed to relax and smile. *This is what life could be like all the time if we were closer to Father.*

When everything was packed up and the children retired for the evening, Peter and Cassandra were alone. Peter said, "Cass, I'm sorry for everything, I want us to be a better family."

"Is there something stopping us from doing that?" Cassandra asked.

"No, you know how it is," Peter said.

"I know," she wanted to tell him everything, "All things are possible with Father, just let Him into your heart, search for Him, express His love for you to the world and you'll see Him in the world."

He didn't say anything but took her hand and kissed her and tried to lead her up the stairs.

"So," she said, "I mean all of this yelling at the children, making negative remarks to them, trying to sue everyone? What is that about? I know you're still drawing up those court papers."

His shoulders dropped and he let her go from his hand.

"C'mon those kids need a little discipline and I'm just having fun with those remarks, and with the lawsuits isn't it our responsibility to make sure that doesn't happen again?"

"But you do those things out of anger and greed. I mean what are you so angry and greedy about? Look at everything we have," she said. "Those things didn't happen to you, and I want to just let it go."

Peter pressed his lips together and looked off, "Marriage has been difficult for me, and I admit I didn't want to be married, and I had dreams of killing you, which obviously I wouldn't do. But, I did have those dreams."

Peter had mentioned these things earlier in their marriage, and they should have ended things at that point because these were the exact same words he spoke years ago – that he had been living with this entire time. Not one thing she changed about herself, or their situation changed his mind one iota when she felt she was working so hard.

He didn't want this life, yet for some reason he couldn't change it. Here was a man so intelligent and capable but lacking the ability to adapt.

"Let Father into your life, Pete. There is nothing else that will help," she said. "I've finally let Father into my life and look at tonight, how it has changed things, tonight was not an accident. Every night could be like this."

"Okay," he said. They turned off the last remaining lights downstairs and Peter waited for her at the bottom of the stairs to walk up together.

Cassandra went over to him and said, "Goodnight, Peter," and hugged him goodnight.

"What? After all that you're not coming up?"

"No," she said and happily took up her bed on the downstairs couch as usual, and he went upstairs alone.

The next day, she woke up early. With Father in your heart, you have a self-assured vantage point from which you are able to see emotions more as a weather pattern outside of your mentation rather than as being part of you. As such, she felt great sorrow for Peter and their situation, with a mix of comfort, warmth and excitement from her time with Father. She prepared a meal for everyone as a way to encourage that warmth in her family, and then skipped out the door as Peter was coming down the stairs, "Aren't you just taking calls from home today?"

"Yes, I'm just running some errands, do you need anything? Also, I made breakfast for everyone."

"No," he said and continued on to the kitchen.

Cassandra went to see Edwin as she planned to field calls from his room today. She wanted to always be with Father.

When she arrived at Edwin's room and walked in, Edwin began to speak without saying hello, "My entire life, I've been looking for you. I didn't quite know what you looked like, because I thought it was you when you were eighteen, but then when you closed yourself off, I thought 'oh, it must not be her.' But I knew that if I continued to hold the feeling of that person in my mind, I knew I would be drawn to her by gravity, by electricity, by the stars, by every possible mechanism conceivable in the universe would fall under my employ and conspire to bring us together. I tried to hasten and to force prophecies and promises sometimes. I knew once I held that person in my arms, then I would know in my heart that which I held in my mind. I held you. Father held you and the journey of three thousand years is complete and God whispers to me from my heart that he sees you now, and last night starlight traveled eight hundred light years just to kiss your cheeks as you slept and the sun rose today just to warm you. I felt so strongly about you, I thought I was imagining you when you walked through the door; almost willing you into existence, because I would see you in the sunrise, the red hair, the transcendent ethereal beauty, the curves of the pale clouds. Your radiant light grows the plants, warms those around you, your light helps others to see Heaven. You heal and electrify, disperse the darkness. You think I'm talking metaphorically, but soon you will see I am not. You are a light closer than death. Two pigeons walking down the street together perched right outside to see this. The eyes of Heaven are upon the Earth and upon us.

"I tried to say I love you that first day we met, caressing and stroking your hair with my breath. Could you hear it, could you feel it in the little red tendrils swaying in the air current? God makes such lovely creatures, whose beauty can't be caught. You are more beautiful than worlds and more heavenly than stars, but all I have are words and all I have are flowers," He handed her a piece of paper with a simple drawing of a tulip and smiled. "Loving you is not an obligation or a job; it's a desire and a privilege."

"Wow, that was beautiful, and I think the kids call that love bombing," Cassandra said.

"Love bombing?" Edwin said, "Yeah, I guess that *would* be a better use for bombs."

"And I look forward very much to this journey we are starting together with Father," she said. "Well, what now? Can I get you anything?"

"Can you drive me to the ocean? I'm almost done healing and I need this little bit to get me over the finish line," he said.

"Sure, right now?"

"Yes," he said as he stood up, and Cassandra thought it was Father coming through Edwin again. But, Edwin then slammed the hard cast around his right arm against the bed frame and then wiggled it off his arm. He then slipped off the loose bandages until he was standing just in his underwear. His abdomen came to a ridge down the center. He was more covered in wounds than in skin. He noticed her shocked expression over the damage to his body. "I heal quickly, don't worry."

After he dressed, she helped him down the stairs and into the passenger seat of the car. They stopped for Cubans. As they drove, Edwin started talking, "Y'know, we are the most primitive species, but there is a special place for us. We have to unlock dimensional travel and warp engines because we're not gonna get very far like this."

He then abruptly stopped talking, turned his head, face blank, eyes wide and he looked at her oddly and looked around the car with the curiosity of a child.

"Edwin?" Cassandra asked.

"Ed?...win?" he said, in an even more confused tone.

"Hello?" She replied.

"Hello!" Edwin said in an excited tone.

"Father?" Cassandra replied in an excited tone. But Edwin then fell asleep as she continued to drive.

They pulled up to the shore, Cassandra woke Edwin.

"Do you remember any of that before you fell asleep?" she asked, "You were acting differently and I asked if it was Father, but then you fell asleep."

"Yeah, I was talking about dimensional travel, because yeah, hand me one of those napkins, I just want to write this down," he said and began to scribble symbols that were foreign to Cassandra. "Where is a safe place to keep this?" and Cassandra pointed to the middle cubby between their two seats, "Okay, ready to go?"

They walked out onto the dock to sit for lunch. There were many boats docked there, their flat decks and pointed masts all forming a clumsy phalanx pointed toward the sky.

"I was born in New York City to two Puerto Rican parents, yet I came out with blue eyes and blonde hair, and my mother joked that I was immaculately conceived, although my father always maintained that they were sexually active, thereby implying that was not the case. And my mother would say, 'I know, I was there, but that boy doesn't look like either one of us." Since I grew up in the city, I became inspired by the bridges, and I wanted to be an engineer and build large bridges – y'know to connect people. However, my first year in college I was having fun, so I didn't get good grades and therefore I dropped out and ended up in the military hoping to help build bridges that way. I showed a knack for that type of work, and I was always so 'lucky' on missions to the point that I felt I was truly protected by Father. I knew because the one mission I didn't take lead, then the point man, a young man like myself at the time was wounded and died in a painful way. So, because of that protection and my ability, I felt it was my responsibility to protect others and therefore I took the most difficult positions in the most difficult missions and had the most success. Yet how could I take any pride in them when it all came from God? I actually did end up being shot during my second tour, I didn't heal as quickly during that time. While recovering, I was planning to get back out there and finish my second tour, yet an Irish Chaplin, after learning my history said, 'You've done enough, you can get back to your life,' Which I intended to do, yet it was not that easy for the higher ranking officers to let me go. At that point I was offered a different kind of military path – which would allow me to both have a life and remain in small military operations, which, at that point, I felt it was my God-given duty to perform. I traveled all over the world, a lot of assignments in Central and South America as well as Africa. Some pockets of Peru are the worst in the world as they have outside influence, meaning the people and population are nice but influence outside the world has collected in that area and there are very evil people down there. That sums up this life and brings us to today. Now, with you here, life is changing and my responsibilities are changing, ever upward. I will go more into consulting for operations, to give us time to be with one another."

Cassandra was still uneasy about her future between Edwin and Peter. It was all happening quickly. Yet she kept it to herself, "Wow, I had no idea. So, these injuries weren't from you in a car accident?"

"Well, I was hit by a car, but it wasn't an accident," he laughed. "Faith is best when actively expressed because in that comes the visible fruits of faith, your reward for trying and therefore need not be blind. God is everywhere, in everything, so to have *faith* in him should then prompt you to act on that faith. I like the term active faith; do those things your mind prompts you to do. I am telling that to you specifically. Active faith has led me to be a level six in the government hierarchy – even some presidents are not that level. They call me the soldier of death."

They continued talking, and after they ate their meal, a large wave seemed to spring up from nowhere and moved toward them, shaking all the boats, the masts swaying in a raucous tumult like an angry mob. After the wave settled against the bank, there were other strange movements from the boats and one by one down a line of boats seemed to be shaken by some large entity underneath the water moving toward them. They both stood up immediately, Edwin pulled Cassandra behind him, and they backed away from the dock and stepped back onto land. "That's enough for today, thank you for bringing me," he said as they got back into Cassandra's car.

On their drive home, Edwin continued talking about various topics. "This monetary system shouldn't exist, and we should just do things for each other. Of course, I am always a good tipper to reward those hard workers. Actually, one time, I gave my last forty dollars to a new

Ecuadorian immigrant in New Brunswick. She had a young child and had to get to social services and had no way to get there and they were going to be closing soon. So, I gave her the money to get a car service because I knew I'd be all right."

"Wait, but don't you get a salary from the government?" Cassandra asked.

"No, I like to put my life at stake just for fun," he said with laughter. "But, no I don't take a salary from them. I do it for free because they put money into your pocket as a way to get you into their pocket. Like a way to have you owe them something. Because sometimes the government doesn't have the best intentions when ordering someone to be killed, yet they will coerce someone like me to just 'do it anyway' because they will say, 'Well, we gave you all that money, now you owe us something,' and that's how the cycle starts. But, since I don't take money, then I can be free to choose my own assignments for God and go about it in my own way."

"So, you don't get anything from these missions?"

"Peace of mind, I guess. Like I said about active faith, it's my duty to do this. God protects me, the government enables me. There isn't much room for money in that cycle if I want to stay true to God. The government *wants* to give me money and has money in some secret account that I have access to, but I have never looked at it or touched it."

"But, aren't you afraid of being killed?" Cassandra asked.

"I'm protected, no," Edwin said. "Now that doesn't mean I can just waltz in somewhere and tell the bad guy, 'Okay, c'mon you're coming with me, our Father said so' and expect everything to be okay. No. It's more like as long as I follow what my mind is telling me, then I am protected. God expects me to follow His instructions, and I have faith that God will protect me. One of my early missions I was hit, and I was down and, I don't know, a leopard or some big cat came out of nowhere and scared the men away. And, actually one of my past lives in Ireland my plane was struck down, and I rammed it into the enemy ship. And, I could have ditched it and been saved, but I was young and hadn't realized my role, and in that moment, I saw my opportunity to destroy the ship."

"Past lives? What do you mean?" she asked.

"Oh, yeah, we all have past lives. Before this was the Irish, they are good people. I see you there too. And for me, because of who I am, I just go right back into a baby, looking at my little fingers."

"Wow, I had no idea," she said.

"But, also, because I've reached such a high connection with Father, I must be even more careful not to abuse it, necessitating I look even more carefully into someone's heart to see if they would benefit from dying. There was one African drug-dealer and warlord that the U.S. wanted eliminated. After I tied him up, I asked him why he did all this. He said that he was extremely poor his whole life. As children, he and his little sister were abandoned and picked through the heaps of trash that you or I wouldn't even want to go near and then linked up with a man who offered him money for distributing drugs which allowed him to afford food for he and his sister. I saw that his life had gotten significantly off track. Yet he loved his sister and he still held that love for her higher than the lifestyle he now inherited from his decisions to try to provide for her. After seeing that love in him, I simply told him to get an honest job and if he dealt with these things anymore in the future then I would be back for him. Therefore, the U.S. gets what they want – the elimination of that drug-dealer and warlord, and God gets what he wants – a man set on a better path. And I haven't needed to go back.

Well, then of course there are some who, even when given a last chance, haven't changed their hearts. One man, a drug lord in South America. The drug lord had a family but had taught and raised his son in a drug lord fashion. He had taught his son to kill other people even when he was much younger than the father. The son first started killing people at fourteen years old. Regardless, I always gave people a chance. So, when I caught the family, I had everyone tied up – wife, son, father and everyone else – and I asked the father to say he loved his wife and tell me a nice love story about her. I told him that he would die if he did not do this. The man refused and said that if I killed him then his son would get revenge down the road. I killed the son because throughout the whole interaction I saw that the son was worse than the father. Then the wife started hissing and saying bad things to me as I was trying to give them a chance, she wouldn't listen to anything, this was after a full mission where everyone, guards, the mother herself were all trying to kill me. So, I killed the wife because there was no good in her either. Still no love story from the father, so after giving the man a chance, I killed him also. But that exemplifies the difference between the ultra-bad people of the world and everyone else – they actively hate love; they see it as a weakness. It is better for themselves and the world that they die as a way to keep both from getting too far away from God. As a way to return them to the spiritual sphere before there is irreparable damage done to the spirit. Being "reset" in a way and once again returning to Earth as a baby, hopefully in a better environment. If your body doesn't honor the soul, then it degrades it."

"Edwin, you might be the most amazing man I've ever met," Cassandra said.

"And you're the most amazing woman! I am just without something when you are not around me. I can already feel it. I can't stand being away from you. And I wait for you to come over every day. I've waited for you every day."

Cassandra couldn't help herself, and she leaned over and hugged him while they were at a stop light, and she basked in their fledgling affection.

"So, the military, that's your Cuban sandwich?" Cassandra laughed, and Edwin laughed as he recalled their earlier conversation from yesterday.

"Well now this is my Cuban sandwich – being with you and eating Cubans," He laughed.

Cassandra thought to herself how everything had reoriented itself since meeting Edwin and Father. Whereas before she had all the material things: money, a family, a big house, good community, comfort, status – yet her heart and soul were not happy. But, now Cassandra was happy in her heart as everything else was now at risk as further distance grew between Peter and what she was beginning to feel as her own "past life".

# 8 – Spirit Machines

*When religion does not describe a person,*
*How then will all the people be parsed?*
*By tendencies in thought*
*And inklings of the heart*

When the day of the next Heis interview came, Cassandra was not able to get tickets. Edwin did not want to travel into New York City, yet he encouraged Cassandra to go in with Marie as she might be able to get tickets somehow. So, without a plan, she and Marie ventured into the city.

They were unsuccessful in finding scalpers, so they doubled down on their gamble by entering into the line for the show without tickets. They asked those around them if anyone was selling or had extra tickets. When everyone said no, Cassandra and Marie then stood to the side of the line, and started waving everyone to go ahead of them, asking each passing person if they had extra tickets. People mistakenly started giving them their tickets, mistaking them for petite security guards. Though tempted to take the tickets, the twins chuckled at the miscommunication and happily gave them their tickets back. Cassandra and Marie soon waved through the last audience members of the line – everyone had now filed past them, the line had ended and they still did not have tickets. Undeterred they tried to feign ignorance and walk in with the rest of the group ahead of them.

"Tickets," the usher said, sticking his arm out and blocking their way.

"Oh," Marie said, shocked as if someone just asked her age, "You need tickets?"

"Yes," the usher said.

"I thought we just pay here," she said as she brought out a wad of money. "Is there someone we pay to get in?"

"Tickets are purchased online beforehand, ma'am," he said.

"Oh, well her name is Cassandra," Marie said. "She was asked to be here, Heis knows her. There is a seat saved for her, I think."

To which the usher replied, "Everyone's name is Cassandra today, ma'am," he said and ushered her out of the line.

Cassandra felt a panic welling up in her, as if all of her plans were crumbling, and she started to cry. The usher, seeing how distraught she was, said, "Just wait here. Maybe there is a free seat, I can't promise anything,"

"Thank you," Cassandra said.

After everyone had gone in, the usher spoke into the comm on his lapel, "Any open seats up there for Armory?"

"One," the voice answered back.

Cassandra and Marie looked wide-eyed at each other in anticipation.

"Go, you go, I'll stay here," Marie said to Cassandra, as they both, in unison turned to the usher and asked, "Is that okay?"

"Yeah, okay follow me," he said and led her deftly through back hallways, up a utility elevator, past the back stage.

"You're getting the grand tour," he said as he then leaned against a metal doorway leading into the large studio hall containing both the studio set and the large audience seating area, where a wall of audience members stared back at them.

A different usher came up to them and in a whisper said, "Hey, what are you doing here? I told you not to come, that open seat was taken," he said.

"I didn't hear anything," the usher said, looking back at Cassandra for confirmation.

"Yeah, I...uh" she said, baffled, shaking her head. They all stared blankly at each other for a moment, deliberating if they should ask her to leave.

"All right, whatever. Just get her a fold-out chair and put it to the side," and Cassandra took her place on a small folding chair on the floor of the studio. Her awkward positioning away from the rest of the audience and her white jacket made her stand out like a white light against a black field from the rest of the crowd. She thought somehow this was destined and this conspicuous seating would present her to Heis and the two would be able to meet on air. As she was waiting for the program to start she texted Marie, "I'm in!"

The program opened on the reporter Veronica Stensi sitting alongside Heis and Dr. Brandenburg.

"Welcome back, to a very special episode of Armory News and we are excited to have back our guests Mr. Heis and Dr. Brandenburg alongside me," Veronica said with a zest of newness and anticipation in her voice, as if she were just as excited as the rest of the audience to see what would unfold tonight. "Last week, Heis claimed to be able to prove the existence of the soul, and furthermore, apply it in new and exciting ways, just as our modern society has harnessed electricity. Is that a fair assessment?"

"Very succinct, yes," Heis nodded.

"Yet, as Carl Sagan said, 'Extraordinary claims require extraordinary evidence. And that is where Dr. Brandenburg has obliged us – a great thinker, rigorously trained at Harvard to apply the scientific method to place the burden of proof on Heis as a way to validate his claims in an honest, fair and acceptable way. Is that a fair assessment of your goals, Dr. Brandenburg?

"Yes," he said.

"Although arguments and antagonisms may arise, we are all working toward the same goal here – to try to understand these new claims Heis is trying to bring to society. If Heis is being truthful, we want to understand him and give him a voice, and if he is being dishonest or fraudulent we want him exposed – God knows the truth. So, please, the floor is yours, Mr. Heis."

Heis smiled, acknowledging the host. "Okay, it is very nice to see you all again and thank you for having me here. So, one reason I first wanted to come on a news program was to get my story out there as a way to act as a character evidence of my genuine desire to help people through their spirit, because the spirit is the prime mover of all things. So, it seems most logical to target that potent energy as a way to achieve a desired downstream result.

Whatever a person may want: more positive thinking, freedom from an illness, a chance encounter with their soulmate. To me it all starts with understanding and developing your spirit.

"I've been in this spiritual device game for a while, so I will share with you the results of some of my other spiritual devices, which operate on the same principles. When used in conjunction with your own inherent spiritual force, it can produce a specific effect. One of which is the interpretation of spiritual force impressions left – via magnetism – upon inanimate objects. Just as you can tell the type of object that left a mark in a tree, whether it's an ax or the knife etchings of young lovers, so too does the spirit of you or I leave an impression on those same objects. I will tell you that periods of intense emotion are also periods of increased spiritual force. In that sense, with the correct device, one can, with patience, see the weight and character of those spiritual forces. Furthermore, marks of any nature of course erode over time, yet some are so forceful that their spark, their expression, created a spiritual impression akin to a hydrogen bomb. And, what person had more spiritual or emotional force – what person had in his left hand one extreme of subservience, docility, kindness and in the other hand, the other extreme of power, regality, stateliness? Who had, in his relationship with people, both personal and impersonality? The extremes of every spectrum existed and were made one in Jesus Christ The Master. No one in history has yet risen to that level. So, I know him by the trees, by the land, and the electrons supplied by the sun producing the wind, he has made his mark plain. So, plainly I will tell you that in Jerusalem, during the life of Jesus, or Ishua – that person was actually referred to by the general community as "Anti-Moses". It was this: the crowd gathered, the population of Jerusalem heard him propound a law different from Moses. That terrified and angered those who expected something else from a savior who, in their minds they wanted him to fulfill that Mosaic law as they saw it – deliver them from the Roman Empire, as Moses did from the Egyptians. But, Christ said no, they were focused on the wrong things. The Kingdom of Heaven is inside, and to master and conquer your own self is more difficult yet more beneficial, than to conquer the world – and Israel is not the twelve tribes, but rather a spiritual state in any person who does the will of God. And, most of the people did not want to hear that, they wanted to be special, nor did they want their children to hear that, and it was by the community's concern for their children being misdirected and adopting ideas that were different from their understanding, and were not what they expected, that eventually galvanized the community against Jesus. So, I give this plain fact to you for us both to dwell on and speak about because how could such a loving person as Jesus be called anti-Moses? It seems ridiculous to our ears, correct? Furthermore, how did I see it? It is there, in the bending boughs of the trees, bowing toward the light. I personally take from this example that we must be wary of both those people that are saying they are the returned Christ and also those that would label someone an "Anti-Christ". Because, while the Bible is a good book, no book is due the reverence that the Bible is given. It does not convey the exact character of Christ, nor the totality of his teachings, and while we should all strive to be like the Christ depicted in the Bible – I would also say that we do not have all the puzzle pieces to most accurately follow Christ's teachings – and therefore a slight misunderstanding of who he is. And, therefore, you can bet that if Christ had come back right now, in the form of a 17-year-old man – palsied, misshapen, balding, yet propounding all the same ideas he proposed 2000 years ago, that some people would call him the antichrist. So, I tell you, think for yourself and come to your own judgment. This is freedom of thought. We must be confident to make up our own minds, which in this new world I talk about. It would rely upon you being yourself and not what others expect of you, but free.

"I have come here to send you facts and direction from the shores of a new frontier expanding outward to encompass even newer and greater aspects of freedom. Like a message in a bottle that does not seek rescue but offers it! Where facts such as the ones I just shared are commonplace. Yet this also I share with you, there are mysterious places where the light of my reason and power of my freedom has not yet penetrated into this unexplored continent, and I really don't know what is out there – maybe in a way it represents my own confusion. Just as you all may be confused about the meaning and purpose of your life in this world or confused about what this or that means – while I know my purpose, still I am confused about things in that other world. So, therefore, when I try to describe this other world, and bring back facts to tell you, there are times that I likewise stumble or make the wrong decision, just as you all also do I presume, and I don't know everything. Which is why I need help – I need *your* help, *you!* I need what everyone needs: God-loving, hard-working, caring, conscientious men and women to help me with this cause – to lace up your bootstraps and press down the dirt of virgin earth and set out on a new adventure of understanding.

"I tell you this because I want us all to become citizens of the same new land, to make progress and industry there, just as we have done here. Just as industry is, in a practical way, venturing now outside Earth, so too, will this new world serve a practical application to the lives of others and warrant its development and refinement through industry.

"In looking back on Jesus' ministry, I see that this new land is exactly what he was trying to facilitate in others, just as I am trying to do, although he was obviously much better at it than I am. He took a much more 'grassroots' approach which is obviously better than my approach. But again, I am not The Master, he was. And, so, what is the difference between this Earth and this new place? Well, mostly people communicate via thoughts. Other than that, it is hard to say sometimes. At one instance it seems like everything is different because the *feeling* is different, and you look at the vibrancy of everything like a child. Like I said, the closeness with the Father is much more palpable as you feel much more as *His* child. Yet when I try to pinpoint the differences further, the specifics almost evaporate or defy vocabulary. There is still gravity and the laws of physics. But, that one thing, that feeling, when you join me there, those short, every day, human interactions to buy coffee or lunch or whatever, those will feel more like jewels within the day rather than annoyances or interruptions *of* the day. Those daily human interactions are more meaningful in the other world."

"How is telepathy happening and human interactions happening if you also say you're the only one there?" asked Dr. Brandenburg.

"I-" Heis began to say but was interrupted.

"And, we'll be right back with that answer after a quick break!" said Veronica and turned to Heis while off air and said with a smile, "Had to get you back for all the times you interrupted me."

"And, I'm sorry again, Veronica," Heis said.

After the break the camera came back to Heis, Brandenburg and Veronica.

"And, we're back. Sorry for the cliff-hanger. We were all waiting for our guest to take a breath," she quipped. "Sorry, that was a joke, and this is a very serious matter. Please go on."

"Well, this would all be much shorter with telepathy in the other world," Heis said. "But anyway, first, I just want to say that skepticism as Dr. Brandenburg is demonstrating; it is a good and necessary thing that we should all adopt. There is healthy skepticism and to be too credulous is exactly what Jesus warned against with the false prophets. I appreciate the work that Dr. Brandenburg is doing, and I agree with you that we are all trying to get to the truth, because among my many faults can be poor communication. So, I appreciate his honing my message to make it clearer and more impactful."

Dr. Brandenburg nodded in silence.

"Okay, but back to your question," Heis said. "I said I was the only person there, but I am not the only *one* there. I did not mention this at first because this is a larger and more difficult thing to convey and comprehend, but there are others there. People just like you and me, who once lived on Earth or other earths and now have reached a level of spiritual development where they were allowed 'out of the play pen' so to speak and let out into the universe now that they had graduated from the infantile into the juvenile soul."

"And who are these people? They were from our Earth?" asked Dr. Brandenburg.

"Some of them, yes, but not a lot. Our Earth seems to be a little more primitive or slower to develop than other earths," Heis said.

"And, have you been to these other earths?" asked Dr. Brandenburg.

"Some of them, well the spiritual phase of them. This here now, us here I'm saying, this is the lower phase of Earth," Heis said.

"So, there is a spiritual phase to our world and all worlds?"

"Yes, sorry, I did say that earlier when I said it was hard to describe what is different about this new place," Heis said.

"And there are others who are right now on this Earth, but just in a higher phase so we cannot interact with them," Brandenburg said.

"Well, we *can* but often our mindset is not receptive enough," Heis said.

"I have so many questions, it is hard for me to know where to even start, but, okay, then let me ask a follow up question. How can we validate any of what you are saying?" asked Dr. Brandenburg.

"There are other records of Christ yet undiscovered existing within the underground vaults of the Vatican. I would start there," Heis said. "They describe as yet unknown information about Jesus. No one knows that fact, I've never been there myself, so that should validate that I have access to other kinds of knowledge. I am not sure, but it may corroborate the story of Christ that I just told, but I'm not specifying the content definitively, I don't know what they say exactly."

"How would you know that?" Dr. Brandenburg said.

"I was thinking about Christ one day – my mind had gone to the other world. There was someone else thinking about Christ in the other world and we were attracted to each other because of that shared interest – yes, that happens – and he'd told me that he was the one who put them down there.

"And, well, let me back up, when you've understood that God talks to us from within ourselves, then it behooves one to tidy up one's thoughts, one's body, to create a more perfect channel through which God may speak to them. However, my body and my mind are not perfect, and I still get imperfect and aberrant impressions presented to my mind that it is difficult to determine their origin. So, there are times when I will push a thought to the side or let it pass by, waiting for the next to float to the surface which I will hopefully be more confident that it had come from God. So, when this thought was relayed to me so beautifully, my heart instantly clung to it as if it were a life raft and I was drifting in an endless sea. Because who am I to receive such beautiful thoughts? I am weak. I am imperfect. I have hateful thoughts sometimes. I eat candy even though I know it's not good for me. And in that sea of constant struggle we call daily living – to be given this gift. Yes, it made quite an impression on me. And when God, through his angels, puts confidence in you to harbor this idea – you better respect and be grateful for that trust and be self-assured in yourself."

Heis paused to think. "Well, not self-assured, but rather *faithful*, as one who carries this special gift. Your assuredness in God and His trust in you, then becomes confidence as a result of gratitude, respect, and humility.

Which is why I present it as a fact right here and now, because that idea assuredly came from God, and it is true. I suppose one might call it intuition, and I think that is fine to convey the idea that it was not a fact that I read in an article by experts, nor have I seen such documents physically. But my one gripe with labeling it as intuitive is that when one has that connection with God – and he will talk with you and encourage you even if you are not perfect – as I said I am far from perfect, but when you have that confidence in God and you understand some of the ways he communicates with you, that, to me is basically an empirical fact which I will stake my reputation upon."

"Well, I suppose I should be thankful that you have given us *some kind* of concrete evidence of your abilities. However, it seems such a herculean task to go into the vaults of the Vatican to validate your story. And it seems suspicious that you put the validation of your ideas behind something you know would not get done," Dr. Brandenburg said.

"Why won't it get done?" Heis said, "Have you tried? God wants us all to be bold. Herculean tasks such as this could be the sole reason and the *soul S-O-U-L reason* – as in body-mind-soul – the soul reason a soul manifests on Earth. Maybe it is now your responsibility. Ask yourself and ask God."

"Well," Brandenburg said. "My only point was that what you did right there is a known tactic used by fraudulent people to circumvent the argument, by championing a fact that is not readily verifiable."

"Understood, so it sounds like you're circumventing the argument yourself right there because you are not directly addressing what I am saying, but rather the same bit of sophistry you accuse me of, you are now employing,"

Heis said with a slight tone of aggression. "I'm sorry, that was wrong of me to say and accuse you. Truly, I appreciate your criticism, and your criticisms are good for the audience as well."

Dr. Brandenburg nodded in agreement and said, "I guess my big concern is that this could all just be a figment of your imagination. Because, again, you have not yet given us concrete evidence of your abilities, and you could be telling us the truth as you understand it and, through no fault of your own, genuinely conveying to us impressions you are getting, but those impressions are not from God. And this place you go to again, it could just be your imagination. As you said, skepticism is a good thing, so if God were working through you, you being his channel, then he would understand that the reasonable skepticism that I am now propounding, and in some way want to allay our justified incredulity and doubt by giving us some kind of evidence. Because, see, by your logic God gave us a thinking mind to employ logic and reason, which is just as important as the intuitive connection which you seem to rely upon. Therefore, being logical and reasonable human beings, I believe that he has not yet given us, through you, enough of a reason to believe you.

"Jesus had people running around in the streets saying he healed this or that person, multiplied the loaves, and he said that even if we do not believe *him* and his words and teachings, then believe the works, or rather the miracles to help convince us that he was sent on behalf of the Father and therefore help others who are struggling to believe what he is saying. So, based on what you have given us, even Jesus would agree with us that we are justified in our disbelief. And, I know there will be millions of people who believe you because of the way you talk, the mysteries you present, the knowledge you claim to have – I mean you are quite convincing. And cults of thousands of people have formed around the personalities of individuals much less convincing and less charismatic than yourself. You are playing on people's hope and desperation, and telling them, somewhat, *what* they want to hear – that we can feel God's love more greatly and hear His voice more clearly, just by doing what you suggest and buying your device.

"Y'know, there are a few medical conditions that produce the exact symptoms that you are describing – hyper religiosity, hearing voices, an intensified internal life, hallucinating they've gone to different places – Geschwind Syndrome being one of them. If you want to convince the audience and myself, then one concrete thing you can do is to see a psychiatrist, get a medical work-up performed and get an MRI of your brain. Does that sound reasonable?"

"If it will help you," Heis said. "And will you grant my request?"

"Investigating the Vatican archives?" Dr. Brandenburg asked.

"Yes," Heis said.

"It is hard for me to agree to something like that. I don't know Latin or Aramaic, I don't know anyone connected with the leadership of the Catholic Church. I'm not particularly religious," Brandenburg said.

"But we are not talking about religion. That's what I am trying to get at. Spirituality is natural, the spirit is real, and therefore I was intending to display facts, ideas and plans that would show evidence of a soul and the spiritual power and energy that can come from that source. What you don't like about religion is probably also what God and Jesus also do not like about religion – those things that most obviously fly in the face of reason. If we stop looking at spiritual topics as religion and start looking at it like a spiritual philosophy – in the sense we are making an objective study of it – it brings in humility. We may be wrong in our study, but this is what we think currently. This mentality will tear down the impregnable walls upon which every religion rebuffs frank inquiry and investigation. Even the greatest medical textbooks understand that half of their information is wrong. They just don't know which half. This would be in the same sense the way the natural philosophers looked at psychology and neurology hundreds of years ago – meaning they didn't have the equipment or the clinical power to yet empirically prove how the psyche worked or how the brain worked – yet they were making early, rough inroads into their understanding, which now modern neuroscience has beautifully elucidated with fMRI and tractography. In that same sense we must understand that spiritual phenomena will one day be understood by science – just as neurology replaced phrenology. But until that day we must do our best to be like natural philosophers of old and act by rudimentary means of correlation. Then the facts of both science and spirituality should agree and reinforce and support one another because God is all, and God is one – spirituality is science and science spirituality.

"In my opinion, organized religion, in attempting to explain spirituality, often does not understand the principles upon which the laws were originally written, and missing the bigger picture, falls into, instead, emphasizing the letter of the law and not the deeper meaning of the law. I agree the story of Adam and Eve – taken literally, is preposterous. I agree that the Earth is countless eons older than what biblical scholars claim it to be. But, I also believe

Jesus was born of a virgin, and he performed those documented miracles. So, where is it that I draw the line when there are no confirmed cases of virgin births in today's world?

"Well, I was volunteering in a hospital one time and, I don't know how I got on the subject, but a colleague had informed me that her friend from high school many years ago, at seventeen years old, had become pregnant without so much as ever kissing a boy. No one believed her. Even the colleague did not believe her. Yet the friend maintained her story. When she was in her twenties, she married a man who had children from a previous marriage, and then they had their own children through intercourse as well. That was thirty years ago. I met that friend, Joanne. She had a healthy child who is now an adult. Yet now, even in her fifties, she still maintained that she never even kissed a boy prior to becoming pregnant with that first child. In seeing how genuine and frankly she spoke, and her story remained consistent, there did not seem to be any holes in the story. Therefore, I believed her. I was tempted to ask her to run a genetic test, but I did not. I should have. So, that story helps me believe that virgin births are possible. But I must admit I believed it even before that interaction. I can almost imagine the way it would happen, scientifically. Though the one thing I get tripped up on in Jesus' case is that men have an XY sex chromosome pairing, while women have an XX pairing – so where did the Y come from? That is the current thought in the back of my mind which I haven't answered yet.

"And, then as far as the miracles of healing – that is not such a stretch for me. When you travel the world and see the various modalities of healing that are being developed – some of those modalities look like the miracles that were spoken of in the Bible. Not only modern medicine, which is a miracle, but for instance, a subtype of hypnosis called magnetism was developed by Franz Mesmer and disproven by Benjamin Franklin and fell out of favor after that. However, before it fell out of favor, the documented everyday miracles of magnetism were impressive – with the ability to spontaneously heal, change a person's physiology, and even enter prophetic states. However, it is probably for the best that it fell out of favor, because it is too much power for the patient to give to the magnetizer and therefore becomes quite dangerous if it were to be employed by the same people who are employing today's health care. Again, modern medicine has its own miracles with advanced surgery, curing some cancers, infectious diseases, autoimmune conditions. So, I am not slighting modern medicine or those who practice it, because I would say the same thing if it were farmers, bankers or playwrights who were doing the magnetism. It's just too dangerous for anyone.

"I am trying to help connect science and spirituality – because often the scientifically-minded have the best empirical, logical and concrete minds. Yet, I feel they do not follow their facts to the correct conclusion because of a faulty priority in their values. For instance, you, Dr. Brandenburg, do not want to look at the vaults of the Vatican, despite my saying that there are records of Jesus in those vaults. This is because you are not humble and possibly a little lazy.

"Similarly, the great empirically minded people focus on comfort, status, money, possessions and the like, which taints a mind devoted to pure reason. But the religiously minded are often no better off than the empirically minded, but for the opposite reason. They often have the correct conclusions as given by Jesus – humility, patience, long-suffering, selflessness and de-emphasis of the material. Yet their reasons for arriving there are often misapprehended, or rather they do not employ logic and reason to help and better express spiritual principles. Rather they just rely on the word of someone else, which is as dangerous as magnetism. So, I say, you have your colleagues at Harvard help you, I'm sure Miss Veronica and Armory News and their parent station now have the proper incentive to help you follow your logic to its conclusion. I will do my part, as you asked of me and we will work together to get to the truth – because if I am crazy, I would also like to know."

"I will see if this is feasible," Brandenburg replied.

Heis continued, "And, again, I am far from knowing everything. But, I am desperate to share this new world with you. I am worried that I am not doing all that I can to help others reach this other place and develop themselves. Yet, with each attempt to unduly coerce people into using this device and dedicating time to it – it always came back around to put me further back from where I started.

"But, you all don't understand that there is some important change coming to the Earth. They call it 'The Light', that will affect not just Earth, and we have been waiting for it a long time. A tide is rising, and I don't know what it is, or what is to occur or when it will come exactly, but I feel these devices – the understanding procured from using them and the self-actualization required to properly use it – they offer a channel to beacon this change and a bulwark or a life-boat to safeguard against the rising tide. It just seems so counterproductive to me to continue to live in this mundane sphere trammeled by doubt, worry and fear.

"Some premonition deep within my soul I'll share; you *may* be stuck here with everyone else who does not embrace this new world. The best of us have moved on, your better selves are waiting for you in that new world. I am usually a very docile and mild-mannered man, but after seeing this new world, you will understand why I act so fervently. It will be worth it. I have been given permission to be forceful now. I wouldn't normally hurt an ant. You don't need to spray them with insecticide you just blow them away with a puff of air and then you spray an acrid substance on surfaces where you do not want them – it doesn't even need to be insecticide, but you can use insecticide, but you spray the substance where they were and they will not go there again – it is funny to see them avoid that area, as if it is water. But, people are closer to me than ants, and therefore I must expect more from a person than I would from an ant – which is why I am being direct with you all. So, what do you have that an ant does not? A full-fledged spirit, soul, mind, and a highly developed system linking these incredible powers to your body. Your body is a spirit machine, driven by and used to individualize an everlasting soul. Your soul is your vehicle in the next world – not this current body.

"You all have aches and pains in your current body, but any illness *can* be overcome simply with the mind/soul. I am not advocating against medical treatment, of course. You should take advice from doctors – they have experience. But rather I say, go to bed thirty minutes earlier tonight, put your phone away, lie there and imagine an intense white light sitting within the body part that is giving you pain or trouble. Move the white light around as if it is giving that localized point in your body an intense energizing massage – almost as if it is electrifying it. For me it is my knee and back muscles that I focus on. Continue using that light within the body part, electrifying it consistently for a solid five minutes, and with that you will feel a pulse generated where the light was, a flow, small fibrillations mount with the persistent focus on that localized part of your body. If it is a muscle or joint you focus on, then also *pretend* your muscle is moving and contracting – but don't actually move or contract it. If you can keep that up for five minutes, you will feel that area come alive – twitching, moving, draining edema, strengthening muscle tone and strengthening nervous connection. It will start small and then if you continue, it will expand outward to the periphery of where you moved the light, and the tissue will organize itself.

"Consciousness, mind, spirit is a self-organizing principle, and by honing it, developing it in these spirit machines, we are offered the chance to make ourselves. And, in the morning you will feel better in proportion to the amount of focus and time you put into that area – that is another piece of evidence for you. Because this is a small sample, this same technique of using your mind as a self-organizing force can be used outside of your body or really with any situation! Get together with others to direct your minds to one purpose and do what you'd like! Some might call it prayer – but it is like prayer on steroids! And, of course steroids are a dangerous substance, so I don't mean it in a bad way, but just that it is very powerful. Using your mind in this way is the start to this journey I speak about – to live more fully, to see God's love more plainly, to build that life-raft, to both take charge and let go all at once! This is you placing a toe on that new continent that I am walking! Continue it and the device will work for you, and you will see what I see and be where I am – knowing the truth yet sounding crazy to thousands of people!"

Dr. Brandenburg shook his head and turned to Veronica and said, "I'm sorry, I can't with this guy."

Heis paused, "I'm sorry, I didn't think and pray about this enough before I came on the show and now, I don't know if I should go into further topics. The conflicting forces being: one, openness and honesty about everything, and two, balancing that honesty with the understanding of graduated truth or progression of facts or a metered understanding. Meaning truth develops new truths like climbing a tree. The bottom branches help you get to the top branches. Meaning, you must learn and implement more rudimentary facts before you can ascend to greater truths. Those higher truths wouldn't be much use unless stacked atop the lower truths. It is as if you brought a cell phone back in time to the middle ages. It's too advanced of a technology to be of any use to anyone, so there must be given time and understanding to build up to greater revelations," Heis said, and he felt their skepticism. "No, this is a real thing out in the universe, I am not just making this up. There are things that have not yet been revealed to me even though I had asked, just like I am not revealing things to you. But anyway, the debate in my mind then being: Is further discussion too high of a spiritual truth to say here and now, or can it be made practical use of? That is what I hadn't prayed enough about."

Heis paused and bowed his head a moment and lifted his hands from the desk; he could nearly see the steam of perspiration venting from the pores in his hands and large dew drops forming on the desk underneath his palms, "I am trying to demonstrate what it means to try with your spirit and to drink water from the cupped hands of your soul. I hope I have done that and I hope I have helped someone. Thank you for this interview. Perhaps we can continue this next week. I am going to go now." And with that he stood up and walked off the set and out of the building.

Veronica allowed for a brief pause before speaking to allow the moment to sink in with the audience. "That will end this segment of Armory news, please stay with us for the next segment."

As the program was fading out, Dr. Brandenburg said, "This is all very interesting, but why did you even have me on the show?"

Cassandra was enlivened by the engaging interview, yet she was expecting him to usher her onto the stage and hold her up to the world and say, "this is the woman who will help us save the world." So, when he abruptly left without any audience interaction, she felt she had missed her opportunity. As she sat, trying to connect with God, she received a call from Marie.

"Oh, Cass," Marie said. Marie was running, "I saw the headset helmet thing," Cassandra could hear the wind blowing through the speaker of the phone, "Hey! Mr. Heis!" Marie said almost in a euphoric laughter. Heis turned to see Marie, "Mr. Heis, I saw your show. My sister is named Cassandra, and it is very important that she speaks with you."

"Okay," Heis said casually, shrugging his shoulders. Fifteen minutes later they were all talking in a secluded back corner of a cafe across the street from the studio building.

# 9 – The Ixoni

*I'm not trying to find my way*
*I'm trying to find Your way*

*But our cells are a strange batch*
*Divine sympathy*
*Hellish anger*
*Spin and stop the Earth with my footsteps*
*I cut too early*
*And therein lies the danger*

Cassandra said, "Mr. Heis, we believe you and we were sent here to help you. My friend is like you in a lot of ways. He and I, well him more than me, have had similar experiences as you have and we all have a common purpose. Please believe me, Mr. Heis. It's such a miracle all of this!"

"Please, just call me Heis. And, okay, please tell me more."

Cassandra went on to explain the past few weeks and what Edwin had told her and shown her. They ended it by saying they wanted to bring Heis and Edwin together at his apartment in New Jersey.

"Okay, let's go," Heis said.

Marie decided to return home to her husband and three children while Edwin, Cassandra and Heis met at Edwin's apartment. Heis had brought up three headsets from his car, one for each of them.

Edwin was curious himself to speak with the young inventor of the soul devices to see how much he knew about the outer worlds. After Heis and Edwin introduced themselves, Edwin said, "You didn't know them."

"What?" Heis asked.

"You couldn't read the people because you didn't know them. You don't realize that you had only read the minds of friends and family – even the reporter you had spent a lot of time with. She became a friend before you tried to read her mind. Also, there was a presiding evil over the environment, and over you as well during the event. Best not to do it in New York City next time."

"Oh, wow. That is very insightful. Usually I'm the one explaining this stuff, but now I'm the one who is baffled. But, what exactly do you mean?"

Edwin waved it off and changed the subject, "Also, what did you mean about 'being given permission'?"

Heis, kicked himself for saying that on camera as he had meant to keep it a secret as he was told, "Oh, that was nothing, just a slip."

Edwin said, "Just be careful in the outer world, you are free to do what you will, and others are free to do what they will, and since you are relatively new to that sphere, you are also the most naive."

No one had ever commented on his behavior in the next sphere; no one had ever given *him* instructions on how to behave in the outer world.

"Wait, so you've been there?" Heis said

"Yeah, and just make sure you are careful, people can pose as others very easily in that place. You have a powerful intellect, and others may seek to take advantage," Edwin said.

"I am a bit befuddled but thank you. I will keep it in mind. Y'know this is how other people must feel when I'm talking to them about the next sphere," Heis said. "You understand – talking in generalities to avoid over influencing them and thereby allowing room for their own soul to handle the specifics of any given situation. It's nice to have you to talk to."

"Yeah," Edwin said, "And Heis, continue to work for good and for enlightenment. We could all work together and it seems fitting and timely to start now."

"Okay, let's do it," Heis said and proposed that they attempt to use the headset to see if they could somehow access that other world together. They agreed, and after they said a prayer, they each put on a headset and laid down on the floor.

Instantly, it was a different type of journey – no gray sea or formless objects – they were transported out into the vast dark expanse existing between worlds. They homed in on one tiny spot of the universe. It was a world with grayish-purple humans that looked vaguely like Cassandra's dream of her great-grandson.

That recognition that Cassandra felt was conveyed to Edwin and Heis, who both quickly realized they were looking through Cassandra's eyes. She felt Edwin's and Heis' thoughts of "It is your intention to be here; you're steering the ship". Yet she herself felt like a passenger, much like in a dream. She felt she was being guided by some unseen hand as a way to show her particular aspects of this civilization.

A feeling of knowing came over her. Those grayish-purple people were called Ixoni simply because they called their own planet Ixon. Three little children lay on a grassy hill and looked at the clouds. The shape of clouds presented to their minds animals, and ships and flying crafts. They had a highly developed mental link with one another, and just as light is perceived through sight and sound through audition, their mental link produced a shared mental space called the enmeshment that was perceived through their cyor. Just as sight senses differences in a small portion of the electromagnetic spectrum, the cyor senses differences in magnetospiritual spectrum. The enmeshment was both a composite of and an emergent phenomenon from the five lower senses. Therefore, Cassandra could understand some aspects of it, but other times she didn't wholly understand what she was experiencing. Like a blind man having no reference for the color red – one must use other ways to describe it. Red is a stimulating color, close in relation to the infrared portion of light which has the greater ability to heat. So too does the red color beget a kind of mental heat and stimulation. A color beloved by lower consciousness beings purely for its excitement.

In the individual mental proclivities, Ixoni were much like people of Earth. However, from their shared mental capacity, that naturally expanded individual mental ability and internal life exponentially. Each Ixoni's stream of consciousness existed, interacted and created within the same mental environment with one another. For instance, when the clouds conjured up those figures in their imagination, the three little children played with them like children play with toys together in their minds. One cloud conjured an animal that resembled a cross between an elephant and cattle and that child held that animal in her mind, while another child conjured up an animal that appeared to have a broad flattened forehead, like a cross between a triceratops and the heavy antlers of a northern elk. Within the enmeshment the two animals sniffed each other, chased each other along the shallow banks of a river and then they fell into a deep part of the river and tried to swim, but they were getting swept away by the current. The third child quickly scanned the clouds for one that looked like a flying craft, that he then conjured in his mind to come and rescue the animals and place them safely back on land. Then the two animals started to dance and bray in appreciation and the children all giggled and continued their afternoon like that.

For the Ixoni, one's mental state contributes both an environment to and a homunculus within the large collective mental expanse of the enmeshment – like adding another room and another person to an expanding house.

Emotional states and impulses that well up in a person are also conveyed to the enmeshment, and nearly the full vulnerability of an individual's intellectual and emotional mind is laid bare as their inner homunculus and environment within the enmeshment. That interaction was necessary for the life and development of an Ixoni, like wind and sunlight to a tree, like sensation to a human.

But all things contain magnetospiritual force and therefore all things contributed to the enmeshment. Natural phenomena transmuted and exerted an influence within the enmeshment just as seasons, asteroids, animals, light and dark have an effect upon our own minds. Everything was connected. The transmuted enmeshed phenomena also contributed their individual and environmental identity to the enmeshment – meaning, a cloud in the sky would also appear as a cloud in the enmeshment. But, Cassandra had difficulty understanding the "environmental identity" as it intermixed with everything else and created and composed myriad phenomena just as individual colors can combine to produce the emergent phenomenon of white light. That intermixing created impulses and tendencies diffusing through that shared space like an atmosphere. The accompanying magnetospiritual force that a specific phenomenon imposed upon the general enmeshment was intuitively measured in a unit of measurements called pirincs. That milieu would produce a force upon each individual Ixoni's internal state which would resonate to variable degree depending on that specific individual. For instance, on Earth some might enjoy a thunderstorm while they sleep, while others are provoked to insomnia with the atmospheric electricity. Such forces would resonate most prominently with an individual who embodied similar receptive proclivities and thus carry the greatest urge for the individual to carry out some impulse. For instance, a dark hoary woods in a deep valley surrounded by crags and cliffs, all might intermix in the enmeshment to impose a feeling of evil in an Ixoni, and, if the pirincs are strong enough then the Ixoni most predisposed to act in such a way might carry out a random assault on a fellow person. Yet everyone would feel some prompting, and even the most highly resonant individuals could resist such forces with an equal amount of willpower to nullify the urge.

    The enmeshment and therefore their society operates on a hierarchy – meaning that those most enlightened, their thoughts brightest and most visited, they mostly associated with one another, and there was a mental distance from those whose thoughts were not as elevated or refined. The most refined were, in a sense, at a higher voltage, or pirinc, and at a higher vantage point and more able to see and sense those in lower positions – and those in lower positions less able to see those more refined. When sentiments shifted from one end, it felt like a wave – pushed outward to the other end. The whole population was one long chain of mental sentiments loosely attaching and interacting with one another in a dynamic reciprocal oscillation.

Light and dark within the enmeshment were ever present in vacillating degrees, similar to cycles of night and day. Yet, they were more a product of mental/emotional states, rather than photons. The light of love, reason, will and wisdom shone within the enmeshment like a sun. Thoughts could be gathered and bundled together and formed into a space within the enmeshment that each person can visit and their most beautiful thoughts were like grand cathedrals, pyramids, skyscrapers and museums.

However, an inverted light, a shadow of ignorance, hate, fear, depravity would ebb and flow like a wind, like a passing thought, an ephemeral breath, that was seen and felt with a sense of place and proximity to it, like the aura of seizure about to happen. If the pirincs of darkness became too great it was as a hurricane or tornado – in the sense that it was highly destructive and disruptive.

The lightness and darkness of the enmeshment was thus categorized into degrees loosely falling into general categories based on severity and character: The light being categorized 1-10 from least to most intense: tujur, suyift, trulw, jandal, vaivt, unhtul, komblich, iljom, Marbhani, Muditadel. The opposite force of dark being categorized from least to most intense: hrast, kortum, imtombi, mivre, tilknon, rikt, aurud, vilram, Oribut, Orshrast. The Orshrast had only been created locally in controlled laboratory settings and had never presided as overarching darkness within the enmeshment.

Cassandra was new to this experience. The tendencies of her mind searched for some physical expression – an artefact of her past life on Earth. She had difficulty keeping her "hands off" the inherent receptive nature of the journey and kept attempting to "take the wheel". In desiring to find that physical expression she was taken to a closer proximity to the Ixoni.

They did not have a hive mind, but in their free will, through their untampered communication through thought, they can almost adopt a hive mind for the purpose of executing the dream of one or a few individuals that they favor. But, if they stayed in that mindset too long or gave too much of their will over, then the tendency started a cycle, and they could lose themselves in other's intentions.

Cassandra was beginning to feel the mental strain to maintain the expedition, and she was encouraged by the others to find their way back to their time on Earth. Within a few seconds they traversed many light years and arrived back at Edwin's apartment.

As they all awoke on the floor, Cassandra asked, "What was that?"

"Given this was your first experience with the headset, that was likely the place and time in the universe to which you are most attracted," Heis said. "In the outer realm, time doesn't exist in the same way as it does here. It is more as Einstein explained and linked to the individual person rather than general shared time, so it is hard for me to say exactly more than that. Right, Edwin?"

They looked at Edwin, sitting in bed, who nodded his head in agreement and said nothing.

Heis started again, "One, I haven't had anyone who has been able to use the device other than me. Two, that was a lot different than what I am used to – that was amazing! Do you know what this means!?" Heis said as he stood up, his arms flailing around in excitement, "I'm not crazy! It works," he shouted as he started to cry, "Its real," he said as Cassandra went over to comfort him. "Please no, it's okay. I'm happy. They're happy tears."

They reviewed the whole experience – everything that was seen and what everyone was feeling throughout that time. During their discussion, Edwin was looking on the whole scene with the same suspicious eyes, the same silence as when Cassandra came to visit him that first day.

"So, can we do this again? This device has unlocked something amazing we can show to others. And, we can understand why Cassandra was attracted to that particular place and time," Heis said.

They looked at Edwin again; he nodded in cautious agreement.

"Okay, please keep these devices with you, and don't mix them up because the internal lattice has become set to your own rhythm. And I don't want to mess with it after getting that kind of amazing result."

As Heis was preparing to leave, he went to shake Edwin's hand, and he saw a small metallic object sticking out of Edwin's ear.

"Oh, what's that?" Heis said.

"It…helps," Edwin said.

"Oh, where did you get it?" Heis asked.

"God, you could say," Edwin said.

"Well, I think I can…" Heis said as he slipped on his headset quickly. Edwin quickly took his own helmet off, but for a split-second Heis gained some semblance of understanding of the internal workings of Edwin. More than that, he saw Edwin as an indescribable electrical pattern and Heis' head was knocked backwards in amazement and he looked at Edwin with the same amazement as the doctor who wanted to study Edwin's heart.

"I...," Heis said as they shared prolonged eye contact between them in silence. Heis stepped backwards from the bed and quickly took his own helmet off, not wanting to expose himself to any possible repercussions. "Well," Heis said, "All the more reason to meet again. You've all given me a lot to think about and a lot of hope within my own soul. I want to help the whole world with this technology – wouldn't that be amazing?"

"Yes, let's do it. Let's change the world!" Cassandra said, sharing his enthusiasm.

"Okay, I have a couple tweaks I am going to make to the helmet which I need to capitalize on before they leave my mind, so do you want to meet again in a few weeks?"

"I think that sounds good, and I'll try to arrange for Edwin and I."

With everyone in agreement, Heis left. Cassandra then turned to Edwin and asked what he thought.

Edwin turned his head down in despair and said, "I messed up, I showed too much. He's not like others. I wasn't expecting that," Edwin said and then he started mumbling to himself and became very angry and punched a hole in the wall, "I'm sorry, Father. I unduly influenced him. He must be given a choice, everyone is given a choice," Edwin said, and started motioning with his hands as if pouring a glass of water. "But, I have to do something now to rectify the competing forces, we will see what it is,"

"What did he see?" Cassandra asked.

Edwin touched his ear and his stomach and said, "They're special. He saw them. They will tip him differently from how he was supposed to be balanced."

## 10 – New Love

*Well I can't sing or play*
*But I got stuff I want to say*
*I like when we laugh so much*
*And every time that we touch*
*Come and take my hand*
*Be my woman I'll be your man*
*We'll be adventurers you and I*
*Traveling upward to the sky*
*We'll see God all through these parts*
*And as we go deeper in our hearts*
*There's so much faith left to explore*
*A brand new world that lays before*
*All I ever want to do*
*Is walk toward that new world with you*

A week later Cassandra was walking through the small dirt parking lot of Edwin's apartment building. She had made a habit of looking up at the sky for some indication, the feeling of some presence from the sun. It was overcast, and the sun beaconed her attention to one particular point in the dense gray sea of cloud coverage. There was something in the subtle contours of the clouds to which her intuition directed her. She attempted to notice some abnormal movement, an abnormal texture or formation, something written in the sky. A feeling of dread overtook her; a feeling of being watched as she thought those people in her vision were coming to invade Earth and she was being directed to the location of their ship hovering over Earth. But, the feeling passed, there was nothing there, and the endless abyss of gray clouds lapped over one another slowly rolling across the landscape as one uniform mass.

She opened the door into Edwin's bedroom and was surprised to see a furnished room with a large tapestry on the near wall, a red leather couch in the middle of the room pointed directly in front of a large TV on the adjacent wall, and a large golden retriever named Astro greeted her at the door, excited for anticipated affection.

"Oh, hello," she said, bending down to pet the dog, "Is this the same apartment? Are you a new roommate?"

Edwin was sitting on the red leather couch; his wounds had long since healed. He tried to laugh, yet there was a large goiter-like mass bulging from his neck, causing his neck to hyperextend and he produced an audible wheeze with every breath.

"Edwin, are you okay? What happened?" she said.

"...share..." Edwin said.

"Share? Share this place with you?" she said and he smiled and nodded. "But what happened to your neck? Do you need to go to the hospital?"

Edwin pointed at the TV. It was an interview with a famous wrestler turned actor, Lucian Rho, who had recently been diagnosed with thyroid cancer that had been put into remission. "...share..." Edwin said, then pointed at the neck mass.

"Share? Share what?" she asked.

"Can..cer," he said.

"You are sharing his thyroid cancer? Like taking that away from him?" she said.

"Yes," Edwin said, still wheezing.

"But, why is it so big? His neck had never gotten that big."

"Take, most…extreme, like pets," he said as the large golden retriever crawled up onto the couch with him and laid his head in his lap and closed its eyes. Cassandra sat down on the couch next to Edwin.

"But you were almost killed two months ago. Aren't you still recovering a little?" Cassandra said.

"Body…heals," he raised up his arms. "God."

"So, are you saying that Lucian Rho had thyroid cancer, then you took the most extreme form of it somehow and you did so because your body knows how to heal more quickly because of your connection with Father?"

Edwin was pleased and he smiled and nodded, "So smart."

"So, he's cured?" she asked.

"Maybe," he said with a shrug, "Given time."

"Oh, because the things that produced the thyroid cancer are still present?"

Edwin gave a subtle nod.

"But, why? There is so much illness in the world," Cassandra said.

"Don't…be…negative," Edwin said.

"Don't be negative? Okay," She replied, "But why him, I guess I was trying to say."

"I like him," Edwin said with a hearty laugh that was subdued by a wheeze and cough.

"So, what happened to you?" Cassandra said

"Few…days," Edwin said, and closed his eyes.

Something about the situation struck her deeply, so she felt compelled to pray over him. She would never do such a thing in the real world, but here and around Edwin she felt accepted and expected to do those things that prompted her mind.

"Dear Father, please watch over and protect Edwin. Please watch over and protect this family, my children and the entire extended family. Please grant us simple, productive, faithful lives and keep the evil and temptation away from us." She also prayed for the Earth and the people of Earth. "Please protect this nation. And please, give me an answer to this feeling of watching the sky."

As she opened her eyes after the prayer, she laid her hands on Edwin. She wanted to help, she wanted to share this with him to alleviate his suffering, but she was scared to take any of that huge mass onto herself.

Edwin, with his eyes closed, took her hand and placed it an inch above his neck like the Reiki practitioners do and swept her hand up and down along the mass.

"That…please." he said, his eyes still closed, reclined on the couch. Cassandra didn't know what she was doing but followed his instructions and clumsily placed her hands just above the mass and traced an outline over his neck and head for a few minutes.

"Thank you," Edwin said in a clear voice.

"You're welcome, do you need more?" Edwin did not reply. Cassandra changed topics, "I texted Heis. He said he was doing well."

Edwin nodded in confirmation.

"I was thinking that we could continue to use the headset. I want to familiarize myself with it, so when we start up our work with Heis I'll be more comfortable with it," Cassandra said, and Edwin nodded.

"Okay, well I feel good and energetic right now. Is now a good time?" Cassandra said, to which Edwin nodded again. When she went to put the headset on Edwin, he held up his hand in a stopping motion.

"Just you," he said.

So, she placed his headset in a cardboard box and slid it under the couch and put on her own headset. She laid backwards on the couch and tried to relax.

After five minutes, she was in a crowd of those same Ixoni. Her eyes were in pain, she couldn't breathe as the city was on fire, with great plumes of smoke billowing up from the city mimicked an Oribut darkness consuming their minds and prompting their hearts into a mass hysteria. Cassandra got away from the city, high up, yet she was still connected mentally to them, and their fear excited her own fear and she saw what they saw. The center of the city was on fire, consuming the large stone edifices. The blaze was spreading to other concentric circles surrounding the city center. As she went further from the scene, she could see the circles were connected to other circles as the landscape and environment would permit and the fire threatened to consume the whole of their small civilization.

An entity dropped down from the sky, floating next to her and looking down on the city. He was a great golden-winged, armor-clad angel, one hundred feet tall hanging in the sky observing the destruction. Its image was perfectly transmuted between the physical sight and the enmeshment – producing a Mutadelic light in all their minds across the whole nation. Then his arm reached forward and was held up as if giving a command. The angel conveyed through its own radiant Mutadelic light from within itself shining down upon the population, reminding them of their own lowly states. *Which light do you follow – the fires of the city or the internal commanding light when both excited fear?* The question was cast to them. The smoke and darkness only served to give better contrast, clarity and resolution to his radiant image in the eyes of those who looked up. A light fell upon the city, multitudes bowed. Other multitudes shouted and made loud noises, crying in desperation and terror and anger.

Leaders had risen in the ages of the Ixoni to "cull the herd" and separate those multiplying dissonant minds that oppressed and clouded the enmeshment with a growing tilknon darkness. They did not have wars over miscommunication or deceit as was often the case of present-day Earth. Rather they had wars simply for outright hate, jealousy, passion, enjoyment, money, power, or land. They had no illusions about these emotions, and they were more open about the reasons behind the warring impetus. *He must be this leader*, the Ixoni thought, *to cull the herd*.

Now, this golden angel beside Cassandra cut the enmeshment down the middle drawing the little homunculi to his light and separating the light from the dark. Yet, it was not the darkness that died.

Thousands of people died en masse in the streets. Cassandra became surprised, and she looked at the angel beside her and saw Edwin's face who was slowly moving away from the city back into the clouds. She became startled and her physical body jerked in the apartment with Edwin. She was half observing the gruesome scene and half in the apartment. With the light gone, the city descended into something past the Oribut darkness into the lowest place their society had ever experienced – the smothering choking stench of the Orshrast. Cassandra, still connected to them in her high emotional state, attempted to give audible language to a population of people that mostly communicated via telepathy, and the guttural sounds which her voice box strained to produce and her abdominal muscle forced out air through, the most taut opening her larynx could produce. She began speaking not for the purpose of communicating information, but rather conveying emotion as their enmeshment sought expression in the Earth, to warn, through her; *hrast oligek cov*, the onslaught of feet pushing a woman down after tripping among a stampeding crowd of people; *asifrit palak vey* the brief feeling of warmth on your face against a large stone pillar as the momentum of the building continues downward falling and crushing a man; *cizkabah ber Orshrast* for the sound of children choking on smoke that blots out their vision in the enmeshment and in the physical world, *Orshrast talenakabatala*, she vomited from the increased intra-abdominal pressure and opened her eyes. Now, firmly grounded in the apartment, she flung off the headset and passed out onto the floor.

 Cassandra awoke in a startle to a darkened bedroom. It was the next morning, perfectly quiet. Edwin had moved her to the bed and pushed the couch next to her where he sat, resting comfortably, his neck mass had substantially subsided. She went down to the kitchen to get a drink of water, still flustered and shaking. A portrait of Jesus stared at her from the kitchen wall. A random thought entered her mind, *dreams and visions are the primitive states of some higher existence.* As if she were learning to walk within some higher plane with this headset. Her whole body felt sore and she went upstairs to lay back down as she waited for Edwin to wake up.

 Edwin awoke an hour later at 4:00 a.m. The sky was still dark. Cassandra asked him, "What was that?"

"The people of the planet were saved," he said.

"So, that was real?" she asked.

"Yes," he said.

"I saw your face. Was that you?"

"Yes."

"How? But, what do you mean they were saved? I saw and felt so many people die," she stated.

"The ones that bowed were saved from that destruction via a near instantaneous death," he said.

"And the others?"

"They were not saved," he said.

"How could you kill all those people?"

"They killed themselves, God just didn't stop it," he said. "That is what happens with all planets, eventually."

"But, why were you there, who are you?"

There was a shift in his demeanor, and a different voice came through, "Edwin is the angel of death," Edwin said as the hairs of his arms stood on end. It was as if he were amassing and concentrating within himself the static electricity of immensity, funneling within himself and refining the power of that point around which the entire universe spun.

She asked, "What does it all mean, Edwin?"

His voice changed back, "There is always a…" he stopped and made a motion with his hand on his chest and then extending outward, "A…herald…coming changes. Always."

"So, what is about to happen?" she asked.

"A winnowing."

"Will you tell people?" she asked.

"That I am the angel of death?"

"Yes."

"Yes," he said.

"What can I do?" she asked.

"Come here," Edwin said. Cassandra was scared to approach him until she saw her own hairs stood on end. She went over to him; a palpable pull of magnetism bent their hairs toward each other and guided their hands like gravity to consummate their love as the electrical breakers in their apartment tripped.

Afterwards, as Cassandra lay next to Edwin, she became frightened and reached over to touch him – she felt his large warm arm, stiff as a board, no pulse. Frightened, she said a prayer, waited a moment and the pulse resumed. The relief she felt in Edwin's pulse acted twofold to also dissipate the fear from her vision, and she relaxed.

"Did you just say a prayer for me?" he asked.

"Yeah," she said.

"Thank you, I don't get many of those prayers," he said.

"You're welcome, Edwin," Cassandra then mentioned that during her walk into the building yesterday it felt like something was calling her out in space. That she was worried about someone off of Earth the way a parent may worry about their child who had gone out for the evening and hadn't returned home on time. She had no idea why or where this feeling was coming from, only that she constantly felt compelled to look up at the sky and the clouds toward some point past the light blue haze of the atmosphere, as if she were waiting at a window for a guest to arrive.

"Just continue to look toward that point," he said.

Cassandra thought that this was to somehow be the future of humanity. That this vision of hers was the heralding sign, the world now warned through her, and that golden angel was a light coming from space approaching the world set to arrive at that future date of ten years. Therefore, to prevent the killing of millions, she felt it would once again come down to her choice to Father.

"Should I be writing this stuff down?" Cassandra asked Edwin.

"Tell the story, but don't write it. That is for another." Edwin said.

She looked at her phone and saw multiple missed calls and text messages from Peter. *Oh, no,* she thought to herself. He would be worried. This was the first time she had not come home.

She could feel the natural course of events drawing her away from Peter with every decision she made. Father continually placed before her a choice, prompting her to choose one way or another. So, now more than ever, she felt an urgency to go through with the plan; she had told Father she would marry Edwin. Yet, Cassandra had kept postponing her talk with Peter to discuss divorcing. She knew people got divorced all the time, yet marriage meant something special to her. This had been her whole life up until a few months ago. She didn't know her past lives, she didn't have instant access to the whole of universal knowledge, as Edwin seemed to. She had doubts, insecurities, and badness in her. As far as she was concerned her whole life was thirty-two years, which is all she knew. She now held it like a marble in her hand to either cast aside or place in her pocket. *But, how am I going to do that? Can't Peter just get sick and die and then that would free me to marry Edwin?* Yet, it was her choice. She had to act on her faith. God doesn't want slaves. He wants willing participants – co-creators in the universe. He would not take it – it must be given willingly and the choice, as with all people, must be their own. Father is the God of all and wills none to die unduly.

# 11 – The Tor

*Elation, fear, greed, charity, dread*
*How do I get out of my head*
*Shortness of breath, tightness in the chest,*
*Heart's beating, breathing, stress*
*I wanna get off*
*Make it stop*
*How to keep it at bay?*
*When you've gone away*

Two months passed as Heis continued to work on adjustments to the helmet and postponed the meeting. Cassandra also postponed using the headset after her last session. In the meantime, the nursing company had reassigned Cassandra to other patients and was not seeing Edwin as a patient any longer. Yet, the two continued to meet for lunch most days and she would visit on the weekends. In the months that passed, Edwin continued to take others' ailments, yet he never complained nor showed the slightest bitterness. It remained his priority to always make Cassandra laugh and feel loved.

"In Heaven, everything is shared," he'd say. He could take anything – angioedema, a broken bone, a tumor, diabetes, dementia, which he did willingly. Even going so far as to take a dog bite that tore the nose of one of Cassandra's nephews. Yet with each illness taken, there seemed to be a minute, long-term diminutive effect, like little etched tally marks in the stone slowly scratching away Edwin's soul and vitality. Cassandra asked him to think of himself, their new family they were attempting to start. He couldn't keep this up. She was afraid she was going to lose him before she even got to know him.

"Ten years. We have ten years. This is my purpose," he'd say. "Leave it to Father. Don't be so negative."

Father would come down to help ease the burden of Edwin's shared illnesses by inhabiting his body and giving Edwin a mental reprieve. Other divine guests would also come through Edwin to help him and to visit with Cassandra. Once, Cassandra's uncle Victor came through Edwin. He recalled how cute the little nine-year-old twins were with their red hair and freckles. The man who designed the Titanic came through to help Edwin and visit Cassandra. He was in a kind of spiritual stasis or purgatory. After their conversation, and in large part due to their conversation and in helping Edwin, he had been able to make it to Heaven. At times, it seemed all of Heaven was propping up Edwin and his health, to keep him going to complete this ten-year mission.

With each person that came through Edwin, his demeanor, facial expressions, sometimes even his physical appearance would change in relation to that person. For instance, Cassandra's aunt Louise was a frequent visitor, and it was obvious she was coming through Edwin because of the way she laughed. During family occasions she would always laugh in a big grand show swaying backward and forward while slapping her knee. But even her perfume scent would come along. Cassandra reasoned that people's appearance and mannerisms during their previous incarnation on Earth was similar to whatever type of body they had among the spiritual states after that earthly life. Because, even the way Aunt Louise pressed her lips together before she spoke, that was also displayed on Edwin's face.

Yet things were also quite different in the spiritual sphere as Louise had been a treasurer for her town throughout her whole life and died in her 80s, yet in the next life she moved on as a 41-year-old interplanetary ambassador to an organization that was like a United Nations for galaxies.

Cassandra was surprised that, in the long list of visitors, she never saw Jesus. So, she reasoned that Edwin might be Jesus coming again. Edwin told her that he was not him, and she conveyed to him her desire to meet him. Edwin said to her that it was not yet time, he was very busy, and she may meet him eventually.

Cassandra wasn't sure where Edwin would "go" during these times when someone else was inhabiting his body – *Was he in there yet suppressed? Was he off somewhere else?* The only thing Cassandra knew was that Edwin never remembered what happened during those times. In a way she felt bad for Edwin, he was either in a state of constant pain in taking others' pain here on Earth, or he was in some kind of death-like sleep where he was not conscious of anything and remembered nothing. Cassandra, like one of the descending heavenly guests, tried to bring comfort to the constant toil of his life.

With her frequent visits, Cassandra noted that Edwin would watch the news constantly and intently. She asked him about that and he said, "I use it mostly to learn what I should pray about from the little scrolling news ticker on the bottom of the screen," he said as he pointed to the bottom of the screen and brief headlines quickly scrolled along the screen: 28 kidnapped in Brazil – Flooding in India kills 134 – California governor declares state of emergency for drought – suspect named in case of missing Idaho woman.

"Yeah, I will pray for each one of those just as soon as they scroll across the screen. It all happens very quickly, but it need not take a long time when genuinely praying. How I do it is I think of only a positive outcome as vividly as I can and try to connect that sentiment and that vision with Father. And, just like the government depositing money in a bank account that I do not touch, I also have a lot of built up 'funds' let's say, with Father – which I *will* use. But, rather than receive those blessings myself, I try to reroute those blessings towards whatever it was I was praying for – like finding that missing Idaho woman."

One evening, they returned to the apartment after spending the afternoon on the windy cliffs of the Twin lighthouses in Navesink. Edwin encouraged Cassandra to try out the headset again if she was willing.

"I don't know if I want to see that again, Edwin," she said, reticent about using the device again. "I was part of them, and I felt what they felt. That is a scary relationship to get into with a population of people that you don't know."

"It's your choice," he said.

Cassandra looked out the apartment window for some guidance from nature and the sky. The light of the reddened evening sun bled into the room, and she stared at it, its pulsations tapping on the glass and beaconing her to come out into the yard. So, she excused herself and walked down to the front lawn to listen to the sun before it set. Now more than ever she would look up at the sky for signs and meaning as she felt it was a communion and communication with Father. Of course, the Father was everywhere, and she felt his presence throughout the day, but she always tried to catch the sunrise and sunset for the little messages he projected in the shadows, the sun and the clouds.

     She analyzed it as if the sky were speaking to her, because, to her eyes, the sun would behave in a way she had heard described only by astronomers. Everyone else saw only a ball of light. To her, the sun actively pulsed and radiated some kind of aura which she could see with the naked eye. And, in looking for the deeper meaning behind it, she could almost discern what it was attempting to communicate. This ability was still new to her, starting when she first started her new job months ago, and since that time the radiations had acted to generally comfort, reassure and invigorate her into a higher spiritual state, thus prompting her visions. However, today, the particular pattern of pulsations radiating from the sun seemed to convey to her, on a subconscious level, a sense of forlorn.

     She continued to stare as the crimson glow lit up her face of freckles, green eyes, and red hair. The tangential sunlight of the setting sun illuminated her white clothing; contrasted with the stark winter landscape gave her the appearance that she was glowing to passing cars. The drivers commuting back from work looked at her standing alone on her lawn catching all the sun's rays. They were initially dumbfounded by the angelic scene but quickly regained their composure and distorted their face into a quizzical look as they felt something was weird and disturbing about her for standing in the cold staring at the sun on a Wednesday afternoon. Her standing alone on the lawn, motionless, staring off – seemingly at nothing – made her an easy target for people's ill-intentioned internal thoughts. She could feel their intentions as they passed as a perceptible aura similar to the sun's radiation, which became magnified by their gaze falling upon her when she wasn't looking. There was a weight to it, barely perceived in the back of her mind, like the force of a small ripple in a pond brushing against the skin. It was that same negativity in the enmeshment that the Ixoni described. She had, in a very crude and primitive sense, learned from the Ixoni how to connect with other's mental states. That mental state was projected onto her by the typical Somerset commuter because her behavior was not typical, and atypical things were a lightning rod for people's attention. And people, at least those left on Earth, in general, often maintained negative internal states while commuting in traffic. She used the primitive enmeshment that she established between herself and the commuters. She could sense that her odd behavior and their negative attention became the same to one another – a general annoyance. She distanced herself from their thoughts and the drivers flipped down their visors to avoid the sunlight she was reflecting.

  It was just prior to dusk, as Cassandra freed herself of their thoughts. The sun was a crimson jewel coloring the voluminous clouds in red, orange violet producing shimmering light projecting and stretching across the sky. The rays of light formed the outstretched fingers of God, as if reminding the Earth that it was in His hand. Cassandra thought to herself that the sun was always setting in one place as it was rising in the other, continually around the Earth. And she imagined those two hands of God were always placed just above the Earth. Just as she had been taught to place her hands just above Edwin's skin to heal him. The scene reassured her against the persistent sense of foreboding that resided in her heart, and she drew strength and fortitude from it.

As the sun continued to descend, she saw the hand God wafted upwards and away to heal some other portion of the Earth. The light was nearly gone now, and the long shadows from the trees lining the yard slowly made their march toward Cassandra. The intense colors in the sky transitioned to more subdued blue and indigo of civil twilight like the austere elegance of an orchid. She hung on to one more grateful moment of light as the shadows engulfed her, her worldly features returned, and a chill fell upon her skin. White stratus and cirrus clouds continued their slow journey across the sky, and she went inside.

As she walked up the steps, she made up a word, "manifestering" as a way to describe what she was currently doing with her dreams. She was *manifestering* her dreams. Meaning, she had every intention of achieving her grand aspirations and goals, but she was also continually delaying their development. She was avoiding talking with Peter, she was worried about what would happen with the divorce and her children, and she was worried about continuing this journey with Edwin and this device. So, when she arrived at the top of the stairs, she texted Peter that she had something important to talk with him about when she got home, and when she walked into Edwin's room she said, "Okay, I'm ready to use the headset."

"The sun sure gave you a pep talk, didn't it?" Edwin said.

She laughed, "That's a good way to put it."

She said a small prayer and placed the helmet on her head. Her vision picked up a few days after the great crisis she witnessed from her last vision. She saw that it was all initiated by a combination of factors starting when their sun stopped producing a specific electromagnetic band as it slowly shifted to the K-type configuration of its own lifespan, which coincided with an increase in infrared output, which caused an increase in temperature on the planet, which then sparked a warming event, producing flooding, destructive weather, increased famine and a more hospitable environment for bacteria and viruses to spread and grow, which then killed much of the population. Then, after the chaos died down, and society reclaimed its composure, the population felt a strong urge to unify their efforts to produce three large space-faring vessels each the size of Manhattan and establish other colonies off of their planet. Which they successfully accomplished after ten years.

    Yet, another problem emerged that started at the same time as that great crisis took place. Prior to the rapture, diffuse emotional and mental states that generally permeated the population would wax and wane with the motion of the universe, their star, the moons, the tide, the Ixoni themselves – all adding a small influence. And, there was an understanding in those days that the kortum and imtombi dark states were transient, instructive, respected – as if it was a stern parent admonishing their behavior and attitude. There was a kind of aloofness from it. However, when the star shifted, and the other Ixoni left, a negative chord reverberated and breathed more fully within the space of the enmeshment and formed a greater presence that generated from itself smaller negative processes, like progeny; like a large vortex that spun off smaller eddy currents – a phenomenon hitherto unbeknownst to any living Ixoni. It was an aurud darkness without entrance and without exit as it was generated, not from the influence of transient external environmental factors, but from within the enmeshment itself – spinning, powerfully fixed, drawing in the eidolon forms of each Ixoni. As if the best of the population that had been raptured had been holding back some pervasive darkness waiting to strike against the general Ixoni population. After those raptured Ixoni left, the billions remaining on Ixon felt alone. They felt as if there was no one left to console them and nurse them back to health, no light, no positivity in the enmeshment, no one to warm and appreciate them; *forlorn*.

    A vicious cycle formed as this imposing pervasive aurud darkness caused a slowly increasing amount of anxiety, fear and impatience. Impatience that the aurud should have been a fleeting vibration to encourage their minds back into a constructive course, yet it became fastened despite their adjustments. Some were driven to lunacy in their futile attempts to placate what was increasingly being seen as an entity sent there to torment them. It began to act like a chronically sore muscle, reaching out and taking root, contorting the enmeshment around itself as the enmeshment tried to balance the new influence. The negativity that was once treated with patience and understanding that it would pass, was now looked upon with fear, that it would stay forever, and grow out of control. That belief itself then fulfilled its own prophecy and allowed that negativity to grow to vilram darkness and take greater hold. That standing dis-ease resonated with many of the Ixoni. It found physical expression as a shared mass psychosomatic manifestation in many of the Ixoni via skin irritations, mental illness, or simply more frequent indigestion.

The polarity flipped as the enmeshment now was not the recipient of outside influence but rather the prompter and the vilram darkness wanted to manifest in the world, and the ships were launched amid riots, rape, war and mass suicides for those who were not chosen to go on this second, man-made rapture.

The vilram pulled at Cassandra to manifest itself and she couldn't bear to remain on Ixon any longer and her subconscious prompted her to follow one of the ships most congenial to her own soul and jumped in time ten years to an Ixoni named Ohinx. Ohinx was the leader of the Northern Crossing expedition, colloquially called the Tor. He looked fifty years old but was around one hundred years old. He appeared to Cassandra as a black and white movie. He was uniformly the same color over his entire body – purplish gray skin, silver hair and beard, pigment absent from the irises and a dark gray uniform. As the Tor moved away from Ixon, they had various devices aboard to help magnify and extend the enmeshment between the ships and Ixon, one of which looked like the device Heis had made. Ohinx looked on in deep remorse as he saw the vilram darkness growing again into the Oribut during the second year of their voyage, and the already faint impressions from Ixon then ceased altogether.

Now ten years after leaving Ixon, Ohinx was dismayed to see the state of their own enmeshment on the ship was little better now than it was when they left Ixon. Ohinx originally thought that only those Ixoni with great hope and therefore great positivity would have the gumption to commit to such an intrepid task as deep space travel. So, in gathering together the positive ones, the negativity should have been left behind when the Tor expedition left the planet, because they presumably had great hope. But the imtombi followed them into the darkness of illimitable space and it became apparent that people left more from fear rather than hope.

To slow its progression and to increase the mission longevity most of the Tor crew were put into stasis prior to departure as a kind of induced coma to help mitigate the damage and hopefully speed recovery from the invasive imtombi. When a Tor was in the induced coma, their presence in the enmeshment was nonexistent. Yet, Ohinx stayed awake over these ten years along with a rotating crew that would take six-month shifts to work the space vessel and then go back into sleep while another crew was awoken. So, Ohinx had ample time to think about the problem.

He and the scientists did not know if the darkness was the Tor themselves or if it was some unknown outside entity sharing their enmeshment producing the withering presence. He saw it shift and oscillate between the kortum and imtombi degrees with each new set of crew members that rotated the work schedule, so it was, at least partly, the Tor themselves.

The ship now far away from any other Ixoni, Ohinx and the Tor saw the waking shift of hundreds of Tor take on a greater portion of the enmeshment, which had originally been sustained by billions of people while on Ixon. Therefore, there were more dynamic fluctuations in the enmeshment as each individual generated a proportionally greater presence and the enmeshment was less "buffered" so to speak from the billions of minds on Ixon. It was almost as if they were slowly discovering a greater degree of individuality and Ohinx started to read the philosophical work of past Ixoni hypothesizing thought experiments of what it would be like if all other Ixoni had died and the enmeshment was reduced to just one person – alone completely from all other's thoughts. Ixoni scientists had documented similar cases, as happens in diseased Ixoni with brain damage – yet those Ixoni could never fully communicate what that feeling was like.

Ohinx wondered how the other expedition groups were doing. The three expeditions had long since separated enmeshments and were now many light years away from each other. There was no way to tell whether the same intensity of negativity was present with the other groups – *was it someone or a group of people in particular which produced this phenomenon which now happened to come with the Tor?*

He contemplated waking up the Tor one by one to get a better sense of where the negativity was originating. He contemplated the morality of introducing this unknown negativity to the collective consciousness of whatever native species was already living upon the new planet they were journeying toward. Like introducing a virus to a species with no immune system to it. Then Ohinx realized what to do with the years left on the ship – with each Tor taking on a greater portion of the enmeshment – he could train himself to become so positive that his contributed presence would partially or totally aid in neutralizing those negative forces which dominated their mental sphere.

After seeing that epiphany, Cassandra was then prompted back into her own body and awoke.

Edwin was sitting on the couch next to her.

She said to him, "Ed, I don't know how much more of these I can take. It is all so sad to see, especially with the headset. It's so much more vivid and real than what I was seeing before the headset."

"It's okay, take a break. You're doing good," he said and the two kissed goodnight and she returned to her own house.

*\*\*\**

She walked through the door to her home with a mounting anxiety. She had texted Peter she wanted to talk and now was the time. God continually, lovingly puts before you choices; the decision coming through your thoughts and actions. While, yes, Cassandra had made a monumental decision in reaching out to God and acting on that faith – it doesn't end there and faith is a continual action. She was pregnant and she saw the subtle signs of fullness in her face. The pregnancy presented the natural impetus to divorce Peter, and she did not want to delay her stepping through this door any longer.

She heard Peter in the upstairs bedroom. Despite knowing what she wanted to do. Despite all her faith, she couldn't get herself to go up the steps to knock on their bedroom door. So, she sat on the couch downstairs resolving herself not to eat or do anything else, unless she spoke with Peter first. As she sat there, a faint noise of video games came from the boys' room; footsteps from Peter moving around the bedroom. He wouldn't come out of the room for the rest of the night. He had begun to spend more time isolated in their room in an attempt to avoid Cassandra. He had suspected she was seeing someone since the board game night when her demeanor changed, and she was spending all of her days out.

While Cassandra was sitting on the couch, she felt numerous times a small voice generate a great wave of energy welling up in her to walk up the stairs, yet she didn't capitalize on it, and the feeling receded. She wanted to be taken over by Father as Edwin could and let him have this conversation with Peter while she went somewhere else only to wake up again with no memory after the conversation was over. She saw that it was herself that was also holding on to something she had held on to from the first few years of their marriage when he first told her that he didn't want to be married – the fear of being a single mother. She sat on the couch for ninety minutes before her hunger, and thus her concern for the nascent pregnancy prompted her to do something, and she tenuously, slowly walked up the steps to the bedroom.

"Peter?" She knocked on his bedroom door. "Can we talk for a moment?" The children had their door closed and were enthralled in their games.

He opened the door, "I guess, yeah okay," he said, as if the sound of her footsteps up the stairs had already broken the news to him.

She had a sheet of points prepared to say to him because she often became nervous during public speaking and these types of interactions. Yet, she instantly saw in his eyes that understanding of what she would say next and she began to cry, "This isn't working, Pete," she said.

"I know," he said, and in that shared sympathy of agreement, he became a friend. She was open with him about everything, about his suspicions, her own unhappiness.

"I feel like I'm leading a double life, I eat with Edwin during the day, and then I come home to you and the kids at night, it's too much."

"I understand," he said.

She didn't plan for it, but she began to tell him even more, about Father, about the oil disappearing from her new pants, about meeting with Uncle Victor, who Peter had also met briefly at their wedding. Peter believed it, she was surprised, and she felt a piece of the original love for him when they were children. "I loved you as best I could, and you loved me, but it's time to divorce, Pete," she said.

"Okay," he said, tears in his eyes.

"We have children together, I want us to still be in each other's lives, this divorce is something we both want. Father has such great plans for you. All of us working together – you, Edwin, me – we can make them happen. We can buy a large property, make a housing development and each house will be different, unique, different eras of American architecture all combined, it will be like a beautiful, living, functional, grand art museum that people will drive through just to look at the houses you made. I was told that," Cassandra said. She knew she was getting ahead of herself, and she felt a pressure on her head that took her out of the moment, "I want you to walk me down the aisle and give me away," she said.

"Okay," he said and they gave each other a large hug and cried together. After it was over, Cassandra ate a small piece of bread and then went down to sleep on the couch, jubilant that it was over.

The next day, Cassandra wanted to keep things moving, so she and Peter spoke with their children, sitting them down in their large living room with high ceilings and large windows. She again felt her nerves well up in her as she walked from the kitchen to the living room. *All part of God's plan*, she reassured herself to combat the little prompting in her heart to take it all back and stay together for the children. And, she reminded herself that 'staying together for the kids' is what she had done for her entire marriage, and she saw the detriment which occurs when Father is not a part of a household.

    Cassandra wished they were a little older to help them better understand. The children were young; eleven, nine and eight; but she did not want to wait any longer. She explained to them the concept of divorce, that they still loved them very much and they were still going to be a family and throughout her talk the three children had much the same stoic acceptance as Peter. Cassandra told them that after this period of adjustment, then a new era would begin if they would trust in Father's grand and beautiful plans laid out specifically for each one of them. She hesitated to tell them too much, yet she wanted to give them a semblance of what this next period would look like; the oldest and the youngest boys would be part of NASA, the youngest would go into space while the oldest coordinated the expeditions – they would create a dynasty within the aerospace industry. The middle girl would go into teaching; attain a doctorate and ascend to the upper echelon of personnel at Rutgers University. She wanted them to feel happy about that, encouraged and inspired, yet they were young and didn't know how to react and what it all meant, and when Cassandra had said all she needed to say and the talk was over, she could tell there was a small sadness in the way they trudged up the stairs; silently back to their rooms – as if she were leaving them. Without saying a word, Peter had also left back to their bedroom. *All part of God's plan*, she reminded herself. Her last test would now be to tell her extended family: her parents and siblings and their spouses the following week. She would also ask Pastor Meyer to attend as a way to balance his spirituality with the doubt and resistance she was sure to encounter from her own family. Pastor Meyer was a close family friend as he preached to their whole family when

Cassandra was a child. His opinion would carry weight with them.

# 12 – Ohinx

*What terrors, what beauties*
*As we loosen the links*
*Wading deeper into faith*
*The heart, the mind race*

*The steps we take*
*To become complete*

The next day Cassandra was energized with a new resolve to blaze a trail deeper into faith as she arrived at Edwin's apartment with coffee and muffins. She ate only a small amount to keep her spiritual awareness keen. Then, she put on the helmet and laid on the couch. She had a routine at this point, and she let her mind both wander and remain blank as she fell asleep.

She was instantly transported to Ohinx and the Tor ship shuttling through the immensity of the universe.

"Ohinx?" Cassandra asked.

Five years had passed for Ohinx since her last visit, and the once youthful and vigorous man had grown thin with fasting, he had long gray hair, his gray-purple skin was radiant and his gray eyes bright with longing to extract from the universe the knowledge of how he might better help his people. He felt as though he was, in bits and pieces, pulling back the curtain of the internal and spiritual machinations of the universe. The Ixoni conception of God was more akin to calling it "The Source" – like a spiritual sun that incessantly and indiscriminately radiated goodness, patience, intelligence and all the positive qualities a person can imagine – just as a physical sun radiated photons, electrons and other high energy particles. To set up that mental link with The Source, one must "clear the obstructions" in their mind. Therefore, Ohinx attempted to set up this mental link with The Source by curating his own thoughts, diet, exercise, air, light, love, willpower, and wisdom. New internal promptings, not from the enmeshment, presented themselves to his mind via a pragmatic intuition that reminded him to check or recheck certain air and water filtration systems on board the ship to promote safer and healthier environmental conditions for those asleep in the pods. The internal promptings of pragmatic intuition showed him simply the next step. Just focus on the next step required and do not worry about the second or third step. Through that simple change in mindset, he was able to set up an active mental link with The Source that continually controlled the very placement of his hand at a particular angle as he would dip a cup into the water filtration to check the pH.

    Establishing that connection to The Source should have taken three years. Yet, his own intermittent laziness, frustration, or simply failing to properly handle his reactions to daily life mired his progress. From those setbacks, that three-year process turned into five years of slow, painful, spiritual progress that was at once both the most difficult to practice, yet the most rewarding in instruction. Enlightenment was a baffling process – how could one understand the little links of cause and effect that started out as a specific physical and mental routine which then produced beautiful spiritual truths? It just worked for some reason.

Some revelations were encouraging: *Those with hope are always in bloom*; while others admonished: *Gifts become curses if used for the wrong purpose.* As he utilized and embodied each new truth, he was then able to reach new fresh ripe truths that he picked from higher branches and lowered them down to share with his brethren. All the revelations were inspiring and insightful, and they all remained cherished gems within his psyche for others to revere, accept and promulgate within the enmeshment.

Each rotation of the few hundred Tor shifting into wakefulness was grateful and excited to witness and visit the begemmed cathedrals Ohinx built within the enmeshment while they slept, and his mere presence in the enmeshment was healing to them. Ohinx never entered into the stasis pods, and therefore also acted as a stalwart sense of memory, continuity and guidance for the fearful and confused space-faring Tor. The dark streams of consciousness he received from his Tor brethren were then lightened and reflected, like an echo, back to them. With each hard-fought truth, he was becoming that natural jandal light within the enmeshment, incrementally combating and staving off the kortum darkness.

The mental lives of his brethren became his utmost priority, and he started to pursue spiritual advancement to the exclusion of bodily needs. He was so busy in the enmeshment maintaining and advancing that light that it became hard for him to come out of meditation to perform his minimal daily functions. He existed as a ghost – spiritually present in the enmeshment, yet with little active physical presence on the ship.

Despite his commitment, he was not where he needed to be spiritually. The Tor would be arriving at the planet Riquay in six months, and it did not seem enough time. *What do I do*, he thought. He had only ascended up through the lower stages of light starting from the nascent tujur, now to the iljom where he received that his final goal would be the Marbhanic light. The Marbhanic light was a little flash of light given off in the enmeshment when someone died and their consciousness was, very briefly, connected with both the enmeshment and the greater heavenly spheres beyond death.

He felt his greatest spiritual development occurred during periods when the fewest and faintest psyches occupied the enmeshment with him – while everyone else slept and he was alone. The subtleties of being alone were mostly foreign to Ixoni because of their mental link – which as a matter of physiology and being alive they were always both receptive and projected themselves to one another. That interaction was like oxygen and lifeblood to their mental states. Yet, he felt, in this instance, with the enmeshment in its torpid kortum state, that it was holding him back. Therefore he did something drastic.

Typically, when there is a crew shift, both shifts are briefly awake at the same time to talk with one another, update the waking shift, and go over further plans. Yet an opportunity now presented itself to Ohinx. The next crew that was scheduled to wake would be that first crew that was awake when the Tor first left Ixon. They had then been asleep for many years and were set to reawake to once again restart the waking cycle. So, they were familiar with their tasks and would not need much updating on their responsibilities. Therefore, Ohinx had ordered the current wake crew to go to hibernation induction prior to the next crew waking up. Ohinx would sign out all updates and responsibilities to the new crew himself. The crew saw what he was trying to do through their enmeshed intentions, and resisted this order for a time, almost to the point of utter refusal and rebellion. Yet, he showed them the beautiful truth that he had received – he was supposed to do this – obtain the Marbhanic light. As evidence, he reminded them of the beautiful places his ideas built within the enmeshment, he showed them the light that was slowly casting out the darkness that plagued their minds. He was the captain, they were compelled to follow his orders, but he wanted to convince them – to see what he saw. After receiving those ideas, they reluctantly supported his plan. Cassandra had continued to observe him throughout this time, though he was not aware of her.

    Sleep induction was scheduled for the morning, and the new crew would not be awake until midday the next day, so he had about eighteen hours for his experiment before he expected to feel the tethers of his fellow shipmates. Ohinx needed as much time as he could to swim out as far away from land as possible. He had glimpses of those who had left Ixon during the rapture, tracking their brief Marbhanic flight from the world, so he had some idea of the path to obtain a similar light within himself.

    A few days later, the day had now come, the final Tor fell asleep in his sleep pod, conveying to Ohinx, the feeling of anesthesia kicking in as the last Tor's consciousness faded from the enmeshment. After the old crew was put to sleep and Ohinx was alone, it felt as if the world had ended and he was the only one left alive, as if the threads connecting him to some anchor had been cut, and he was now spinning, dizzy, disoriented, moving aimlessly through a void. A void which had always been there, the terror, it had all been there all along, only it was covered by others, and he only noticed it now. It was as if all his senses had been turned off. His mind became confused and rebelled against an unknown threat, and it lashed out against his own psyche – some shapeless black entity writhed and wiggled toward him, and he started to lose his sanity – MELODY, MADNESS, CHISEL, CHEST. OH, OH, OH THE PRIMBAL CHANT. AH, LA LA, FOR FATE RENEW TODAY AS MY DEATH. INTO DEATH. SURGE POWER REVEL ROAM. Little specks of cognition peeled back little curtains in space and spoke mysterious words – a myriad of little pieces of consciousness opened little doors each of which opened and spoke a little mystery into his thousands of ears – each one a different species. They communicated with him via the sound of his own – IT WAS THE SOUND OF HIS OWN MIND CRACKING he learned and watched it happen – splatter against the rigid ridges of stars glistening in the distance. "NOT HERE LITTLE ONE," THEY GIGGLED, faces in the blackness of space, he could hear them GIGGLING – their little eyes, their eyes were NOTHING IN THEIR GRIN WAS NOTHING, yet HE COULD FEEL THEM. IT WAS AN AUDIENCE OF THEM, ALL IN ONE, they had been watching him his whole life, laughing the whole time at his dreams, but this was a dream? The voices, LAUGHING IN THE SOUND OF HIS OWN VOICE, he was himself, peeling, cracking away from himself – separating itself and looking back at him, laughing, the voices in the blackness, he rolled on the floor of his room, his hands in his hair, which of the thousands of scattered eyes, skies, minds were his. His hands didn't work in the coldness of space and he struggled in a panic to grasp at himself, he was their play thing in this state of panic which increased his panic and he's picking at the little marbles rolling away from him, and he hid among the little bright consciousnesses opening the doors as if he were hiding in a school of fish. He was terrified and all the little bright lights fell away from him and there was no obscurity to protect him – and he saw. EYES OPEN, eyes closed, it was the image in his head he could not stop seeing. WHY DID THEY LAUGH? THEY LAUGHED AT HIS DREAMS – AT WHAT HE WAS! NO CONCEPT, NOTHING, TERRIFIED and HUNG INTO NOTHING WITH NOTHING AND NOTHING, but his own Awareness. THERE WAS NO TIME, NO BODY, but HE AND THE VOID AND THE VOICES OF TORMENT CACKLING BEHIND THE BLACK CURTAIN of the universe and all existence was a slow torment by a man laughing behind the – some featureless figure was darting and tip toeing behind THE BLACK CURTAIN slapping at it, making a lot of noise, tiptoeing toward him – outlined faint hunch-backed decrepit body crept, I SEE YOU he shouted, the thing's legs sticking out from beneath the curtain. HE DIDN'T WANT TO EXIST ANYMORE; how does a consciousness exist against infinity – it can't. He was being overcome by infinite space and infinite time, and the only way out was out of existence, and all of death was his to die – HE WANTED TO SLEEP, THE ONLY WAY TO STOP HIMSELF FROM GOING INSANE – IN SAME – was out – TAME – CAME – LAME. HOW DOES IT FEEL TO BECOME A ROCK? HE WAS DANGLING IN THE UNIVERSE, ABOUT TO DROP, TRYING HARD NOT TO BE SMEARED ACROSS THE STARS like a spilled glass – keep the consciousness in the brain – it was going to fall out. HE TWISTED AND CONTORTED INTO EVERY SHAPE rolling around spasmodic epileptic on the floor, HE WANTED TO BREAK HIS OWN BODY AND DESTROY HIS OWN MIND RATHER THAN FACE THAT SHADOW BEHIND THE UNIVERSE AND THOSE WHO DWELT BEFORE HIM. MILLIONS IN THE UNDULATING MADNESS OF PEOPLE DARTING BEHIND A

CURTAIN coercing his mind to tip off balance, "tip, tip little one, tip the glass," FACES TORMENTING HIM, HE ASKED FOR HELP, BUT WHO WAS TO HELP HIM? ALL WERE ASLEEP OR FAR AWAY. HE WAS LOST CLENCHING HIS TEETH AND HIS TEETH SHATTERED AND DROVE THEIR JAGGED ENDS UP INTO HIS GUMS, HE HAD NO ONE BUT THEM, THEIR MINDS MELDED WITH HIS AND THEM. *Why build these cathedrals in your mind?* Now them being him used his self to kill HIMSELF AND JOIN THEM, THE TARP THEY HID BEHIND WAS NOW INVERTED AND COVERED HIM AND THEY WERE FREE TO ROAM AND GIGGLE AND PLAY AND HE WAS THE ONE BEHIND THE SHEET NOW CONTAINED – THE OUTBREATH his lungs collapsed into dense sponges and ringed clean all the air, HIS OWN MUSCLES WERE TETHERS THAT CONSTRICTED HIM – HE ASKED FOR HELP FROM THE SOURCE OF GOODNESS, CALLING OUT FOR A FATHER to protect him. Cassandra observed flashes of these moments and reached her hand out to him. She was then transported back to Earth and awoke from the vision.

    Ohinx continued. Urt? Cass? A light in the darkness, Urth? A valve had opened and a torrent of fluid electricity was passing through his body. He cried out in pain. "A Father…" he eeked out of his lungs as he had forgotten to breathe. The pores cleansed his skin, burning away every thick oil which sat upon the surface, the pores of his bowels shuttered the dross and effluvium purified – everything which held him back. A drop of light fell from a radiating mass, undulating like a living sun, burning white hot and when he looked at the immeasurable mass every possible eventuality lent itself to his mind, everything, unspeakable beasts, the holy form propagated across all space. The holy form was a living shape which could contain a spirit within the living mass of light: the form of a person, was that him, who was he? He looked down at his own hand. Every possible event existed within this sphere – and then it exploded, seeding each possibility throughout endless space. He saw himself fly past his own eyes, retracing his journey to his current destination. Hearts beating underneath blankets saying things to each other which wouldn't fit into a planet, electrons rebelling, planets colliding into each other and new forms growing from the scattered matter, and one piece of that shattered mass dripped a drop off of the new form not yet created and fell transiently toward his forehead and christened him in its cooling water and extinguished his molten body and the vapors which arose from the heat presented as pictures to his mind – a new race already present in the holographic two dimensional planes where all things exist in thought, but waiting to be brought into existence. A voice said to him: *The Tor colony and the Human species must come together as the present state of the universe is about to take on a new form and they would need each other in that new era.* A Holy Spirit does not repeat herself, and there would be a winnowing, as the universe develops itself, some forms get left behind like a shuttered carapace less suitable to receive that greater bounty taken from that formless infinite principality which through the material universe, it bestows its own brilliancy patiently, urgently filling and emptying vessels. New vessels would be soon developed.

    Entity tears, tearing, a teething, a seed, growing roots, six tree rings, a spiral of light lighting fires, but different kinds of fire – first mass, then heat, then light, then electricity, then magnetism, then spirit, then a seventh spiral further out from the others, all built upon one another, what would that seventh force be? A toroid ceaselessly celestially spinning and developing matter. *But does it stop there? Is that the shape of the universe?*

*No, no, one thing at a time – there would be time for that – what was in that drop? The image slipped* away from him like a dream as his body began to wake up and became less rigid. He couldn't remember and he just needed one piece of that mission to anchor him into the whole series of visions. It was the vision of his daughter, who didn't exist at the time which indelibly burned itself into his mind and he wouldn't forget for the rest of his life that mysterious form yet so pleasing to his mind and soul.

*But what was that other species?* he thought.

Their representation among the spiritual sphere represented a single note in the symphony of the heavens – Vi. Vi, Veye, Vie, Vy – VI, VEYE, VIE, VY – Vi, Vi, Vi, Vi. He was remembering – the Ixoni who had traveled away from their planet was Tor expedition – the heavenly spheres referred to them as such – A box opened, Tor, no music, their spiritual sphere note was not mentioned – *Why was it not mentioned?* T…T…T, nothing.

He saw faint rays of light reaching out to him like a phalanx of spears driving against the dark. THE Light against the dark allowed some contrast and he was cognizant enough to be able to turn away from the dark curtain. The light gathered in one location, as if billions of faint small light sources converged upon one location and glowed – a beautiful white, blue, and green object hanging in the darkness. It seemed only a few steps that he took to get there. It looked like his daughter, but different – a woman Ixoni – No, the new sound, Vi – the connection was unusual – she didn't seem to have any awareness of him, and he was able to observe her through a keyhole without the typical sympathetic connection being established. *I must be dead*, acting as a guiding angel to this woman, and so he watched her, her whole life in a matter of moments, and he grew to love her, and now that he died, all his internal being was presented to her like a proud child showing his mother his art work. There was no reticence, no hesitation, no fear to show her who he was. The woman then aged backwards, as if her life was in reverse, as if he could see all the forces which brought her to that moment in perfect clarity. But, he could not place her. A kind of sympathetic connection was created only after he saw her whole life, but it was not like the usual sympathetic connection. It was almost as if he had to look at it only tangentially to feel it. He was tempted to form a greater connection and stay with her, but then he saw other lights, like stars scattered across the expansive void of the universe. How does one describe everything? He felt they beckoned him. They were other worlds, other beings within the universe and then the whole universe, every molecule was instantly before him, the soil, stones, the air, every molecule was aware of him and rejoiced in his presence. Every molecule lit up like one great star and there was no blackness between the dots, as if every object had an internal light radiating forth. He could see infinitely far and infinitely close with infinite clarity down to the very building blocks of the universe because he could feel them. But how did they behave – in particles or in waves?

  He was lectured to by the heavenly bodies – the planets, the comets, the suns, the black holes – all judiciously instructing him. The Vi were the people of Earth, just as the Tor were people from Ixon. The Vi and the Tor represent two opposite principles within the universe. They represent the two opposite forces of the universe which live on opposite sides of the universe which separated themselves in the beginning of this present state of the universe. A singular wave now bouncing back, reverberating, as if they were each a wave out in the ocean, rippling around the spherical universe and once again headed toward each other drawing again to how it started with one single annihilating point.

The forces are not good and evil, for good and evil exist within each of the two forces. Rather, the forces are negative and positive, male and female. But much more than those stereotypical trappings typically assigned to those roles. Because male and female of any holy form should not idealize becoming just male or just female attributes within those forces, because that would not be a fulfilling purpose. For the best of us are masters of each and highly expressive of both their male and female ideals. Good and evil forces exist within the forces of negative and positive. Both the negative force and positive force have within their midst those who are ignorant and those who are wise; those who love and hate or are indifferent.

He also received knowledge of his own race, from the perspective of an objective observer. Given that the Tor are intimately connected in thought, it is necessary to explain some of these mechanisms. The mind is unable to annihilate a thought. The effort to do so will only create more attention to that thought. But, the mind can ignore a thought, push it away, and it will naturally move on to another thought for the entity's consideration. It is this exercise of ignoring thoughts and allowing the internal force to present another thought which allows the Tor to maintain their own thoughts and thus their own identities, otherwise they would return to the archaic period of sharing a mind with one another without individuality – as it had been in what the spirits termed the Ixoni's archaic history. Ohinx was shown that the Ixoni were originally derived from a hive-mind and the masses bent to the will of other more powerful individuals and lost their own identity. But, that was the past. Pushing a thought away is second nature to Ixoni, but Ohinx had to understand that the Vi do not know the pitfalls of collective thought.

Ohinx was shown other things from the Vi on Earth. They did not have an enmeshment, but they had a primitive communication through their breath and conveyed through the eyes. For instance, a mob mentality was a collective consciousness based on fear and security similar to the kortum darkness presiding over the Tor enmeshment. Physical societies of the Vi were beautified, while their thoughts were often unrefined – which was opposite the Tor who attempted to beautify their thoughts, but their physical buildings were humble. The Vi species was born of individualism while the Tor started out in a collective. As the universe progresses, the Vi are now headed toward collectivism while the Tor are headed toward individuality. The Tor's consciousness started at the other end of the spectrum from their Vi counterpart, the Vi's early history reflects people whose thoughts and feelings were so dissimilar from one another that Ohinx was surprised they could even communicate through a singing wind, or the breaths – they called talking. The unification of Tor and Vi will be required to maintain the positive aspects of collectivism and individuality, while also protecting against the dangers of the same. They are two waves headed toward each other. As the waves collide some will be pushed higher before the two waves pass each other and go in opposite directions.

As he familiarized himself with the Vi, he was accustomed to being intimately connected with his own race; he did not know universal etiquette for relationships. So, he often came across as being too attached to whomever he made contact because that was what he was used to. On Ixon, he was able to know most everyone's thoughts, hopes, dreams, fears, sexual fantasies, toileting habits – none of it was more or less polite or proper than any other topic. It was a shock for him to come from that environment, and then to be exposed to entities across the universe with other thinking customs. It created tension. Most of the Vi he connected with preferred talking about some topics more than other topics, and some topics remained in total obscurity – so he had to adjust.

    Ohinx was currently acting as a discarnate entity minimally attached to his physical body, and when finding a receiving vessel to commune with among the Vi, he immediately sought to know everything about that other entity and his overflowing interest sometimes had the opposite effect of what he intended, and that communing entity became closed off, suspicious, and withdrawn to his intense interest in them. But this itself proved to be beneficial to Ohinx's education in that he realized that not every entity he came upon was one he should become familiar with. He was told all these things by the guiding spirits but did not heed their warning readily and a few times some ill-tempered discarnate entities sought to distract him, misguide him, or outright trace their fingers along that fine tether leading back to his physical body and possess him. Luckily, he was with company and was shown how to wisely conduct himself. It was these types of entities that now surrounded the Tor ship and reinforced the imtombi darkness – but he was told not to fixate on them, and he would get more information on them later.

    "What do you want to do now?" they asked him. He had finished their initial tutorial of the cosmos and now he could decide what to do.

    "I want to find that woman who saved me from the darkness of my own mind; name of "Cas?" he said and thought of her image. He found her among a star the Vi of Earth affectionately referred to as *their* sun. The first words, the first idea he wanted to convey to her was that moment she saved him and what she meant to him. Because this was the most important thing to him and thus, he wanted to say that thing first. *You saved me – I love you!* he wanted to express to her. But, as he moved he found himself not conversing with her, but with a male figure named Edwin that was in spatial proximity to her and acting like a look-out, a guard with wings with a spear of light just like those spears that drove back the figures in the void, just like that angel that hung over Ixon many years ago. That man was welcoming, and Ohinx saw through his eyes, and felt what he felt. It was almost as if that same link which existed between Ixoni was now accepted by this stranger. And, in an instant the two knew each other. Cassandra was driving a car. He was preparing to be her husband.

Ohinx learned what a husband was. The Vi, by intention, choose with whom they wanted to intimately consociate and procreate, whereas the Tor perform that task (or rather have that task performed for them) automatically, naturally, rather than making that decision themselves – as the Vi would do. So, he became confused momentarily, one because of the mating customs of the Vi, and two because he was expecting to interact directly with this woman, so when she looked at him and said "Edwin?" and Ohinx repeated, "Ed…win?" with a vibration conveyed to the oral cavity he said it as a question. He hoped for a better explanation, just as those universal guiding spirits had explained to him whatever he wanted to know just with one thought.

However, Cassandra, oblivious to Ohinx's expectations, only said, "Hello?"

"Hello!" he said. He was about to say that very thing he had prepared. But, before he could do that he was politely asked to leave by the entity Edwin who originally resided in that vessel. And he returned to the open streams of the universe.

And, soon he did not realize that he had his eyes open and he was in his ship. He had a body; his whole body was sore. He looked at the time – it had been half an hour, and he was profusely bleeding from his mouth. He reoriented himself, and thought, *our new destination will not be Riquay, but rather we will join the Vi on Earth.*

As his spiritual advisors withdrew to attend to other seeking minds, he was left alone to explore and contemplate the expansive trails of the universe nearing infinity. The universe is wondrous and the gems of creation lie in our own appreciation more than in that which is appreciated – that is the evolution of the universe. He looked upon the universe like a parent looks upon a child. Ohinx, became somewhat worried about going back to the Tor connections. He was afraid that he would become bored with that mundane existence and the Tor, in general, would hold him back from ascending to further realms of wonder. The truths he had received were building blocks that incrementally brought him to greater realms, and in coming back down to the Tor, those fine, intricate, delicate truths would be useless in lower rudimental realms of existence. He could see why philosophers, of any species of the holy form, they tried to distance themselves from the external stimuli to transcend to greater planes of thought and it was a pure connection with that infinite source of all, becoming a receptacle of pure inspiration received from that infinite sun which was the pursuit of every philosopher.

Would that mundane plane of existence upon which he used to tread, would it move too slowly? Would the steady stream of excitement become deprecated amid the monotony of typical existence? Would all sensations be privations compared to where his mind was now? Would the enmeshment feel like a prison? He didn't want to forget this feeling – that there were invisible forces connecting every living being in the universe. How could he express that connection within the small portion of existence in which they conducted their business. He wondered how he could have ever been afraid of eternity. Now he needed it, and that rudimental plane was not the plane that he wanted to remain upon for any appreciable amount of time. There was nothing for him back there, that slow plane represented one part of existence, while he was more preoccupied now with the realm of the mind, of dreams, of spirit which represented the other plane of existence. It is within the realm of mind and spirit that all his challenges would now lie. He wanted to vanish from the craft – hide his material body squirreled away in some hidden recess where no one would ever look within this vast floating city and from there, as his body desiccated, birth a new form, or take a sleep pod and lie in it indefinitely as he traveled spiritually through that congenial bearded soul in charge of travel and launched on his next vivid adventure within the mind and spirit. He had access to it. The universe was all there waiting for him, the actions, the events, the efforts of his heart's content.

    Trifles, all small trifles, scrambling and squabbling and clamoring back in the previous sphere antagonistically vying for space. He saw all of it, it was not the soul or spirit that became tired, but rather the means by which the spirit/soul interacted with the physical body which became depleted by hitherto unknown laws of nature, which now seemed so obvious. How did material existence become backwards, become antithetical to that original beautiful vantage point? How could antagonisms be fervently sustained in an overwhelmingly beautiful universe?

Out there he seeded the minds of artists, inspired writers, gave clarity to engineers and mathematicians – they all felt like his brothers, sisters, daughters, sons and their joy gave him joy and inspiration, gave him inspiration and pushed him closer to the next spheres of existence. There was no loss that wasn't wanted, no gain that wasn't stepped toward. He was part of vivifying the universe to life – bathing it in beauty. But soon, amid the glory draped over his shoulders, parading around his love, he knew he had to turn back – the watch was set, and this beautiful existence would mean nothing, this splendor would fade if he did not remember those privileged words spoken to him in a song by the universal spirit – "Vi". He alone heard that sound, and ascending so high his own spiritual voice became a hymn to guide him which said to him, "Nature does not repeat herself" and time in that physical sphere was essential. So, he was torn, he could go back so easily if the universe weren't so beautiful and inspiring, if the dichotomy between these two worlds weren't so great. He felt like he was forcing himself to go back to a willing banishment from Heaven – as if there were at an impasse.

He was quickly reminded by some passing spiritual friend that it was his choice. He could stay and that would be okay – the universe is too beautiful for confusion. Ohinx stayed relatively close to Cassandra, and he observed their planet Jupiter. It circled *their* sun, its ring would one day become a moon, it would one day have beautiful life on its surface – all according to the laws of the universe. Ohinx had his own instructions, and he remembered the original purpose that motivated him to attain enlightenment in the first place – to help the Tor. Therefore, he reasoned, there are realms above this present state of even more resplendence, opulence and joy, and above those too, where new eyes and ears would be needed just to taste the euphoric heights of sensation – all radiating outward infinitely from the universal spirit, who spoke to him – "Vi". The roads to higher spheres lie in executing the will of the infinite source, which now rewarded him with what he wanted – a way to help his people. The creator of all splendor is able to perform all these tasks on his own, and The Source was not so weak that he "needed" Ohinx to do anything – all was choice. He realized his path to those greater spheres lay, paradoxically, in the voluntary subjugation of his own free will in abeyance with The Source to once again occupy his physical body. Ohinx need not be conflicted, this task was for his own benefit, if he so chose, but what could he have left to learn back in that sphere?

Who could be his confidante among his own people to replenish his soul and stay the degradation? It was the man who asked him to leave – Edwin, and his wife, free from that imtombi darkness. They could be the key to those greater spheres. If he could meet them, then a bulwark of divine inspiration could be established between them and, if they facilitated and cultivated that divine bliss, then the three of them could slowly extend that sphere to encompass the whole community of Vi and Tor to raise their planet to the next sphere. They could be an example of divine beauty and if they stayed true to themselves then others would catch on.

He didn't know how much time he had left before the other crew awoke, so he returned to Edwin. Even though they were intimately connected they didn't think the same way. So, he knew what he wanted to say, but the words and ideas did not flow readily and did not convey their true meaning. He had trouble controlling Edwin's body, and the constant pain of being in his body did not dissuade him from being able to look directly at Cassandra. He smiled, and she smiled back at him, as she walked in the door. He wanted to say something, but it felt like moving hard clay around. He didn't know if he would get the chance again, so he blurted out, "Yo…yo…Yosemite!" *No, that's not right,* he thought. It felt like he was experiencing sleep paralysis – his mind was awake, but he couldn't move his body, which terrified him, as if he would be trapped here indefinitely and he'd forget how to get out. *Let's try that again.* "Youu…" he sounded like an old man's last words – *that's all right, they'll be my last words then.* "You saved me!" he said with every muscle in his body contracted to try to coordinate phonation, and let his muscles loosen and he was exhausted and the media through which his spirit interacted with this body quickly exhausted itself and by a change in polarity another magnetic force created a static bond with the body and as the two forces briefly touched, Ohinx mentally conveyed his plan to Edwin.

"If Father wills it," Edwin said.

Then, Ohinx also attempted to contact other Vi through the enmeshment, but they weren't listening and their cyor seemed undeveloped as a child's. The beta frequency of their mind was too dense to facilitate a receptive mindset. They had a faint presence in the enmeshment, during their sleeping hours or briefly in deep meditation, and more so with the females. Yet interaction remained difficult and often they only became engaged and paid attention when Ohinx relayed to them the most awesome of visual scenes that he could remember of his own planet of battles, animals, flying ships in the air, the rapture on his planet, which Vi mistook as vivid dreams, rather than actual scenes from a far off planet. So, Ohinx became receptive to humans projecting outward their intentions and actions during the day as a way to continue to learn about them.

# 13 – Relkiv

*Now it all comes toppling over*
*Tipping, crashing, then compressed*
*It's all scattered now*
*All you've built*

*Faith is the principle*
*That rallies to it a scattered sum*
*All the power of many suns*
*Or just a few twigs*
*Or a tattered one*

*Stand up from death*
*Use what is left*
*another breath, another breath*

On Earth, Cassandra had once again put the device on her head and entered into her visions. She had not seen Ohinx ascend to the Marbhanic light. She now picked up with him just after he had awoken from that ascension.

Ohinx had finished eighteen hours of meditation and saw the little nascent lights of his brethren emerging from their sleep and forming in the enmeshment. Ohinx was surprised to feel excited to once again connect with his

Tor brethren after the many arduous years of focusing on isolated meditation.

Relkiv was the first to awake, and he awoke to Ohinx as the only one with whom he could mentally converse. Ohinx was superiorly situated and naturally presented to Relkiv a Marbhanic light. Relkiv, being a pragmatic man with a large ego and retaining the vestiges of the imtombi-riddled enmeshment, now came to tentatively commingle with Ohinx's reformed enmeshment. Ohinx perceived Relkiv as a small wisp of smoke coming into the enmeshment and diffusing into the spacious environment of their mental location.

It started with their personal and professional relationship, then expanded until it became a magnificent connection of divine beauty, love, warmth, light. He was showing Relkiv that Relkiv could form similar relationships with the universe and with the source of all goodness. The waking Relkiv, disoriented, just pulling back the cover from his mind as he awoke, was receptive and had the proper mental reaction as Ohinx had hoped for.

"Good, Good," Ohinx thought. Currently, it was only Relkiv and Ohinx and their personal relationship now expanded to form the whole of the enmeshment. So, Relkiv, through Ohinx also had a touch of the infinite sun which produced a permeating force which was the building block of all other natural forces. Ohinx's ascendancy raised Relkiv's perception simply by osmosis and proximity. Ohinx's five-year plan was working: his light was driving out the pervasive Imtombi darkness, he would once again establish a proper enmeshment. As Relkiv continued to wake, he was in a kind of expedient upward fall as he felt alone – perceiving Ohinx only as a Marbhanic light. So, Relkiv thought he was dying all alone in space because the Marbhanic light, as the last action of all dying Ixoni, was therefore indelibly linked with death to all Ixoni. Relkiv misinterpreted the sensations and the feeling of being alone to an Ixoni reinforced the feeling of death and each one must overcome it in their own way as Ohinx had. For Relkiv, the emptiness of space was an echo chamber for his own thoughts projecting out and back onto him his own large ego in the form of wild panicking tentacles writhing in the darkness, scrambling for something to latch onto. It was a kind of suffocation, like a fish attempting to flop around to get back to the ocean.

But, then in utter blackness of space, Relkiv saw that the pervasive darkness was partly himself. He did not like what he saw, and he could not let go of that Imtombi force to face himself and the tentacles clung more tightly to his "self". He could not let go of the fear of letting that self become discarded. He did not want his "self" to die. There is a little light in everyone's "self", which, similar to the central spiritual sun shining and lighting everything in the universe, however, someone like Relkiv, at such a junction in their spiritual development must, at least momentarily douse the light of their own ego to be able to appreciate the subtle, all-pervading light of the central spiritual sun to see the beauty in the blackness of space teeming with life. Yet, Relkiv hadn't practiced. He was struggling at this time to make such a transition, and Ohinx watched carefully as Relkiv struggled with the choice. Ohinx offered a hand, which Relkiv could not see, all he saw was the void between worlds, an Oributh darkness, a purgatory between lands, where all other senses were shut off. Ohinx was gravitating toward the darkness with which he was more familiar simply as a means of survival to attempt to hold something in the dead of space. Space to him was death, with all his senses off, he sensed something else, someone else. It was his own ego, the only light that he could see. It also acted like a beacon for other entities roaming the void who were also unable to transition and continually stuck and clung to anything they could sense, anything that would allow them to delight in sensation.

Everything became so bright that Relkiv couldn't see. He had no physiological mechanism with which to resolve the blinding light. And, in grasping for definition, one of the creatures wound its way along the tendrils leading back to his body and Relkiv grabbed onto it. Ohinx was rebuffed in his attempts to shoo the creature away. Ohinx saw the creatures that had followed them into the voids of space. They had been allowed to be released on Ixon – most of those creatures were still there. They traveled the universe waiting to prey on those spiritual children and pillage everything that was good. Ohinx could now see the evil lurking in the universe. He had been so wrong as a young man – he thought the only evil was ignorance – but no, there was intentional evil waiting for him. There are spiritual parasites and soul viruses. How can entities exist within the universe which spit at the source of all creation, prey upon the light and exist in darkness past the Oribut – UMVOC they called itself and it reached now for Relkiv. How can anything anathema to The Source be contained within the universe which was created by that Source? The creature reached deep down into Relkiv's heart and touched the seat of his spirit and a coldness imprinted itself onto him. A thought of conquest excited Relkiv's mind, and salivation watered from his mouth before he could balance incoming sensations with his own inherent proclivities of goodness.

Ohinx's outstretched arm was crowded out as Relkiv became inundated with discarnate entities and they clung to him with an intuitive flattery of his ego. Relkiv wanted them. They used that flattery to gain his unconscious confidence, and he became confused about which one was him. That confusion at this critical junction magnified itself and mirrors crashed into his consciousness, and he tried to pick up the shattered glass only to cut himself on the shards. He thought the mirror was himself and he attempted to force his ego back into what he knew it was. He was trying to go back to himself. "We can share," they whispered to himself as a duality formed – dual consciousness, a phenomenon only speculated by the Ixoni spiritual scientists. Relkiv had learned about it as a child. A concept so dear and tantalizing in his early development, now he nearly went mad with elation being given the opportunity to achieve it through what he thought were angelic beings and his own spiritual advisors. They told him he had also become enlightened and this was his gift, yet Relkiv could not see that the light they reflected was that of Ohinx and of Relkiv's own light and goodness now deluded itself covering the grotesque forms of these beings. Being his own light and therefore a comforting familiar sight to himself, he found contentment in the current state of things, not wanting to expand his mind again and was dismissive to the promptings of his soul and of Ohinx.

Relkiv, now possessing a dual consciousness, one hemisphere of his mind connected to the umvoc and with the other hemisphere he formed a tenuous relationship with Ohinx. But Ohinx was too high for Relkiv to ascend without causing himself pain. With his umvoc hemisphere, Relkiv projected a similar type of imtombi enmeshment as a way to weigh himself down. Other Tor then arrived to the enmeshment, still dazed from their anesthesia wearing off. The first to awake were Wentre, Alcor, then Vaish. Relkiv, in having his thoughts once again connected to those who had awoken, he felt a pain or stiffness. Ohinx once again tried to associate with those waking Tor, but he seemed not a person, but a distant Marbhanic light, which to the Tor, meant death.

Relkiv saw that Wentre gravitated toward the artificial enmeshment that Relkiv created because it felt more familiar. Ohinx tried to push out his hand to him, but Wentre didn't recognize him because Ohinx was a completely different person compared to when they went to sleep fifteen years ago. Wentre, by his own choice associated with Relkiv's enmeshment and perceived Ohinx simply as an influence like the sun.

Relkiv felt less pain as he was weighed down further by associating with Wentre's own imtombi influence. Simply as an act of survival, Relkiv sought to entwine others in the artificial enmeshment and divert the Tor down a misguided fork in the road, a bend in the natural evolution of the Tor expedition, and a new idea coincidentally opened up to Relkiv, and he felt pleasure, power and passion for conquest – when for so long he had felt fear, as all Ixoni had. Relkiv knew there was some accidental yet powerful opportunity happening within himself and he wanted to exploit it.

The natural enmeshment was just a part of nature. Its progression was guided by nature slowly developing that environment. Yet, Relkiv now set up a division within the Tor which had never existed prior to him creating it now. He was now the first to do this. That natural enmeshment, now being co-opted by a dark force through Relkiv, became artificial and unnatural. Nature's guiding influence was now usurped and governed by Relkiv and the creatures that helped him – and all the Tor were in jeopardy of being willing captives. With each pulse, push, pull propagating from the intention of those few beings, now Relkiv could see Wentre and Vaish unknowingly submit to the artificial enmeshment as if it were the natural prompting of nature.

This power was new to Relkiv and he used it clumsily and with great pain to his mind as he felt his mind splitting down the center. Having a dual consciousness, he did not use his cyor with as much alacrity as previously. Relkiv was no longer as perceptive and discerning as he deluded himself also. Ohinx had ascended so high and the others now so low that Ohinx saw Relkiv as a little reptile on a rock preaching to other little reptiles, scarcely aware of their own captive state.

Then Alcor awoke. Ohinx had a previous affection for the female Alcor and it was from the previously developed genuine love toward her, that when she woke, though Ohinx was almost a completely different entity – that love that he felt for her persisted like a father reuniting with his daughter. In the endless, dizzying sphere of the universe, among the grandeur of the spiritual citizens, love is a real force. When all semblance of ignorance and falsehood fall away as one's spirit is developed, still, that love remains. Anyone can love, and start accumulating love, adding love to others, sharing love, developing it in themselves like packing a backpack for your long future journey into the universe for when you depart your present rudimental plane. Don't be afraid of the many mistakes that you will make in this journey because love will eventually triumph and the sting of mistakes, the sting of little deaths, the sting of lost ego, physical and financial hardship will bloom into something greater than love, which you will know, which you will realize only if you love. Because genuine love the two shared, though somewhat eccentric and unbalanced, was enough to give her a chance. She could see Ohinx as a person – as others ignored that Marbhanic light he expressed, she realized that light was Ohinx.

Alcor was out of sync, and when presented with Relkiv's enmeshment she did not react in the same way as Wentre and Vaish who readily associated with it. With the various waves, whirls, emanating from Relkiv he could see that artificial enmeshment fall upon her, yet her cyor was more perceptive than her male counterparts, and her perception and her body held against that threatening tide like a breakwater. He was not able to see inside the harbor of her heart as he was able to see into Vaish and Wentre. Previously, all Tor were intimately connected, yet with this unnatural enmeshment that they existed in, it did not encompass, extend and pervade all aspects of Alcor as her sympathetic nervous system warned her of something amiss.

Relkiv continued to attempt to subdue and overwhelm her heart as she awoke, presenting to her wandering eyes little shadows peeking out from behind objects, lights appearing brighter than normal saturating her vision and causing her cyor to "squint" and "wince" from an unknown feeling of sadness. In subtle ways he tried to coerce her and trick her cyor to give up a greater portion of herself. Yet, if he was not able to reach her, then he was going to get rid of her.

Vaish and Wentre conveyed streams of consciousness amid themselves as a form of conversation – yet everything in this new enmeshment was run through Relkiv now. So, he told them to stop because it was distracting to him. Relkiv didn't know where Alcor was physically on the ship amid the myriads of sleep pods – he had to focus. He sent Vaish and Wentre to find her.

Ohinx saw everything as clear as day. Ohinx tried once again to commune with Vaish and Wentre as they were no longer in close proximity to Relkiv – yet they continued to be scarcely aware of him. That small connection Ohinx held with Alcor gave her a hazy impression of something being wrong as she now sat up in her sleep pod. There were always dark waves within the enmeshment like phases of night and day. This particular instance of darkness was difficult for her, and she felt as if she were dying, losing her ability to fully sense the enmeshment, because the false enmeshment that presented to her was not as vivid and visceral as it was previously on Ixon. She saw Vaish, Wentre and Relkiv, but they looked and felt different in the enmeshment, out of proportion – larger. The thought entered her mind that she was going to die. And the enmeshment became drowned and saturated with one kind of sound and the volume of that sound increased. The other three did not seem to hear it. She closed her eyes and looked forward to the next phase of life through the door of death to Ohinx's Marbhanic light that seemed to beacon her from the other side. She had dreams, she was the same person in the physical world as in the enmeshment, where did she go wrong? She wanted to help children. What would now happen to those dreams? Who would help the children? There did not seem to be one to whom she could pass her torch of purpose amid a suffocating darkness. Her heart was filled with confusion and a finger thumbed the string of her soul like a hand strumming one string of a guitar – the sound was deafening – DUM, DUM, the vibration of her soul hit against a hard portion, muted, and it was not allowed to ring out in perfect harmony with nature as it usually was and dissonance filled her ears – DUM, DOOM, DOOM, DOOM, *The Source* she thought, DOOM she said, OOOOOM, she felt nauseous as if she were slowly lowering herself into her own grave. She felt a pressure sensation on her forehead. DOOOM, DOOM, *the light*, she thought, and a faint light danced in her heart amid the DOOM DOOM DOOM. This was it. I must be dying. This must be what death feels like. The Marbhanic light awaiting her like a lighthouse showing her passage appearing as Ohinx who always felt like a Father. DOOM DOOM, "Father…I need you" DOOM DOOM DOOM, "Father, I need you," and the dancing light increased in size, until it was upon her like a speeding object and wrapped his arms around her, a brilliant familiar face entered her volition with an even greater brilliancy and splendor she was accustomed to seeing – the clear smiling face of Ohinx wrapped in bliss dripping from his brow that he was able to reach her; now able to hold his daughter, quieting the tone in her mind, altering it to remove the dissonance, and he spoke to her with the voice of The Source, "My daughter."

She must be dead, that familiar Marbhanic light ushered her into Heaven. She could feel more love than had existed in the varying degrees of darkness since the rapture.

Relkiv saw her slipping from his grasp, as if he at once held the whole world in his hands with his new enmeshment, and that was now slipping from him as she slipped toward the other enmeshment occupied now by Ohinx. He was so close to holding all thoughts, all actions of others within his own domain, like a black hole, pulling everything in and presenting it back to him as a two-dimensional surface which he could read and know everything – every thought, every influence. He was not going to let that get away from him. He was going to find her and, by whatever means, bring her back, or snuff out her light. But she was slipping away from him as she followed that other path, and he was having trouble placing her physical body.

On her part, she was still weak, barely able to take possession of her own mind and it floated like driftwood where two waters of different temperatures and salinity meet and she was tossed and turned as the two waters fought to engulf her – two living waters which sought balance, yet did not want to concede any position to the other. Funnels and vortices tossed her mind around; she was a link between the two enmeshments. It was too painful; she couldn't let go of or hold on to either one of them.

"Release the others, quickly now," Ohinx conveyed to her, "It's the only way."

Relkiv combed through the records of the ship to find her pod as he canceled the wake protocol for the other hundreds of Tor that were scheduled to wake. Alcor could barely move as she struggled to regain her strength. Her goal was to manually release the rest of the Tor from their slumber and the collective pressure of the waking minds naturally gravitating toward Ohinx and the natural enmeshment would overwhelm the artificial enmeshment.

After ten minutes of feeling lost and torn asunder between two oceans, she gained enough strength to stand on her own with wobbling legs. The added strength of her waking mind unfortunately acted like a greater beacon for Relkiv to approximate her physical location. She manually unlocked the pod next to her and then went down the line. She had unlocked ten pods when Relkiv rushed into the pod hanger.

"Stop that," he conveyed. The umvoc, through instantaneous flashes, used Relkiv's half mind to convey to Alcor every type of insanity to falsely stop her from unlocking the other sleep pod.

"No," she conveyed.

Relkiv lunged at her and took hold of her and wrestled her to the ground. He shoved her to the ground and, with half of his mind he entered into a deep trance and tried to connect with that piece of his enmeshment that still touched her nervous system. She was not as perfect as Ohinx, part of her wanted that artificial enmeshment as Wentre and Vaish did. She had participated in some of those wars after the rapture. She had been excited by all the violence. A series of random pictures alternating between the two enmeshments flipped in her vision. The heavy-handed nature of this interaction betrayed its own intentions as she was now able to more concretely feel and perceive that amorphous presence of the artificial enmeshment.

Relkiv, seeing Alcor's realization, frustrated by his own misstep, became ever more angry. Relkiv preferred to add Alcor to his enmeshment as she was beautiful and more pure, and to subvert that kind of spirit would all the more easily bring others to his side.

As they struggled with each other, Alcor reached for a small piece of furniture to use as a weapon against Relkiv. The Tor in the sleep pod next to her, Lairu, began to wake.

"1-2-3-4" Lairu conveyed through her cyor, "1-2" she was counting breaths as she was doing in the moments before she was put to sleep. Her loving presence was felt immediately. She was a teacher back on Ixon and, from that profession developed the skill of keeping herself separate from the young children that she taught, and she acted as an instructive influence for the young ones to follow. She treated this artificial enmeshment in the same way she behaved in response to the many errors the children would make in their behavior. As she slowly awoke, she giggled at the funny sensation that was attempting to overwhelm her. She immediately rejected the artificial enmeshment and joined the natural one. Vaish and Wentre were a few minutes behind Relkiv and they immediately took up a utility ax and swung it into the pod, breaking through the outer protective layer and plunged it into Lariu's chest and she collapsed in the pod and her blood pooled to fill the lower portion of the stasis cylinder. Her last thoughts were an explosive symphony of electrical discharges of Marbhanic light that, combined with Ohinx, momentarily brought Vaish and Wentre to their senses.

    Despite Alcor's sympathy toward Ohinx and the gravitation toward his celestial office, she continued to feel some similar feeling toward Relkiv. Some of those feelings in him were also in her and she felt she was neither as good as Ohinx nor as bad as Relkiv.

    The other nine waking Tor, the flash of Marbhanic light, Vaish and Wentre gravitating toward Ohinx all distracted Relkiv and he became a catatonic weight atop Alcor, as Relkiv used all of his focus to reestablish the false enmeshment. Alcor had the opportunity to use the piece of furniture to hit him off of her and he rolled away stiff as a board.

    Alcor limped away into a half run and then in her weakened state her muscles failed her and her forward momentum tipped past her center of gravity and she fell forward into a roll, and she toppled over onto her right side once again on the ground. Relkiv reestablished the artificial enmeshment and subdued Vaish and Wentre. Relkiv was now observing the internal processes of Alcor's mind with delight as he realized that the more she panicked, the more she became defenseless to his mental incursion and each time she blinked, each time she became dizzy another false sensation was presented to her cyor unbeknownst to her – similar to when one is tired and the mind plays tricks through quick flashes of dreams to divert one's attention into a dream to trick you into sleep by thinking you are still awake. However, the tense situation also betrayed this false sense that Relkiv was attempting to place in her head. He could not convince her that she was not under attack and she resisted sleep. Wentre and Vaish cornered her, and in her confusion a pearl of light, reminded her that these were once her close brethren. She held onto that thought and tried to express it in her thoughts, with her actions, demeanor, the way she moved across the floor as she backed up to the walls, "My sweet brothers" and those sentiments flew past their awareness with a flicker of their eyelids. Her back was now pressed against a cold metal wall and the heat from her back was instantly conducted into the ship and taken from her body.

"Brother..." she conveyed to them as tears welled up in her eyes and poured from her heart, "Brothers," She focused, imbued with the purest and brightest crystal of sentiment she showed to the approaching assailants. "Father..." She conveyed to Ohinx as they took hold of her limbs and held her to the ground. Relkiv assumed a meditative position. It wasn't real, she thought, or was it real, she couldn't remember which was real and which was artificial – what was dark and what was light. It felt like someone was hitting the thoughts out of her mind and she was beginning to lose consciousness. She could feel Relkiv, a shadow in her thoughts approaching the seat of her autonomy, her consciousness. She had to resist, if she lost her consciousness, she was not sure where it would end up, what would be real.

Relkiv lost patience and now stood up and took hold of the ax and walked over to her. He got on top of her, straddled her torso and held the handle of the ax against her neck. That same sensation of dying in the enmeshment was now recurring, Relkiv wanted to recreate that feeling of dying and that it was Relkiv, and not the light from before that was her only way out, only way through to life was by Relkiv's hand. The revelations of light which once lit her cyor was now being suppressed as she became suspicious of the entire material world. The pain was too much. She wished she was stronger. She didn't want to die, she wanted to care for children, and by exploiting that desire Relkiv could feel darkness reach into her heart, which had resisted him so diligently, she lost faith, and the creative light dimmed. No sentry on the parapet held its post to keep out the enemies from her heart. Relkiv assumed her own voice and told her to let go as dark tentacles appeared to slither into her heart and wrapped around it like a snake. Its tendrils were like roots that subverted her own sensations, thoughts, unconscious promptings, and that celestial infinity that exists within all sentient beings then offered itself up to what it thought was its master, that place reserved for The Source now seated some unknown entity – and Alcor's tense muscles relaxed and she fell into a deep sleep. With Alcor asleep, the other pods that she had opened were once again closed and the passengers put back to sleep.

The darkness was partly with the Tor when they left their world, and Relkiv was looking for those darkest people to wake them first and recruit them. He saw that if he woke everyone at the same time then he would lose his grip. Relkiv took the plans that Ohinx had developed to root out the darkness, by waking everyone one by one and now use it as a means to promote it. He would wake the darkest among them; they would be most easily recruited. Relkiv would use them to support, sustain and proliferate the false enmeshment. He would keep those bright lights in stasis until he could build enough force to compel them.

It was terrible. Someone was murdered. And, one of the Tor is now holding everyone else hostage," Cassandra said. She felt all of it reaching into her own heart. "Not again. The violence, the hate. Every time I put on the headset there was another monumental tragedy to witness. I never want to use the headset again. I was helpless. I was no use."

"You did help Ohinx." Edwin said. And, she realized the pain and torment she felt – that is what Edwin experiences every moment of every day. Her reprieve was removing the headset, but Edwin had no reprieve save for Father and the angels of Heaven. This is what she said "yes" to for Father. This is what would, in some unknown spiritual way, save the Earth.

As Cassandra calmed down, she and Edwin looked at each other, both were baffled, and Edwin said, "that wasn't supposed to happen."

# 14 – The Singing Garden

*What does the future hold?*
*So much is unknown*
*So just tread lightly*
*In body and in soul*

Heis had been adjusting his device for the past several months, and now completed, his mental energy expended, he pushed himself away from his desk, rubbing his eyes. He was a paradoxical mix of fatigue and hypervigilance as he had been fasting for the past week. His hands shook as he took out a pocket-size black notebook he kept in his back pocket. It was filled with otherworldly devices which had no known earthly similarity. They were all inspired by the one-on-one millisecond flash of connection he had with Edwin. As if Heis had reached his hand directly into Heaven and pulled from there twelve devices – the purposes for which he was not sure. The impressions he was given that night he faithfully transcribed, filling twelve notebooks – one notebook for each device. Now, as he thumbed through the pages, he didn't know whether to burn them, patent them or keep them to himself. They made all his inventions look like children's toys and he was now beginning to lose enthusiasm for his own creations.

Heis had been fasting for extended periods intermittently throughout these few months. He did it for multiple purposes; to keep himself clear headed, sharp and focused while he tweaked his device and wrote down the other twelve devices; and as a small sacrifice in deference to these beautiful devices which he was shown. Before he broke his fast, he wanted to celebrate by visiting the new Zizuri Aria Choral Gardens. This respite would act synergistically with his fasting state as his sense of smell was now highly attuned, and he anticipated that the smells, sights and sounds of the singing gardens combined with his increased olfactory acuity would almost rival the sensations of the heavenly outer world.

Unfortunately, the opposite was also true, and the fasting state caused him to detest many of the scents of the city, his building and even his own apartment. Any little bit of grime on his keyboard, his desk, on the walls and edifices of the city became abhorrent to him. He had to cut a piece of lemon and hold it close to his nose as he walked through the city to the botanical garden.

The Zizuri Aria Choral Garden was the first botanical garden of its kind – a great clear, domed structure hermetically sealed to prevent the escape of the genetically modified plants. The ease of gene modification had recently risen to the capability of allowing the artistically minded to easily express their creativity using the genetic code of plants as a medium. Within the Aria were the biomes: Tropical, Desert/Chaparral, Temperate, Grassland, Alpine and Aquatic. Within each large biome were fifty musicians and singers each walking the path on their own individually. Each individual strolled along the garden playing and singing, the sheet music fed into their augmented reality glasses. As they circulated, the glasses also directed them where to walk and when to stop so that small ephemeral nodes of 4-6 musical performers would briefly form like old friends catching up on each other's lives. Patrons close to a node would hear that specific melody, which, when the node dispersed, each performer continued to play and the music turned into a large amorphous, yet beautiful choral choir, ringing in harmony with one another against the domed clear walls of the biome.

    When Heis entered the aural and olfactory excitement of the singing gardens, he threw away the lemon and gingerly ambled along the garden path appreciating the aromatic vapor emanating from each engineered plant like a prayer to his nose. With each new step, a new and different proportion of plant scents combined within his nostrils. There were tiger shark lilies whose flowers felt like the skin of a shark, Viet Mint – a Vietnamese creation with vanilla-mint pine aroma, Daphne-dil a combination of Daphne and daffodil, Maplesuckle that produced nectar tasting like maple syrup. Orange Birch was commissioned by the North Carolina Botanical Society for submission to this exhibit as it combined all the fragrant trees native to that U.S. state. One plant was a rendition of catnip called Human-nip. He stopped a moment – this was the spot in the room that was his favorite scent – the Viet mint five steps away, the Orange Birch ten steps away, the Corelits ten steps away, and all the hundreds of other plants contributing subtle notes into a perfume that naturally culminated just beneath his nose. He lavished in this rare and ephemeral sensation that it would never be bottled, and one step in any direction and the proportions would change. He closed his eyes and breathed it in deeply and loudly through his nose without regard to those passing him, letting out an audible sigh.

Musical performers walked by him, the cadence of their singing or instruments played in long drawn-out notes that created a local musical phenomenon but also lent their notes to the greater sound reverberating all around the enclosure. It was the perfect volume of background music. The movement of the performers to his closed eyes enchanted and disoriented him into an ecstasy that wiped away every worry that plagued him over the last few months. He let down his guard and allowed himself to fall in love with it all.

He then continued along his path. There were immense varieties of unknown flowers, trees and shrubs, each compelling one's attention and filling one's senses in new and interesting ways. In his weakened fasting state, Heis was completely enthralled and felt he was floating and being wafted carelessly and delightfully from one biome to the next. He bent down to stick his nose into each new plant and appreciate each passing song. He enjoyed himself so much that he wanted to shake every hand of the teams of artists, scientists and musicians that poured their effort into this intrepid and glorious accomplishment.

The choral procession was just hitting the zenith of their performance as a well-dressed man walked up alongside Heis as Heis had his nose squarely embedded in the aromatic foliage of yellow flowers, head engulfed by its leaves. Heis was completely unaware of the man's presence.

"Golden Ansels," the man said loudly.

"What? Golden angels?" Heis said, as he was taken out of the moment and pushed the leaves of the plant aside to see the man who was talking to him.

"An...sels," he enunciated more clearly, "Golden Ansels. I'm just reading the plant label here. It sounded nice so I said it out loud."

"Oh, their smell is amazing," Heis said as he stood up and wistfully walked off to enjoy another plant.

The man caught up with him again. "Sorry to bother you, but I saw your interview. It was quite interesting."

"And your name?"

"Mark Herent," he said.

"Oh, very good, Mark. Yes, it was for me as well. I hope to get back there soon," Heis said, as he knelt down to usher a bug off of the walking path and into the flower bed, "Come, come, it is dangerous here, what would you be?"

Heis then turned to the stranger and said, "They'll probably kill him after this is over, so he doesn't escape and potentially pose an ecological threat with the pollen or seeds from these plants. *You've seen too much,*" he said jokingly. "But, I'll give him a chance. We all just want to feel we've been given a chance."

"You think so?" Mark said.

"Yes, don't you?"

"I don't know what they'll do with them," Mark said.

"Just a thought," Heis said as he stood up and walked away, carefully looking for other bugs that might be on his path.

"I would like to help you," the man said, attempting to engage Heis more earnestly.

Heis stopped and turned, "Give me a chance, you mean?" Heis said, laughing at this new inside joke between them.

"Yes, I can help invest in your devices to disseminate and spread and sell them. Y'know get them out there in the hands of more people – perhaps help produce a tutorial on how to use it to better guide people to that place you spoke about," he said.

"Well, that is very generous of you – thank you. I appreciate the offer, and of course I would like all the help I can get. As I said in the interview, they don't sell well. So, I'm not sure it would be a sound investment, and therefore I would not feel comfortable allowing such an investment," Heis said.

"I would not be doing it for money, but rather, as you said, the humanitarian aspect – helping others."

"My empirically minded man, what would make you want to do such a thing?" Heis said.

"Because I believe you."

"Believe me?" Heis became confused by the contrast between the man's words and the general gestalt the man projected during their brief interaction. The dichotomy identified, Heis began weighing everything related to the man to put it on one side of the balance or the other – hair, hair style, eyes, eye color, countenance, clothes, tone of voice, etc.

"And, tell me, do you have the device yourself?" Heis said.

"I do not," Mark said.

"Yes, that seems right," Heis said making fly judgements about the man, "And so, what is it you believe about me?" Heis said.

"You, in general, your intentions and your goals," Mark said.

"Hmm, and you saw my interview?" Heis said.

"Yes," Mark said.

"So, I just asked for people to meet me over there in that other plane," Heis said.

"No, you asked for help, too," Mark said.

"Hmm, okay, okay. Yes, you're right," Heis said, "Would you want to get the device and have me help you train with it?"

"Uh," Mark took a long time to think, "Yeah."

"Doesn't sound like you're too interested," Heis said, "Which is okay, I was just trying to see where you were coming from."

"Okay let me explain. I was sent on behalf of an organization that is interested in your work," Mark said.

"I see, so you are not interested in it for yourself? Again, no condemnation, I'm just getting to know you," Heis said.

"I struggle with matters of the spirit," Mark said.

"We all do, that's kind of the point," Heis said, "Jesus struggled."

"Well, I just wanted to say that my organization has already invested heavily in a man that is working exactly on your same type of device, but approaching it from a slightly different angle. Between the two of you, you both could scientifically map this new emerging discipline. We have money and finances to fund your research."

"What is his name?"

"Hm, I don't know if I am allowed to give out his name," Mark said.

"Okay, I understand. I thought you might be talking about someone I met recently," Heis said.

"Would you be interested in simply meeting with him? No command performance required. He would be able to answer all of your questions," Mark said.

Heis thought back to God's words to him. *It was time.* He had kept everything so close to his chest over the years. Now that his project was televised and his thoughts were now out there, further secrecy would be of little value. He had to risk it all at some point if he wanted to let the project fly and take wing. He could wait his whole life for the situation to be perfect. He desperately wanted a more ardent study of spirituality, to trade ideas and collaborate.

"Okay," Heis said.

After the Zizuri Aria Botanic Garden, Mark and Heis spoke for an hour at a cafe. Heis spoke with Redd via secured channel virtual reality headset and was shown around the new lab in Peru.

"So, would you like to meet in person? Again, no command performance, just a meeting," Mark said.

"Okay," Heis said, "I will meet him in Peru."

# 15 – Telling the Family

*They call you crazy, for seeing what could be*
*Let them laugh, they're out of key*
*They're out there, and I'm with me*
*They're out there, and I'm with Thee*

The Sunday of her family meeting came. Cassandra had asked everyone to meet at her parents' house. She arrived early to help with any last minute clean up her parents might need. There was very little talk while they cleaned and beautified the living room. Her parents viewed the meeting with a vague suspicion, which was compounded by Cassandra's own discomfort and anxiety, so they cleaned in silence. Her father was a taciturn man by nature, having grown up in a difficult environment, so the silence in the house was almost natural. As they cleaned, her mother could see Cassandra had a little fullness in the face and neck which was unusual as she was typically very thin; a residual propensity after having experienced anorexia during childhood.

*This was the last challenge*, Cassandra thought. She had met every other challenge. She told her husband, her children, she had changed jobs, she had agreed to marry

Edwin – she erected all these pillars of faith she was now using to build the foundation of this new life she was attempting to grasp. This last meeting was the last hewn stone pillar from the unyielding mountain of her former life.

She wanted it done as soon as possible – she had delayed long enough. Things were moving forward, and she needed to move forward to meet them. She could feel a piece of her mind becoming snagged on this last mooring line before she could set out into the open ocean of faith. She didn't know what was going to happen in the future, she might in some way be called away altogether from her family and so she wanted to have that closure between them.

Everyone was arriving and she was relieved to see Pastor Meyer had come. He joined everyone else gathering in the small living room. There was a tense and mysterious atmosphere that filled the room as everyone waited for Cassandra to share her news. Just a month ago the living room was used for a family party; a happy occasion where all the grandchildren joyfully laid on the floor and played board games after having run around outside. Now, that all seemed a distant memory as Cassandra looked around the room. On the far wall of the living room was a fireplace with exposed brick chimney which opposed the large wooden hutch across the room containing family pictures, mementos and heirlooms of bygone generations, where sat the purple and gold crusading knight of the family crest.

Her brother Danny, oldest sister Sadie, Sadie's husband Conrad shared the couch while Peter, her parents, Pastor Meyer, Marie and her husband Emmett, sat in the individual chairs that lined the perimeter of the room. She had the impression that she was a speaker talking to an audience, which made her nervous, and when everyone settled in, her father said from his large, cushioned chair, "Okay, Cassandra, the floor is yours."

"Okay, thank you for coming everyone," she said as she looked down at her paper filled with bullet points of things she wanted to mention. Marie was saying a small prayer in her head. *A choice is a prayer.* Cassandra continued, "There is a thread of goodness that has wound its way through this family and through the life of each member of the family. A seed, growing over centuries and generations, passed one to the next, sheltered and nursed. Something greater than any one of us. That is why I called you all here today, because I see it growing and beginning to now bloom," she said as she held her belly. "Peter and I have decided to divorce. We both agreed to it and we both have wanted it for a long time now. I feel I've been living a double life as I've fallen in love with another man named Edwin, who I met six months ago. He is a custodian at the hospital, and he is the kindest man I've ever known, and we have since fallen in love. I've been spending my days with him and then I come home to Peter and the children in the evening. But, I can't keep up this double life, so Edwin and I have decided to start a life together. I've told the children who I think they understand, and I want us to continue to all be a family. This doesn't have to change the good parts of being a family, but we've been suffering for a while now, and I hope this new phase will ameliorate those issues and enhance our relationships and our connection with God, with Father. Peter and I do not work as husband and wife. With that ending, it is both of our hope that we will be better separately yet continue to parent together and support each other harmoniously. Most importantly, it is God's plan for Edwin and I to marry and to have children. I was told this by God himself, who I've spoken to. I've spoken to Uncle Victor and Aunt Louise. I've spoken to so many other people that have passed away. I've seen whole worlds of other people just like you and I, with the same concerns as you and I, but also very different in a lot of ways."

"Ho, ho, hold on," her father interrupted, "Cassandra, what are you saying? You spoke with God?"

"Yes, I spoke with Father, he told me about myself and things that had happened in my past that Edwin could not have known. But more importantly, he told me about the great plans he has for the family, each one of you." She said, "Dad, you and mom will stay healthy into old age, enjoy your retirement and this budding family. Sadie—"

"Cass, you can't really believe this, can you?" Sadie said, she was the eldest sibling, and she had a good relationship with Peter. She felt that divorce was akin to death and an affront to God, and as the eldest she felt the need to protect everyone from this terrible fate.

"I do, I spoke with Uncle Victor and Aunt Louise," Cassandra pleaded, she felt herself becoming more anxious as she sensed the tide of opinion in the room mounting against her, eroding her wish for everyone to embrace this new man in her life and believe.

"This is all crazy, I don't know who this man is, but you have to stop seeing him and focus on your marriage," Sadie said.

"Sadie, there is no more marriage, we agreed to get divorced," she said and they all looked to Peter, who had been silent.

Peter, now seeing how the family leaned in his favor, felt he was now entitled to be angry. "Well, I mean, look at her, she's pregnant," he said, shrugging his shoulders. "What was I supposed to do?"

"Oh my God," Sadie said, struggling to contain her outrage, "No, Cassandra, this man seems dangerous and he's lying to you, and he's going to ruin your life as he is doing right now."

"Life is something different to me now. I was not happy in our marriage. Peter himself said he didn't want to be married just two years after we married. I've been working on things for the past eight years, God was not in our life, I was tired, he was suffering. God has given me a different path now."

"Cass," her brother said, "I'm divorced, I'm glad you two are in agreement with how things are to proceed, but my concern is for you. I am worried for your safety because we've never met this man and all we know about him is that he is a custodian. It is possible that he is just taking advantage of you. You know this happens to married men and women, especially since you've been under a lot of stress for such a long time and now this guy comes along and seems to answer all your questions and concerns and put you at ease – that can be a dangerous situation. He could be lying about all this."

Cassandra had hoped Danny would understand, having been divorced, and he had some similar visions himself in the past. Now, with that small hope doused, she became more intimidated by the mounting doubt toward her story; *where was Edwin to show them*, Cassandra thought to herself, *this was not going as planned*. Why did she have to involve her extended family, her own family accepted it well enough, she could have kept it at that.

"But, how do you explain Uncle Victor, Aunt Louise and God knowing about my past?" Cassandra said.

"Well, everything is online now, he could have just scoured the internet," her brother said.

They all looked to Marie, who had remained quiet and listening throughout this time. Marie was in a precarious situation because she knew the family was looking at her because of her close relationship with Cassandra to persuade Cassandra to stop seeing Edwin. Marie said, "Hey, if I couldn't persuade her to stop seeing Peter when we were children, then I really could not hope to change her mind now. It's her choice."

"So, you believe all this that she is saying? Talking to the dead, talking to God, *aliens*?" Sadie said.

"Cassandra believes it, and I believe her. So, I'm open to it. We learn of miracles and amazing visions in the Bible, so it's not unheard of. I was with her when we went to go see the Armory interview with Heis – and it was a miracle that she got in, that I saw him after the show to talk to him. And, now they're all trying to help each other to do God's will. That doesn't seem like a bad thing."

"Heis? You mean that guy from the interviews who wants to explore the Vatican and says he can read minds but wasn't able to?" Danny said, letting out a small chuckle.

"Yeah, we were there during his last interview and we spoke with him and they all used that device that he was talking about. No one else had been able to use it, but Cassandra did. That must mean something. That in itself seems miraculous," Marie said. Marie did not really know how much she herself believed about what Edwin had said or what was happening with the spiritual device, but she was open to the idea and believed all things were possible.

At the mention of Marie and Heis meeting, the group all collectively had the same thought, that somehow this strange man was going to try to convince Marie to leave her husband Emmett.

"And, Emmett, what do you think of all this?" her father asked.

"Listen, I trust my wife, we have a great marriage and three beautiful children. What do I have to be suspicious of?" Emmett said.

There was a brief silence as the group had reached an impasse. Pastor Meyer had been silent. He learned to say little during these types of discussions and allow each side to air all their grievances as part of the process to move forward, yet he could not hold his tongue any longer. "Cassandra you have committed one of the most despicable and sacrilegious acts a person can perform against the church. That connection with the Father has already been established by Jesus. Jesus' willingness to give up his life on the cross and atone for our own sins, he has only strengthened that connection. We are different from the Catholic church because we say we can establish that connection with God without the necessity of an intermediary such as a priest or bishop. Yet, that connection with the Father is made through Jesus – *I am the way, the truth, and the life; no man cometh unto the Father, but by me* – Jesus himself said. So, no man can see the Father except through Jesus, which this man Edwin claims to do. The greatest saints of the church, giving up all material comforts to follow Christ and Father have not spoken directly with God. St. Stephen, the first martyr for Christ, the namesake of the church you grew up in, had not been able to attain such a spiritual connection with the Father as a reminder to us all that Jesus is our advocate," Pastor Meyer said and he quickly went into saying a prayer for her because she had committed an unimaginable crime against the church and her family. He treated her as if she was bereft of her reason, as if she was possessed by some demon.

While he was saying the prayer, Cassandra began to cry, mortified that the man she had invited to be her greatest advocate had become her biggest opponent. It was all upside down.

After the prayer, her father said, "Cassandra, I can't endorse, I can't support this behavior. You've only known him for a short time."

Sadie chimed in again and said, "And, Cass, you tell this man to watch his back, I know some people in the police force, okay. His record better be clean as a whistle."

"Sadie, that's not necessary. Don't threaten things like that." Cassandra said

"It's already done Cass, it's already done. I'm sorry, I'm sorry you matter to me," Sadie said.

"I matter to you, but what I want doesn't matter to you?" Cassandra said, "This is what I want."

"I'm the oldest, I have a say in this, I am trying to protect you," she said.

Cassandra put her head down and tried to remain peaceful in the face of flaring emotions. She said, "Things have not gone how I wanted them to go, it was supposed to be a difficult yet happy moment for everyone, as it was with Peter and I when I told him. Yes, it was a happy moment for us, because he wanted all of this just like me. He agreed to walk me down the aisle at the wedding."

"Cass, I'm telling you right now, I'm not going to any wedding," Sadie said.

"You haven't even met him yet. You don't know anything about it," Cassandra said.

"I know he impregnated a married woman. That doesn't sound like something God would endorse," Sadie said.

Cassandra tried to calm herself and not fall into needless argument. She reminded herself that she was a tool for Father, and he was using her as a way to reach them and she had to keep going – think and believe her way forward – show them what God showed her – give them that choice that he gave her – challenge their faith to rise higher. "Send me to a psychiatrist if you want to make sure that I'm not crazy or possessed or schizophrenic. So that I would be able to, at the very least, convince you that I understand the choice I am making. And, perhaps the psychiatrist would have a different understanding of things."

"I think that's a good plan" her father said, "Everyone in this room wants what's best for you and you are a grown woman. Things seem to be moving very fast between you two, a baby, a divorce, a marriage. Additionally, would you agree to forty days without seeing each other? If this is real between you two and you want to spend the rest of your lives together, then forty days is nothing. But, if there is some kind of hold he has on you, or he himself is not patient enough to wait for you, then things like that would make themselves known in that time spent apart. Then, if after forty days, you two still want to be together then I will meet him. In the meantime, we can have the opinion of the psychiatrist, but, until we can settle this, would you agree not to see him for now? Not forever, but just for now?"

Sadie interjected, "Well, I agree that I think we need to put her in a mental institution if she's going to be believing this nonsense," she said, turning to the family. "I don't feel comfortable with her being out in the world, much less around him."

Her brother in a calm tone said, "Cass, this is just all very odd to us. We haven't seen the things that you have. There are real medical conditions that can produce – I think they call it adjustment disorder or very brief psychosis," her brother said. "So, I would agree with the psychiatric evaluation because, let's say this is all from stress, which we all know you are under a lot, the adjustment disorders can play tricks on you. A professional would be able to tease that out."

"I would be fine with the psychiatric evaluation as long as it is paid for in cash so there's no record of it," she said.

She almost pushed back on the forty-day separation – she didn't think it was necessary. Things were actively happening of which she would need to be a part, and the separation might interrupt this grand plan. But, then she thought Edwin had just left for South America and he would be away for two weeks, so she wouldn't see him for fourteen days anyway. So that could be used toward these forty days. She'd really only have to be away from him for three more weeks.

"Okay, and we can do the forty-day separation," she said. "But today counts as the first day because I did not see him today," and she took out her phone to look at a calendar.

"And, no communication whatsoever – phone calls, texts, emails, whatever," Sadie said.

"Oh, wow, would you look at that, forty days ends on Easter!" Cassandra said, feeling reassured in the serendipity of the moment that it was something that God wanted, "Yes, I understand, no communication. But, I will call him once to tell him about the forty-day hiatus."

    The conversation had now gone on for an hour and was now concluding as everyone had reached some agreement. They got their things together, hugged and kissed goodbye. The psychiatric evaluation would take place next week and Cassandra walked away feeling disappointed with the response. Only Marie supported her, everyone else did not believe and even Peter changed his mind about the situation.

# 16 – Field Mission

*You're not afraid of death*
*Nor loneliness*
*Once preferred being alone*
*Clawing to God's throne*
*You idolized dying*
*The cold vivifying*

*The austerity reminded*
*To reach what was behind it*
*That was the toll*
*To stay focused on your goals*

*Leaving little to chance*
*Carrying the heavy lance*
*Pain, pain, a little more pain*
*Holding to the purpose for which you came*

*You refused to break*
*You refused to take*
*That easier path*
*For our sake*

Edwin wished he could have been there to support Cassandra, but he took this assignment because he unduly influenced Heis and was therefore indirectly responsible for the decision he was about to make. So, after saying goodbye to Cassandra, Edwin took a taxi down to the Elizabeth industrial port after dark, made his way over to the Arthur Kill waterfront and walked out to a small, dilapidated utility shed in an isolated wooded area. Inside were dirty shovels, rakes, old rafting equipment, spare wooden planks leaning against the walls. There was a hole built by a family of groundhogs that poked out from beneath the side of the shed. The thought flashed across his mind: last summer, a young child had wandered off from his parents exploring the nature preserve and reached his hand in the hole only to be nipped on the finger by the mother rodent and from that developed a small fear of dark holes that would persist into his adult life. Edwin approached that same small hole and stuck his hand deep within, all the way to the back, past the furry critters, they stayed docile while he found a rusted nail jutting out from beneath the wood boards and pushed it away from himself. He pulled his arm out and stood up, walking over to a small ramp leading up to the front entrance of the shed. He moved aside the small ramp to reveal a crevice nestled between the dirt and the shed. He held his breath as he wiggled into it, feet first. As he stuck his feet in, he felt a lubricated loose plastic sleeve that stuck to his skin, and after he got his large belly past the edge of the shed, he fell into the plastic sleeve that spat him out in a pitch-black cavity beneath the shed.

    "Edwin Vega," he said into the darkness, expecting the room to light up, yet nothing happened. While inactive, the room was filled with nitrogen as a suffocation deterrent for possible interlopers.

"Edwin Vega!" he shouted, feeling a faint burning in his lungs. Still nothing. He tried breathing the nitrogen-filled room, yet it only intensified the suffocation as the residual oxygen from his lungs leeched out into the room. He started fumbling around for a spare canister of oxygen, but they had been removed. *This is ridiculous,* he thought and tore a hole in the plastic sleeve that brought him into the room and let fresh air roll in. He turned on his small light on his phone. He saw that the shed had no power to it. He climbed out, got on a government motorcycle parked at the dock in one of the shipping containers, then raced down the road to another safe house. On the way he called the Aether group, the call was connected without an answer.

"Where is he?" Edwin said.

"En route to Peru, estimating about eighteen hours until he arrives," the operator said.

The Aether group emerged during the internal struggle between Blue Light and Delta Force in the 1970s. When Delta became operational, their command structure, operational culture and recruitment tactics were unpopular among most of the existing Blue Light members. So, the military branched the teams to set up a rivalry between them, while also assigning general specialties to each group. The rivalry between them was intense as each vied for supremacy and government funding. Delta became the officially acknowledged special forces unit while the Aether group became decentralized and unacknowledged for when the U.S. wanted no link back to itself.

"Pick me up at my location," Edwin said.

"Copy, sending transport now," the operator said.

Heis was being brought to a secret Peruvian scientific compound as part of The Island's expansion and their first branch into the continental market. Yet, given the powerful and evil off-world influence which plagued the unassuming nation, a problematic partnership developed between that bad influence and the scientific influence of the island which culminated in amoral research performed on human life without regard to the soul within. People were treated like lab rats and regularly sacrificed to study the effects of various biologic ballistics, pathogen vectors, and highly invasive and experimental surgical procedures. Thus, given the nature of Redd's experiments, he was sent to the Peruvian facility because it offered a more robust pipeline for human experimentation.

This compound had been on the U.S. hit list for over two years, yet all missions to destroy the compound were unsuccessful, the agents were never heard from again, and the compound quickly followed the legend of the unicorn as something unattainable and foolish to pursue. Edwin had now taken the mission as a way to prevent the exponentially multiplying negative eventualities that will have emerged from Heis' involvement in such a facility. Therefore, his mission would be to render in some way the facility inoperable and fiscally unviable for future restoration.

Heis could not fall under the influence of outside forces at his present state of nascent spirituality. He had neither the incredulity, guile, or fortitude to understand what was good and what was evil. He had already been tricked into thinking he had spoken to God which had partially sent him on this course to this facility. His choice was being taken away from him, and he did not know it. Evil wants to coerce you into thinking their choice is your choice while goodness protects as much of your free will as you can assume. If Heis wanted such scientific capabilities at his disposal (as was the choice that he made) then he must go to the relatively more moral Island facility from which Redd had emerged. Heis was supposed to go to the island, yet an evil force residing in the Draco nebula, caught the unsuspecting Heis in their web around the star Thuban, and the umvoc force 150 light years away became cognizant of Earth.

The business model of the Peruvian site was the same as The Island. Yet, given their willingness for human experimentation, their isolated facility was beginning to overtake the parent Island facility in revenue, which compelled their own internal rivalry. The U.S. government themselves had, on the one hand, purchased the results that came out of that lab, while on the other hand had financed missions to destroy the facility. The forces controlling the facility knew of the military incursions yet still dealt honestly with the U.S. in business and science as they didn't want to lose their largest client. Thus, the Peruvian facility became a quagmire of international relations.

When Edwin was picked up, he saw three other specialists who were brought on to the team. He had worked with two of the men, James and Torrence, but he did not know the woman.

Without greeting the others, Edwin instantly said, "No, I will be working alone, drop them off here."

"Not this time, it is too important," James said.

"That is why I will be working alone," Edwin said.

"Sorry, my good man, we all requested working alone, that is why they brought us together," Torrence said.

"Drop the guys off here and drop that woman off in the next state and then head to Peru."

"No time, you'll have to work together," the mission sponsor said.

"Listen, I don't take a salary, I don't have to follow these rules you set in place to gamble on lives," Edwin said. The mission sponsor was the agent who put up the government financing for the mission. The sponsor was in charge of setting up the mission until the mission became "active" at which time the mission leader, which was always Edwin, would take command.

"Until we get to Peru and the mission starts, you are not yet in charge," the sponsor said.

"Okay, Let James drive," Edwin said without hesitation, "it will give him something to do aside from trying to kill me in my own shed," Edwin said.

"Come now, Paps," James said, "there is no reason to make unsubstantiated accusations. Besides we all know you've had a difficult life, so is dying really so bad? You've done enough – isn't that what the chaplain told you back in the war?" Edwin said nothing during this tirade and James continued, "You know I didn't want to kill you, I was just keeping you on your toes – like a litmus test – if you survived then you've still got it, if you didn't then probably best you weren't a part of this team. And, you really have done enough. Maybe it's time to let it go and let me take over with fresh blood…but, yeah, I will drive."

They filed into the van, James in the driver seat, while Edwin, Torrence and a new teammate named Amina sat across from each other on two benches that ran lengthwise along the walls of the van. Torrence was a familiar face to Edwin. He was thirty-five years old, and being closer in age to Edwin who was forty-one, knew that he likely was not going to ever be the leader of Aether, because that compulsion to dominate, that antagonistic relationship, particularly men of that profession feel toward one another – that was all subdued in Torrence seven years ago when Torrence was nipping at Edwin's heels much in the same way James was now acting. At that time, Torrence and Edwin's relationship had their own seminal moment. Torrence had been shot and left by the other team members. Torrence himself had left behind maimed team members the same way on other missions, so he was ready to die or to be captured. Men of that profession were singularly minded as dogs chasing prey, primal and inordinately focused on completing the task and returning home. But, Edwin went back for him. Edwin carried him on his shoulders through the jungle. Torrence had fainted as he was being carried and woke up while on a transport shuttle out of the country, Edwin sitting across from him, blood spilling out from a large gash across his stomach from a machete. That moment changed Torrence, but it was six months later when they were in the changing room that Torrence saw that Edwin had no residual scar from that deep machete wound, and Torrence understood. At that moment Torrence realized that Edwin was not human. He didn't know what he was, but no human heals like that. Torrence realized the magnitude of Edwin's beneficence – not only toward him, but as a protector of all that was good, and a champion for God and the lights of the world.

  James sped down the highway and the light from the passing streetlamps bled in through the tinted windows of the backseat where Edwin, Torrence and the woman sat. Their bodies jostled with every quick turn, yet Edwin and the woman did not break eye contact with each other. There was no one he loved more than Cassandra. He told everyone that, and Cassandra was always on his lips when they were apart, "I am without something when I am not with her." But, there was something attractive about this woman besides the physical beauty of her appearance. It was in the eyes. They communicated without words and had an entire conversation about their lives as he traced the edges of her iris which were always in all people, a slightly different color than the rest of the iris. However, while most people had lighter edges, hers were darker on the periphery. He noticed that her eyes were focused specifically on his left eye. When streetlights repeatedly passed, he saw her pupil rhythmically dilate and contract in response to the shifting light. But, there was another movement in her eyes, a quivering of the zonules superimposed upon the reaction to the light and dark. There was something in her sympathetic nervous system – or she was engineered. He counted the pulsations, and it seemed to coincide with the heartbeat he saw in her thin neck as the van stopped.

"We're here, get out," James said.

A medical officer named Reid was waiting for them at the large entrance of an old barn.

"Come qui–" Reid started to say.

"There is no time for this, come with us on the ship," Edwin said.

"Sure," Reid said and quickly wheeled his small portable lab onto the ship as the tailgate lifted and closed behind him. The Lorentz electromagnetic shuttle took off, silently, speedily into the night sky.

"Well, thank you, it's nice to be in the presence of such highly motivated individuals at the peak of their physical abilities," Reid said.

"Except for Paps," James said. Yet, Edwin again said nothing and James continued, "He is so out of shape, he looks like someone who hasn't exercised in the past twenty years. He looks like all of those fat slobs at the diabetes clinic. I'm surprised he can get out of bed, nevertheless complete a mission. You know what though, I really was expecting you'd die in that shed and then we wouldn't have all the constant issues you cause within this division. I'm asking you as a friend now, please retire."

"You're talking so poorly of him," Amina said, "Doesn't that look bad on you? Please we are all in this together, there is nothing you can change about that now."

"I could kill him right now, that would be changing something," James said, "Or, I could kill you right now. No one even knows who you are."

A creaking sound came from Edwin, like an old house whose pipes were expanding against the cold, and wooden columns were straining under the weight of the house.

James looked at him in disgust, "Your body sounds even older than it looks. You're too old, I'm leading this mission now." He pointed at the two other members of the team, "you and you listen to me now and while we are out there in the shit," He turned to berate Edwin once again, "Spics typically have a lower intelligence than whites, Asians and Jews. So, I bet you didn't even get out of the shed, you probably were never able to get in there you're so fat. So, this is me saving your life, okay," he started to talk slowly, as if talking to a cognitively impaired person, "Sooo…dooon't…gooooo…innnn…your…sheddd. If you are ever able to fit into there again, it will end your life. You're not—"

"That is enough," Edwin said. Edwin was conflicted as to how he should respond. On the one hand it is not good to have this degree of insolence brooding among the team against their leader, yet Edwin knew that he was himself protected by God, so in a personal sense, it did not matter what James said to him. The ramifications of James's own negativity, resistance, and anger would be brought down on his own head and on the head of the teammates. This is why Edwin preferred to work alone – teammates made things messy. He looked deeply into James's eyes, tried to interpolate his words to see the man behind the bravado. Edwin had the benefit of experience, and the many years that he spent in the military brought within himself many of the same feelings of frustration that James felt – it was about control. Yet James added overconfidence to his desire to be 'top dog'.

"What, you can't think of a response?" James asked, "that's what I'm saying, you're too old, you don't have that heat in your blood—"

"We will speak later," Edwin interrupted.

James shook his head in frustration, disregarding Edwin's comment and then took a seat.

The plane landed and James pointed to the others and said, "Remember, you follow me."

Then, everyone got up to leave, and Edwin in a soft voice said, "One second, one second James, hold on one second," James did not listen and kept walking. Edwin took the back of his neck and slammed him down into a chair. James was disoriented by the magnitude of force which unexpectedly pulled him backwards and down and tried to look for what he had gotten hit by, and the room spun around him until the first thing he was able to focus on was Edwin's gaze.

Edwin's soft voice was gone and the levies broke which held back the immense power of his anger and personality, and a large bear's paw of Edwin's hand wrapped around James's neck, "We have a mission, I am your leader, you do what I tell you to do. You are a good teammate. I don't want to kill you. But, I will if you become a threat," and his hand squeezed James's trachea as James tried every tactic to get out of his grip, twisting toward the thumb, trying to bend the elbow, kicking him in the testicle. It only fueled the madness in Edwin's eyes, made him more powerful and the sequence of events ending James's life flashed before Edwin's eyes, and Edwin saw this thought and relaxed his grip.

James caught his breath and rubbed his neck which was still deformed in the shape of Edwin's grip – his neck felt raw, as if sandpaper had twisted around it.

"Now, do you want to be part of this mission or not?" Edwin said.

A singular nod expressed James's understanding. Edwin, satisfied, helped him up and said, "Doc, give him some of that booster fuel."

"I actually call it Snake oil because it is good for everything, but I don't want *that* to happen to me so, sure, we can call it booster fuel," The doctor said attempting to use levity to break the tension, "Actually, it's mostly cocaine and amphetamines, I should just call it coc-etamine."

"Well, James was a snake, but not anymore, now he's destined to live among the stars!" Edwin exclaimed, "So, I like snake oil, too."

The doctor bent down to look at the neck, and after a moment's study said, "Well, you can certainly count your lucky stars. Another pound of force and you would have been popped like a pimple, and there ain't enough snake oi- I mean booster fuel that could have fixed that."

James was still attempting to understand what had just happened, he became flush, then pale, lightheaded and then the doctor's hand caught his head as he briefly lost consciousness. He then came back to consciousness quickly.

"James, his hand is no longer around your neck, why are you passing out?" the doctor joked.

Edwin came closer to James, "James, that is more of an opportunity than you gave me to survive."

James said nothing, his head still whirling.

"Now you're the one not saying anything, James?" the doctor said. "Looks like you really *are* learning from Ed here."

Edwin said, "He still looks rough. Try some of your concoction, and if it works, he can come along. If it does not then drop him off."

"Okay," the doctor said, as he removed a flask from his pouch and handed it to James, "Now don't you worry, yes, I have tried it many, many times on myself."

James took a swig and handed it back to the doctor.

The doctor, seeing an orange label said, "Oh actually this one is mostly amphetamine and tropane derivatives…er…" Reid took a swig himself, "Oh no, actually there *is* cocaine in there," he said with a wink to Edwin, and then turned to James and said, "Don't worry, there's some other things to nullify the side effects, so just…enjoy."

James still was not looking well, and Edwin now regretted his decision to use force to get his point across.

"Okay, keep him with you, don't drop him off with us," Edwin said.

"...I...I want to go," James said, obviously causing great pain to speak.

"You will stay here," Edwin said, turned, and joined Amina and Torrence.

Edwin was relieved that James was not going because he could see that James's mind was agitated to such an extent that he would have done something rash, foolish or harmful. But, it was not enough, he saw deep into James's heart and these small concessions that momentarily indicated a change of heart were superficial and fleeting changes which would revert back to his normal spiteful and domineering behavior after he left this environment and re-entered a community in which he was the best. It was not enough, the amount of time his hand laid around his neck, yet any longer or any stronger would have led to serious and permanent injury – which, paradoxically, would likely have humbled him enough to make him a better teammate and better operative. Edwin would not do that though, he took all the vengeance except for that last bit, he left that to God – the meaningful changes had to come from the temple of James' own body from that portion of God vibrating with the same love, creativity, will and wisdom that Father demonstrates toward us. Yet, men in general were the least likely to acknowledge that humility.

It was not enough; all the team members should be sidelined. Edwin could see all of it – they would die. Heis was too important to this group of people. This group of people were vicious, relentless, they had no spirituality about them. They thought that this world, this plane of existence was all there was and there was no ascension beyond Earth for which they were preparing. As such they wanted to fully enjoy this experience as much as possible and in neglecting their spirit, neglecting that part of themselves that gives true satisfaction, their earthly appetites became intrepid experiments in depravity all to substitute Earth for Heaven, creating an artificial heaven. As that group of people have aged they draw closer to the end of their world, the end of their existence – and so it will be – because that is what they believe and what they have consistently demonstrated in their actions over their entire lives – Heaven does not exist for them. They felt, in some way, the collaboration between Heis and Redd would act as the conduit – the key to the development of their sadistic aspirations and prolong their life or offer them a way out.

A call came through his deep ear comm, "We have a replacement for James. Don't worry, you have worked with him in the past."

"No, we are moving out now. There is no more time." Edwin shook his head in exasperation, he obviously had no control over the number of operatives, and this mission was important enough to potentially expend all of their lives. *How much was the government paying them to essentially kill themselves?*

"He is already here, he is the doctor, take him with you," the operator said.

Edwin looked over to Reid who was tending to James. Reid briefly touched his ear to muffle the outside noise. Reid was currently being told that he was going with the rest of the crew. It would be four of them.

"He is taking care of James, he can't go," Edwin said.

"Don't worry about James, worry about the mission," the operator said.

*Enough talk,* Edwin thought. "We are moving out all the same." He turned and motioned to Reid who walked over to Edwin.

"I don't *only* specialize in saving lives – I am also handy in taking them! I am like a God!" Reid said jokingly.

"You want to go?" Edwin said.

"Yes," Reid said.

"Okay, from now until we have brought Heis back to this location, follow me," Edwin said.

"Yes," Reid said.

Edwin turned to walk, yet Reid did not follow, and Edwin turned back around to look at Reid expectantly.

"...Oh, okay one second I have some gifts and special things I had wanted to give the gro-"

Edwin did not answer but only spun around in expectation that Reid would follow.

"Yes, of course, coming now, well I only need my juice anyway."

They mounted four hoverbikes disguised as motorcycles and rode off.

"The mission has started, I am in control, God is with you," Edwin said as if it were to be the last words spoken to these people. He said it with the intonation of the chaplain that visited him while he was sick and comforted him. "They've already gone into Peru; we cannot use the Lorentz aerial anymore."

The four of them passed the Ecuador-Peruvian border, "They are going to Chavin de Huantar, underneath the archeological site," the operator said.

"If they bring him to that underground facility then it could mean very bad things for the world. And, Heis himself will be miserable and confused," Edwin said.

They were about one hour from the Chavin site. However, they were waiting in a small town for darkness to come before going further. The small town was safe as it was a local associate outpost – a congregation of foreign espionage agents hoping to get "in" with the American government. The town was on the outskirts of the mountainous woods, and any further advancement would be met with many guards along the various inroads in broad daylight. During this time, they were told that the convoy holding Heis had also stopped somewhere outside of Lima.

While scouting the town, something felt off to Edwin. Torrence was on the highest rooftop of a hotel. Amina was down on the ground, pretending to be a tourist at a local fountain.

Edwin had taken a construction hazard vest and started walking purposefully around town acting like one of the locals. He was Hispanic and fit in more than the other three who put a pigment on their skin to blend in. Despite the various skin pigment augmentation methods, they still looked white based on other physical characteristics in the face, eyes, and build. Edwin did not suffer from those issues, he was a large man, and no one would suspect him an agent, he spoke perfect Spanish tailored to the local dialect.

A voice came over the comm, "Move to San Marcos, coordinates 9°31'28.0"S 77°09'25.0"W".

Edwin said over the comm, "Stay where you are, I will go by myself on the bike."

While wearing the construction vest, he moved purposefully as if he were actually a construction worker begrudgingly attempting to get done with his work so that he could get home. His bike was hidden in an empty metal shed. As he opened the door, the bike was gone, the shed was empty, a bullet sunk into his back as he dropped the construction equipment he was holding.

Chaos ensued as Torrence said from the top of the roof, "Shit, they found me," followed by a loud buzz and distant gunfire. Drones whizzed overhead like hornets, tracking their every movement.

"I was shot, not sure from where," Edwin said.

Indistinct background voices came through Torrence's comm as the gunfire intensified.

Edwin said, "They know we are here. Don't go to the San Marcos coordinates, go to where we were when Reid stopped to piss."

More gunfire erupted in the small town as local associates of the U.S. hoped to prove themselves and engaged whatever mysterious force was attempting to kill the mission operatives.

"Torrence was just thrown from the rooftop," Amina said, "I suspect they also know where I am. The local agents are providing some room to move. I will make my way."

As Edwin was shot, he rolled into the shed so that anyone would need to get close before firing again. He laid there. Every second he could stay alive brought with it an increasing likelihood that he would survive. He could feel the fragments of the hollow point bullet fanning out just below the skin. Edwin had a thicker layer of keratinized skin, giving it a higher hardness factor, coupled with higher threading of connective tissue, and blood as a non-Newtonian fluid, expressed the higher degree of rouleaux stacking – all of which acted as a thicker shield. Already he could feel the deep wells of nutritive blood mobilizing from the azygos vein, the sympathetics fine and minute tendrils coordinating the body to compel it to reject the shards and return the structure and function to its original form.

A grenade entered the shed next to Edwin and he batted it back out the door.

He heard a voice from outside the door, "Hold it for exactly one second longer and then throw it to the far side of the shed," someone said in an American accent.

"James?!" Edwin shouted.

"Here let me do it," the voice outside said. "Like this." And the grenade plopped into a far crevice of the opposite wall, slightly on a down slope where sand had accumulated. Edwin quickly threw the construction equipment he had been carrying on to it and the grenade exploded while the equipment was in midair – giving a margin of protection as the grenade sprayed shrapnel around the shed and embedded itself into Edwin's back, buttocks, and feet.

"All right, you go in first. He is dead and then we will give his body over to Burandano for the reward after we get the rest of them," the voice said. Footsteps cautiously walked toward the shed and a shadow darkened the doorway, but he didn't step in. Rather, the nozzle of a rifle poked out from the edge of the door frame to scout the inside of the shed. He shot a few times haphazardly around the shed and the nozzle withdrew quickly back behind the door.

Then, in an attempt to confuse Edwin, the man laid down and quickly peeked his head around the bottom of the frame to see if Edwin was dead. Just as a substantial portion of the man's head emerged from the bottom corner of the frame, Edwin fired his rifle and the bullet first grazed the edge of the doorway, attempting to get as close to the center of the man's head as possible to deliver a killing blow. And just as the sound and flash of the ignited bullet left the gun, the body in the doorway slumped onto the ground without another word.

"James?!" Edwin said, yet no one answered back. "James, you're making a mistake." Yet, whoever was out there only answered back with the sound of the pin being pulled from a grenade. As it was thrown, Edwin pulled the dead body into the shed and hid from the explosion. It acted like a concussion grenade in the confined space and Edwin was beginning to lose his hearing – he wouldn't be able to hear the pin-spoon-ignition anymore. The next grenade was thrown with a greater amount of force to bounce off the far wall toward Edwin and the explosion nearly ripped through the corpse shielding him.

Edwin just had to bide his time and something would happen, patience, goodness and faith bide their time while evil, hate and ignorance couldn't comprehend the utilization of time, and lash out haplessly. The man outside knew he needed to kill Edwin now, while he was isolated, trapped, alone – there would not be a better chance. The man knew Edwin was lying against the corner of the shed. Explosions and gunfire continued in distant parts of the small town.

Edwin heard footsteps slowly circling the metal shed and then stopped on the opposite side of the corrugated wall – the two men were inches from each other. The heat of Edwin's body was permeating through to the outside of the shed giving him away, so he shifted away from the wall. A quick burst of gunfire slapped at the wall that Edwin had been leaning against and punched a large dent into the side – yet it didn't pierce the structure. Then, as the man continued to circle to the far side of the shed, Edwin quickly took up the slack in their game of squirrel and inched closer to the opening of the shed, dragging the corpse with him for cover.

Edwin was forty-one years old, when he first turned thirty-eight, having served nineteen years in the military, he was feeling he was past his prime and awaiting the day that he would give his life for Father and for America; and that the woman he was looking for his whole life must have died from some accident and he was looking forward to meeting her in Heaven when he also died if there was anytime between being reinserted into a baby. So, Edwin had wanted to spend the remaining years consulting for the military and devote a larger amount of time taking on the ailments of others. He had planned for a final grand jubilant celebration of his life and death by giving life back to some seventeen-year-old child with osteosarcoma, lying on their death bed, body overcome with tumors, thin, cachectic and in pain, morphine dulling the senses as she gave up her last breath. Yet, Edwin would give his life to her, death would be a relief to him, and he would die in joyous laughter.

But, that is when he started to change. He had always healed quickly, been protected by God, picked up and retained information and used that information creatively. But in his thirty-eighth year, something different started to happen and information was given to him. He lost vast stretches of time and soon realized that his prayers had been answered, and he may once again find that woman he was looking for and the ebbing tide of his vitality again sung vigorously in his neurovascular bundles communicating this new song to the rest of his body.

In the thirty-ninth year, he was told that he himself was a principle in the sense that he was something existing outside yet in conjunction with nature and the material universe, also known as an angel; the angel of death via the intermediary soul willing its way, flooding great plains, and pressing down adamantine mountain, allowed to walk freely among the Earth.

While lying in that metal shed, an influx of energy overwhelmed Edwin while he was thinking of his son, growing within Cassandra. The fine tendrils of the sympathetic nervous system tapped electrical reserves stored within the vast quartz veins for which Peru was coveted and typically used by the off world forces, and he used it himself, strengthening his muscles and lighting the phosphorus of his mind as if he were being electrocuted. Yet he could divert the electricity to his own will and via mass activation of his entire body snapped his muscles into tight tension and he rolled over and tore through the many bodily alarm bells assaulting his brain to stay still. There was no pain in staying still – yet there was death. He took into himself all the mental insanities plaguing the local population influenced by evil outside forces – to use 'fire against fire' now that he had found the right moment to 'lash out'. And, the mental docility the town felt was contrasted by the natural equivalent of phencyclidine (PCP) saturating Edwin's mind with NMDA blockades and dopamine and norepinephrine rushes. Angry, excited, in pain, maddening – he had to hurt something and release this static charge. He sprinted out the door, and the unexpectedly sudden sight of Edwin quickly approaching from around the corner of the door took James off guard. Edwin carried the dead man as a shield as James shot into the dead body. As a reflex, James flipped a switch in his body suit, which unleashed a flash, smoke and a loud noise, and Edwin was blinded but he kept in his mind James' position, dropped the dead body and lunged at him. At the same time, in the midst of the smoke, James blindly dove to the left and nearly cleared the open arms of Edwin already in midair. Edwin caught James's ankle and the familiar feeling of Edwin's grip caused James to let out a loud yell. James pushed another button to electrify the surrounding air as he hit the ground, yet the voltage was not high enough to stun and overcome the ferocity and vengeance which possessed Edwin. The circuits within Edwin's brain usually held at bay all the terrible thoughts which incessantly presented themselves to Edwin's mind. The part of his will that kept those circuits active were now disengaged and the dormant depraved portions of his brain became unhinged, and a small seizure was now depolarizing and putting into overaction those deep terrible thoughts and that small dark portion then spread to other cortical areas and the countenance of his face changed to a different person and James, if it hadn't been for that familiar grip now clawing up his legs like an animal, he would have thought it was a completely different person attacking him. Edwin's face became gaunt, long, sullen, rigid, angular, dark eyes, his very eyebrows lost their gradual arch and flared up at their apex and at an abrupt angle fell toward the sides of his face. His entire being was shrouded in a hazy darkness, flashes of electricity crawled across the atmosphere surrounding him. Edwin sunk his hands into James's clothes, feeling the many electrical wires beneath his shirt and tore it off, snapping the fine wires. A small armada of reflex explosions and discharges erupted in a flurry and Edwin and James were both consumed in a blast of smoke, gravel, sand, dirt flinging up from the ground. When it settled, James' body was full of small holes pouring out blood and he was once again a small fragile, pale child at the mercy of Edwin. James was completely incapacitated and the tempo of the situation slowed down. Edwin rolled off of James and knelt next to him. They looked each other in the eyes. Edwin, knowing the end was near, said, "My brother," and smiled at him.

The sun was setting and Edwin would need to be moving soon. Edwin never noticed the sunset and sunrise like Cassandra did, yet as he sat there with James, her sentiment seemed to pour through his own being. "You see the fingers, the hand of Father?" Edwin said to James. "He reaches out to you, brother," as the spears of light danced and cascaded within the terse clouds meandering through the sky. "You'll go to Heaven, brother. It was not all your fault. You had a hard life and that is the environment we operate in now, we get used. I don't want my children going into this line of work for that same reason." Edwin said to James, "But, you took it too far, and you were given chances to change. Therefore, when you come back to Earth to meet these same issues, you will largely be in the same environment as you started. You will have a hard life. Is that what you wanted from all of this? To get nowhere? You will be here again, and that is all the punishment I wish for you. Whatever I can forgive, is forgiven." Dusk covered the cold mountainous landscape, and the cooler air made visible wisps of steam smoldering upward from James' dead body, like a soul leaving its domicile.

It was time to continue onward. His sympathetic nervous system was still bursting with energy, and the demons were still dancing in his brain, lighting fires, razing and tearing through the docile demeanor he tried so hard to develop and maintain in civilian life. He needed something else to fuck or kill to exercise and expel this feeling. He got up to run toward the gunfire. While he was running, he doubled over and put his hand on a tree for support. This side of him was like a cancer and diverted all bodily resources to sustaining itself to the exclusion of the rest of his psyche and reasoning faculties. The parading demons plucked his strings of pain and laughed at his anguish, his body became rigid, his fingers dug into the tree, his fingernails peeled off against the bark, he clenched his teeth around a small branch, he clenched his other fist and his nails dug into his palms. He could see the face of that demon becoming him and beaconing him to let his resistance end and give in to the passion of destruction – each wound singing praise to death, each avulsion praying for more pain, excitement, euphoria through domination or death. Any action no matter how appalling could be justified by a man in the throes of ecstasy without any mind to the repercussions.

"Where is everyone?!" he shouted into the comm.

"Torrence assumed dead, Amina severely injured, Reid moving to a previous location on foot. Local forces cannot get to Amina, please proceed to her expediently, she's in a drainage ditch, a culvert north of your location," the operator said.

The insane energy still coursing through Edwin prompted him to sprint like a madman toward her location, almost tearing at his own flesh in the process, leaving a trail of blood behind him leading back to James. His eyes dilated to full bore, panting heavily to throw off the carbonic acid accumulating in his blood and restore the electricity. Three assailants surrounded the culvert, and one local force operator on a rooftop tried to check their advancement, yet there were two more assailants walking up the stairs behind him. The closest assailant to Edwin was preoccupied by the rooftop and the culvert. He heard Edwin's panting and footsteps too late as Edwin sprinted faster the closer he approached. Edwin lunged at him, nearly tearing through him and breaking his spine with his weight, and they rolled on the ground. Edwin then got on top and with one large swift blow with the man's own rifle and he was dead. Yet, it wasn't enough to satisfy his appetite, and his mind was tipping into a place where he wouldn't know friend from enemy and the whole world would become something he had to subdue and dominate.

He quickly stood and broke the straps that secured the rifle to the dead man. Edwin then held the dead man as a shield as he ran toward the other two men who now directed their fire at him. He again started to run manically, feeling the clunk of bullets hit himself and the dead man. Edwin fired wildly toward the other man as he ran. There was no patience, no caution or intelligence in his approach; a wild rabid animal seeking death. He and every other man could not exist in the same world. There was no reason. He was going to kill every male – not to save anyone, not to fight for the light, but as competition and pleasure rolled into one. The two men started to fall back and run away. Edwin caught up to one and held him down as he shot the other in the back. *Please let this be the end of it* he thought as he then killed the man under him.

There was a brief stay of his madness after killing the two men, but then the dissonant cord welled up in him again with a crazed excitement and he now looked to the local force man on the roof to quell this passion before it overtook him. The local force man waved to him as Edwin aimed his gun upward at him and started shooting. Edwin couldn't hold it back; he could only tip his hand this or that way as he started to fire wildly at him and ran toward him. The local force operator, confused, took cover flat against the roof. Then, as Edwin leapt the drainage ditch to run to the man on the roof Edwin glanced at Amina lying in the large culvert, and without hesitation he dropped everything and ran to the culvert and crawled toward her. He tore off her pants, and her bloodied arm extended a welcoming hand that touched his face and invited him to continue – and the madness was soon satiated – his reason, docility, and composure soon returned.

Without wasting time, he said to her "Stay here." The local force man on the roof was pinned down by the two other men. They were stuck in the stairwell as the local man watched the door to prevent their advance. Edwin quickly entered the building, quietly walked up the steps, maimed and subdued the two men, tying them up and leaving them to that local force man – it would be his ticket up the ranks. He saw one man who was shot, incapacitated on the floor. He saw the rest of his life, a beggar on the streets because of the wounds he now sustained – that would be enough to atone for the killing he had done throughout his life.

Afterwards, Edwin returned to Amina, giving her a pair of the assailant's pants, then lifted her upon his shoulders and carried her to the street. He stopped a car, leaned into the passenger side window. "Give me your license!" Edwin said, while holding a gun.

"I need it," the driver timidly said.

"I will send it back to you tomorrow, here is a thousand dollars. If anything happens to her, I will kill you and your family, others will kill you and your family. Drop her off at this location, one second," Edwin said and turned away from the car, "What are the coordinates of Reid?...Okay thank you," and turned back toward the car, snatching the man's phone from its dashboard mount and typing in the coordinates. They will give you another two thousand dollars when you arrive. If you do not, then you will die," Edwin said as the driver handed over the license. Edwin noted the license plate – COA-78P-NR5.

All the fighting in the city had died down, the car drove off. Edwin was far behind schedule. This all could have been avoided if they had just allowed him to work alone. He was angry with himself for allowing it to happen; for allowing himself to be convinced. His uncertainty got others killed when he should have been more forceful in acting on his thoughts.

The operator spoke to Edwin, anticipating his needs, "Amina's bike is in the garage in front of you. Go back for Reid and then continue on the mission," she said. It was tempting for operators to act as if the field agents were simply pieces on a chess board they were controlling. This was especially true in those retired field agents who never became 'top dog' and now sought to satisfy their authoritarian impulse in the operator role. Edwin did not want to act that way when he became an operator. Edwin subscribed to "the man in the ring" mentality; giving great liberty and forgiveness to those in the field who were risking their lives; responding and reacting to a dynamic, ever-changing environment often mixed with fear, excitement, and clumsiness. That was the way God viewed the children of Earth, so that is how he wanted to act. Operators, sitting comfortably in their command module had vast information at their fingertips should, at best, only ascend to the level of being a helpful resource to the field agents. Aether group also subscribed to this philosophy and mission leads continued to be the field agents – though this was mostly to retain good field agents in the field rather than behind a desk.

"No, have *them* catch up with me. We've lost too much time. Why didn't you know about this ambush?!" Edwin yelled through the comm.

"The convoy is about an hour from the destination," the operator said in a calm, steady tone. Yet Edwin could sense the subtle change toward a submissive attitude and an acknowledgment in her overstepping her role.

Edwin rode south on the hoverbike at a blistering speed through the mountainous and mesmerizing Peruvian cloud jungles. He had wanted to visit the Peruvian Andes willfully under different circumstances and dreamt of a world in which his services would not be needed. This whole region of Chavin de Huantar, if excavated, could bring a whole new understanding to world history. The large stone pillars buried underneath these archeological sites were the prototype of the totem pole. And, the recently excavated platform mounds marked the first evidence of the mysterious Mound Builders whose structures strung their way north into central and then North America as monuments to God. He knew where all of them were located, or he could figure out where they were. That would be a dream for when he retired – he wanted to search for this buried treasure with Cassandra's father as a way to connect with him. Cassandra's father, now in his sixties, was a standoffish man out of love for his daughter and from his own difficult upbringing. Edwin hoped that such a trip would warm him and give him a taste of adventure and enlighten the preconceived notions to which his soul clung. Edwin hoped to spur a similar transformation in Cassandra's father as had happened to Edwin at thirty eight – to show him the wonder of the world and touch that spirit of childhood that he was partly denied when he started working at an early age, as was the custom during that time of American history.

Edwin's spiritual connection with his spiritual Father was profound, and he could see the strings of the world preventing others from establishing that same connection with their heavenly Father the same way Relkiv created a false enmeshment to the other Tor. Relkiv played on their fear, superstition and confusion. Edwin felt both an obligation and a pleasure to help others ease and willingly relinquish those earthly tethers and replace them with a connection with Father in the same way Ohinx was attempting to do with his people. The Tor referred to God as The Source, in the same way Earth referred to him with many different names depending on the spiritual philosophy, but God himself wanted to be known as their Father. When the Tor arrive at Earth, that lexical difference would be another unnecessary source of contention and confusion, just as it had been on Earth for many generations. The people of Earth had a very primitive type of enmeshment and each one, through that invisible channel of inspiration, could thereupon manifest Heaven in this world within their sphere of influence as one flame ignited another struggling wick until the entire world's population relinquished pettiness and saw how direct light in pictures obscured, erased and drowned the hardened features of their face and clothed them in radiance and beauty and one could not tell if you were sixty-five, forty-five or twenty-five. He could see those walking flames in his everyday life, scarcely aware of their own celestial beauty, some half ignited, some fully aflame. The greatest among them being Cassandra.

  As he rode, the waning moon was a shadow of itself, and the landscape nearly pitched black to conceal his movement. He switched to his night vision glasses, flipped a switch on the bike to remove the motor sound and wheel display, so that it hovered silently along the ground, all lights on the machine were turned off. There were many checkpoints with national guards who were employed by the same bad people who owned the science facility. So, he did not engage them, and he passed by them like a wraith with only the scattering of birds to cause any alarm, of which they only took notice after he had already quickly passed them. They did not call in the rustling of birds as an intrusion for fear of reprisal and in their mind they instantly came up with their story of plausible deniability, "no one came this way" they would say. Edwin saw all of this in their minds as he passed. They wanted the money, but they didn't want the responsibility to be the ones to engage any enemy combatants. It was not difficult to read other people's minds or even read the minds of animals. It only took practice, like learning another language. Some had more propensity than others with this practice, yet nearly anyone could learn. But, like their connection with the Father, their worldly connections often obscured the many miracles waiting within this reality. It is how the angels communicate, it is how people will communicate in the future, it is how other species within the universe communicate – by the eyes, by the intention and the thoughts.

Yet, there were things Edwin did not know – one of which was who would take Father's place after he relinquishes the post to another. Edwin supposed it would be Jesus, yet based on the upward trajectory of Jesus' soul, Jesus was destined for another purpose. Which was also, something Edwin did not know – what would be the ultimate purpose of Jesus' soul. Currently, Jesus was acting as a guide for others, not as a reformer, because the denizens of the spiritual universe were not in need of that same spiritual reformation that Jesus brought to Earth. No, those other spiritual denizens, like Jesus, were patiently and joyously raising the vibration of their souls as they went about their daily tasks and their business – sometimes helping the crying worlds, sometimes traveling for work and pleasure. It was in this latter aspect that Jesus held dominion. He, in some way, managed the comings and goings, the means of travel by which those souls traveled in thought throughout the universe.

Edwin silently passed another checkpoint. It was for everyone's benefit that the guards not see him, that they don't set off alarms as he slipped past, that he be allowed to go about his business uninterrupted because he held in his mind the sanctity of all human life, more so than any other person in the Earth could possibly hold in their own utilitarian and conflicted soul. It was why he chose to associate with Cassandra's family – despite their unwillingness to embrace him – they were a group of the best people in the entire world, quietly going about their business, positively influencing others through their actions – now in small deeds, later in grand actions. So too are the spiritual spheres of the heavens constructed and advised to behave – to influence, but not unduly impress as to possess or take away a person's decision. Seek your own level and repel by natural tendency those not on the same level. Yet the Earth was different, all levels commingled. Two parents who raised four children, they only planned for three, but the third were twins, then the four were each supposed to have three, making twelve and then each of those to have three adding up to thirty-six and that great family – not in physicality but as physical representations of the principle of goodness rippling outward into a bigger circle. But a terrible event interrupted those plans and there were only ten, not the intended twelve, leaving two seats. That is one of the many perfect reasons which compelled Edwin to seek Cassandra – to offer replacement and balance to restore the growing circle to twelve. It was for every perfectly culminating reason why Edwin sought Cassandra.

He slipped past the third checkpoint noiselessly and without alarm. However, that same logic would not work as he approached the final destination where he was to destroy the compound. Those who more closely guarded the throne of depravity were not misguided souls mired in the dredge of circumstantiality tepidly limping toward Heaven – they were the inner guards of the evil cabal. They were not ignorant, they were not weak, nor weak-minded, they were not lazy. It was out of intellect and their own conscious decisions that they craftily designed the inner defensive system like the sympathetic nervous system itself, meaning if one checkpoint failed then they would all be punished, so a guard letting a specter slip past the checkpoint could not overlook the issue and hide within plausible deniability because there was no hiding from the ramifications of those actions – they all had families and children and of each would be required a human sacrifice if someone got through. A human sacrifice like the ancient Chavin, Nazca and Inca of this land, misdirected by evil outer influence even in those primitive early days.

That evil cabal was composed of some of the most brilliant minds, yet they rejected their own spirit and therefore had no appreciation, no understanding, no willingness for spiritual principles. There was no spiritual longing in their soul – they had relinquished it with each new earthly gratification. And, seeking greater wonders of the Earth soon amalgamated one with another to take advantage of their group intellect and their positions to further that gratification.

Edwin was fatiguing, the loose demons of his mind now having chewed up all available resources. His large belly was now smaller as his high metabolism fueled the chaos of his mind. The electrical supply lines, the blood rich in fat, protein, glucose had all spent their efforts and those once bustling avenues bounding with life were now thin, sparse and thready, and they strained to uphold their offices. He became more reliant on the air to contain enough charge to sustain his mental and physical activities. One device in his liver helped to nullify the rising pH as he continued to breathe heavily the electrical mountain atmosphere.

The cloud jungle was becoming more dense, fewer roads and trails, and despite his silent vehicle the very leaves of the jungle acted as alarms signaling that an interloper was approaching. The internal gyro attracted the flow of electricity to itself and from there spun and acted as a refining station for that raw undeveloped electricity and turned it into pure magnetism, warm, healing, rebuilding the torn portions of his body. He had long since stopped bleeding from grievous wounds as the gyro, built specifically for Edwin to produce a magnetic field that reinforced the natural function and structure of his body. So that any one malpositioned tendon, muscle or bone; or any open wound, cut nerve would naturally act as a magnetic sink and, because that injured portion offered the most resistance to the spinning vortex of his natural magnetic body, would therefore be given the most magnetic pressure, to rebuild itself and once again sing harmoniously with the greater body. But, Edwin was even more special than that beautiful piece of technology, because his body communed with the stars, with the life on other planets, with the Earth and that spinning vortex of refined magnetism we call spirit. He had many refined spiritual vines reaching out and shaking hands with all of nature and the central whirlpool that was named Edwin was, in a way, a force that could, like an infinite series of gear trains reinforcing everyone and each action, generate a torque to move the entire universe. From the beginning of time, he tried always to be humble and responsible with this power – because if he was not, then God's confidence in him would change. He would feel the change, he wanted to always earn God's trust, and if he did something to threaten that trust then Edwin would fear that there would be another individual to act as a more congenial outlet for God's plan on Earth. Edwin, being who he was, always wanted to be leader of God's pack.

Another checkpoint approached. He tried to slip past the guard as he had always done. Five men watched for him and had seen him coming from trail cameras set along all the roads. They monitored the trail cameras coming online in a series, closer and closer to their checkpoint. They calculated and anticipated his likely route and trained their night vision sight on the dark roads in the jungle brush. They all had comparable high-tech equipment to Edwin, anticipating this, seeing in their minds his own movement on the screens. He went up above the tree line during areas of higher guard concentration. He then showed up on radar briefly as an angel echo, as it is termed in the industry.

As he got closer to the compound, there was less distance between guard stations, and if he stayed above tree line then he wouldn't have the cover of trees and therefore they would have a clear shot at him from automated anti-air ballistics. Time was the factor as he knew God would protect him, so as a way to rectify both the urgency of the situation and the danger, he ducked down below the tree line and sped 70 miles per hour through the thick jungle, weaving and hugging the trees, feeling great centripetal force as he curved quickly around large boulders. Five men heard the cracking of branches and flapping of leaves progressing through the jungle. They were too slow to react to the speed of his bike; the automated firing turrets were not calibrated for such velocity. The jungle itself offered its own dangers as well. He was weaving around trees and through dense brush, and he had to maintain a high velocity to overpower the vines that rose up to snag him, or a thick cluster of branches would briefly divert his steering and nearly throw him off his bike. But his arms overpowered them and speed, 80 miles per hour now, increasingly became his only defense.

As he passed the next checkpoint, there was now a quarter mile until the next checkpoint. All the guards could do with their high-tech equipment was see that some ghost was moving through the trees at a worrying speed. Their only defense was to fire all weapons into the jungle as a way to save their own lives – shooting at nothing in particular, hoping Edwin would run into one of their bullets. If someone got past them then they would not live much longer. The bullets flapped past Edwin, slapping the leaves, cracking the branches, thuds into the bark and he cleared them.

A guard, seeing the entity speed off past them communicated to the central hub, "Fuck, we have a breach." Some men, seeing the futility of their actions to stop the intruder, quickly abandoned their posts. They feared punishment and ran home to take their family away from Peru and move to another country to start a new life.

Edwin threaded the needle, zipping through the dense jungle and he suddenly burst out into a cleared landing strip. He tripped the infrared beams of motion sensing spotlights. But, they did not activate in time to capture the invader, and the spotlights followed a trail of empty grass and dirt just behind Edwin. He could usually see and feel a few steps in front of his current step, yet now he could not see, mentally, as far in front of him – he could not anticipate, and he began reacting to gun fire and explosions as the small army surrounding the facility and archeological site fired wildly into the night shooting at a ghost. The defensive guards acted as though there was an entire army of special forces invading the compound and the gates of hell were actively opening up to their location.

The guards' faces with gritted teeth conveyed a crazed excitement from an unknown enemy. Edwin could feel their dispositions; they were both thrilled and fearful of this imposing invisible army. In their minds the enemy was everywhere and nowhere, and they had long given up their poise and their reason for excitement, anger, and fear.

Edwin was trying to trip as many alarms and explosives as possible to create as much confusion as possible. It is not that he wanted to risk his life in that way, but rather, it was his only chance to get close enough to the compound. He had to facilitate and develop an air of panic in their hearts. The small army was retreating and had coalesced like a school of fish around the entrance of the compound in anticipation of receiving the fast-approaching convoy carrying Heis. Edwin would briefly pause in the dark spots between the light and steady a rifle on his bike handles. He fired on fully automatic and unleashed ten steady explosive bullets into the group and small fires began to kindle within the group, alighting the silhouettes of those enemy soldiers. But he wouldn't sit to follow the kill, he had to continue to move swiftly. Some bullets, some shrapnel grazed him, tore his clothes, lodged in his skull, struck out his teeth. Each hit to his body, each tear in his skin made his thoughts move more swiftly, slowly feeling the demon emerge to kill himself and everyone else, gripping more tightly the handles of his bike. He circled the group to maximize the confusion and maximize the friendly fire and then he would double back and circle them the other way. He launched a smart grenade into the group – which had different stages – first flash and concussion, while it sprayed smaller frag and incendiary grenades to encompass a larger area. He had to maintain his stealth, and firing from a location would give away his spot. Fifty men were reduced to thirty-five.

Edwin had no disdain in his heart for the men who were trying to kill him. They were ruthless, petty, conniving, violent and delighted in pain. He received aromatic emanations of their character through the sounds of their footfalls, through the way they searched for him, through their own thoughts which Edwin, when he chose, received impressions of those thoughts. Most of them were products of their environment and therefore a passive type of ruthless piracy in that they behaved the way they did because that is what they learned from others and therefore passive, like animals, subject to making decisions based on obtaining comfort and security. But, there were some, the most intelligent of the group who were actively, positively, knowingly ruthless, clever. They were the ones that were the most dangerous. They made decisions based on an internal desire to cause pain, rather than give themselves comfort – similar in character to that administrative and higher-level group that held Heis.

Another pass did not produce additional casualties. They were well trained, yet he could see their willpower failing in response to a growing fear of repercussions from their masters. Their own denial of their soul made them sheep, acting against their own instincts. Edwin tightened his circle – putting him more at risk of direct hit, yet again he was following the guiding thought in his mind to destroy the compound before Heis arrived. He just had to be patient and persevere; he could feel the pressure mounting in the situation, in the hearts of the men, their ammo decreasing and having to break formation and get more ammunition. He saw it, they looked every which way, the opening in the group, they still did not know exactly where he was. Speed, movement, motion and patience were the kings of war – demons whispered to him and fiery thoughts passed his mind. It was time, a 110-mph dash through the opening and into the group, he wanted them to turn on themselves – they would shoot out of fear. He let loose every weapon that his fingers could push as he maintained his grip. Grenades dropped, side mounted machine guns brought the weaponry of an entire battalion down upon those men defending the position. He cleared a hole for himself to flee and circle back around and that is when a large caliber bullet passed through his leg and damaged his bike. It moved erratically now, and he knew escape would be impossible and he jumped from his bike without engaging the safety, so that when he jumped it would activate a failsafe originally intended to prevent other countries from stealing the technology. And, so he rammed the bike into the largest group he could find, about five men, and it burst into an electrical explosion that charred the unsuspecting men – eighteen left. He sought cover with only his rifle and side arm, the men now seeing him run clear as day, directly in front of them unloaded their bullets into Edwin as he jumped behind the corner of the facility, circled around the other side of the building, then went up a utility ladder and drawing them away from the opening. They released the dogs to find him, so he jumped into a dumpster of garbage to conceal his own scent. Edwin closed the lid, wiggled down to the very bottom of the dumpster and lowered his body temperature to avoid IR vision. They would probably find him. There was a lot of yelling and commotion during that time. The unsuspecting dogs sniffed past the garbage and hurriedly kept on their way with their noses to the ground.

    At the bottom of the dumpster, bags of hot garbage from baking in the sun sat upon him, their weight hugged him. One bullet had hit an artery, and the twenty bullet wounds now spilled blood lining and pooling at the bottom of the metal dumpster upon which Edwin lay. He was quickly succumbing to hemorrhagic shock, and the muscle of the heart lost its load and beat rapidly out of control. Out of control the gyro of his abdomen, drawing power from the mineral veins in the mountain, attempted to divert resources across the body, yet it wobbled out of sync from the intended rhythm and sputtered at a frail RPM. REM sleep presented pictures of Cassandra to his eyes like a blanket to a shivering body. His body was shutting down, and he would be dead in a minute. Ants crawled up on his face and into his ears. Edwin was confused. *I thought I was going to die laughing*...and the gyro in his stomach stopped spinning – the magnetic field was gone; the body no longer fit for habitation.

***

    The inherent upward physical and spiritual refinement of all environments on Earth was, as mentioned, somewhat bogged down within the confines of Peru by beings outside of Earth. That area retaining a growing preponderance of the negative force now caught the attention of a being who had made it his life's work to nullify such forces among his own people. The spiritual connection between these beings having been established during Ohinx's enlightenment now necessitated his involvement in the events of both the Tor and the Vi civilizations as an arbiter and judge; as one who would be responsible when, at the end of his life, he unclasped his hands and presented his work to the Lord of Life. Father and the Holy Spirit had now given Ohinx another chance to do what he had been unable to do among his own people – nullify the darkness and put his light to constructive use. The opportunity now given, the responsibility now lay with Ohinx in attempting to establish a more full and robust connection with Edwin.

    Balance; Ohinx used the universal and spiritual law of reciprocation as a way to appropriately judge Edwin. Ohinx saw Edwin through the lens of how Edwin looked at

Heis. Ohinx saw the long string of connections of people giving their life for a God-given purpose; for a goodness greater than themselves, so they themselves could reach up to that purpose and become greater. Quizzically, in the fading light of Edwin's soul reflecting on itself, Ohinx saw flashes of his own purpose. He saw the seventeen-year-old girl for whom Edwin wanted to die. He saw the face of Cassandra, the light that saved him. So moved and enraptured by these visions, Ohinx did not know if he was looking at Edwin's dreams or his own and, in the confusion, Ohinx nearly lost himself, and he was now Edwin and Edwin was him. The spiritual link fully established, the pain excruciating. His thoughts, his will fleeting and Ohinx started the death process a second time as this physical body acted in recalcitrant subjugation succumbing to the lacerations of Edwin's failing body. *If it would be allowed, then I will die for him*, Ohinx thought, *that is just.* The static medium through which Ohinx's soul associated with Edwin's body mobilized and utilized every resource to create a spark to start the heart and the gyro. Bullet wounds and deep lacerations formed on Ohinx's own body many light years away – he comparatively weaker and could not handle a fraction of the bodily damage which now consumed Edwin – *it just needs to be enough*, Ohinx thought. Ohinx diverted more of his attention to Edwin's body; face down, he saw blood spilling out of himself, so he drank his own blood, licking it up from the bottom of the dumpster tasting the acrid residue lining the rusted metal. He pierced bags of garbage to drink the liquid accumulated on the bottom corner of the bags in an attempt to refill the volume of his arteries. He punched his own stomach to reset the gyro to correct the rotation, distributing the magnetic warmth over his cold, numb body. Feeling and sensation returned, thoughts returned, Edwin's soul at once being let free now descended back down into the flesh. Ohinx had learned of the Vi's conception of *God, called him Father, meaning a protector and provider.* The magnetism through which the soul interacts with a body was now fully consumed and Ohinx was spit out from the body, *I hope it is enough.*

Edwin regained consciousness thirty minutes later, he had never been unconscious for such a long time while inhabited by a heavenly force, and there were residual thoughts of being Ohinx, as if Ohinx were a wind that blew in through a house and kicked up the curtains and rustled the loose hanging tablecloth as Edwin, just catching the last fitful movement of the drapes before Ohinx closed the windows behind him. Ohinx's thoughts seemed like that of a child's, curious and loving without duplicity, but lacking wisdom, and therefore his thoughts were eccentric, profuse, fleeting, and each new sensation of this new body was to him a new world which set off a million new thoughts.

Edwin was again functional in spite of his grave wounds. He looked at his watch: 4 a.m. The transport holding Heis had already entered the facility; Edwin had failed. It was time for him to return.

"Is he in?" Edwin said over the comm.

"Yes, move forward with destruction of the facility," the operator said.

"No, Heis is in there, that wasn't part of the mission. He's a U.S. citizen," Edwin said.

The last time Edwin had failed was September 9, 2001, when he failed to stop the assassination of the Lion of Panjshir. Edwin could hear the guards now walking sluggishly, still patrolling the area. He could hear the exhaustion in their footsteps moving slowly, not fully picking up their feet, their posture was poor and they slumped over slightly and everything they carried hung and swung off the front of their bodies as they slouched forward. Edwin had nothing left in his arsenal except for his handgun. It would be light soon and he wouldn't make it out when the sun was up.

He slid out of the dumpster unseen. The facility was built into an archeological site and Edwin retreated below ground to the ruins. The underground ruins were not patrolled heavily. Edwin limped along the underground tunnels built by the pre-Nazca Chavin culture and came across the Lanzón – the human-animal hybrid fanged deity. It was the axis mundi of Chavin de Huantar, a singular pillar representing the link between the spiritual world and the physical. The facility was built there to honor that pre-Spaniard civilization that was originally destined to produce something grand on the Earth, just as the European, Asian, and ancient Middle Eastern civilizations had flourished and secured their place among the fruitful history of Earth. Yet, the indigenous of the Americas were denied that chance to hold the torch of civilization.

Edwin quickly made his way to the nearby airstrip. He crouched behind a dirt pile adjacent to the field. There was fifty meters of open field and multiple guard towers surrounding the strip separating him from the nearest Cessna. It would still be dark for another hour. He crawled slowly through the field, he could hear the casual conversation of the guards, talking about the attempt to infiltrate the compound "I must have shot him three times at point blank range, now we just have to find the body," and they were excited to change shifts at 6 a.m.

As he reached the airplane, he quietly opened the door and rolled in. Light was just breaking in the East. He ripped open the control panel, connected the battery to the fuel pump and the fan. Lights from inside the cockpit flickered on. He grazed the ignition to the battery wire and the propeller started. Edwin heard shouting from the nearby guards. He quickly got the plane moving down the runway. After twenty seconds of steady acceleration, he lifted off to the sound of gunfire pelting the exterior. In his haste he forgot to check the fuel gauge, and he was out of gas while still descending from the mountains. Luckily, coming from the high altitude allowed him to use the plane like a hang glider. He was able to reach far into the unguarded open waters of the Southern Pacific before he dumped the plane. He deployed the life raft as the operator in his ear told him there was a nearby American ship coming to pick him up. He sent out a flare to alert the ship where he was, and he was retrieved from the ocean.

    When he boarded the ship, despite his failure, he was given a hero's welcome and that night he was invited to sleep in the officers' quarters. Yet he preferred to sleep among the racks of the berthing with the sailors.

## 17 – Diagnosis

*God help me see the things that I don't see*
*Love, patience, grace*
*God tell me what I want to be*
*Love, patience, grace*

Cassandra's husband, the family and the church all starkly opposed Cassandra after the family meeting. It was only Marie who lent her support through their daily morning calls, staying open-minded about Edwin and actively taking an interest in him. Marie saw the positive change that Edwin's presence had on Cassandra. Yet, the family, seeing Marie's support toward her twin, continued to put pressure on her to convince Cassandra she was making a mistake.

Marie had her own internal struggles about Edwin and prayed to God to tell her if this was real or not. That question was in her mind one day as she was picking up clothes for her children at the mall. *What was going on? How could God break up a marriage? The Bible writes that marriage is a sacrament, one flesh, what God has joined together, let not man separate.* Then, after picking out clothing and paying for them, she went to exit the store. The bright afternoon sun poured into the dimly lit clothing section from the glass doors that led to the large parking lot. She squinted her eyes as she walked and didn't pay much attention to a perfume saleswomen misting fragrance through the air who handed Marie a sample of the perfume. Marie was still deep in thought, ruminating on her quandary, as she exited the store and walked through the parking lot. When she got to her car she moved the shopping bags over to one arm, and while attempting to dig the keys out from her purse she opened her hand to show the title of the sample perfume, "Miracle" written in purple and gold. *Miracle?* She thought. *Is this a miracle?* Her own internal voice prompted the question. And, during her drive home she reinterpreted Jesus' words: *What God has joined together, let no man separate – but God could.*

So, she felt that was a little, yet very meaningful sign to her, encouraging her to believe Cassandra and this situation in general. *Small things should not be overlooked because they are small.* Marie quickly called Cassandra, who was overjoyed to hear that. Marie told the rest of the family about the answer that God had given to her – and said that if they only asked for His guidance, they might get a sign as well. But, they did not share in her epiphany and remained unconvinced and doubtful of its significance. *Miracles or signs mean very little unless witnessed*, Marie thought, it must happen to them to ascribe any meaning to it as her own little miracle did little to convince anyone of anything besides herself. *But, how could it happen to them if they weren't at least open to such an occurrence?* Marie tried to tell her eldest son who was fifteen years old and old enough to understand, yet he too seemed to get angry and stormed out of the kitchen when she told him. As he stormed out, she saw her youngest son coming down the stairs, watching, confused by the residual echoes of the scene and the foot stomping, attempting to interpolate what had happened.

The situation at Cassandra's house also became more negative as Peter, now acting as a lightning rod for the family's outrage, allowed evil to creep into his heart and expressed extreme bitterness, callousness, and at times, an overt hatred toward the mother of his children.

"The witch is coming home kids, make sure she doesn't try to abduct you," he laughed at their confused and frightened faces.

When she was home, he continued to avoid her, disdaining her being at the house, and asked her to move out immediately.

"Where am I supposed to go, Pete? You all wanted this forty-day hiatus," she said.

"No, see, you've gotta find a new place. All that with you and Edwin is going to end during this forty-day hiatus when you realize he's been lying to you the whole time," Peter explained.

"Pete, you don't have to be so malicious about all this, I know this is what you want as well," Cassandra said, "And, you don't have to actively try to turn the children against me. You said we would continue to co-parent."

"Oh, I realized how crazy you were," he said, "and I didn't want the children around that kind of insanity. And, if there is a wedding, which I don't think there will be, then I'm not going to walk you down the aisle. And, with you out of the house, I'm going to file for child support, so just be ready for that."

They had agreed to not sell the house in the divorce and that she would move out, so that the children could stay in the house and remain as minimally impacted as possible. She wanted to stay in the house with her children and have

Peter move out – and she knew that is what he wanted as well. Yet, spite became a powerful motive in Peter's heart, and he now wanted everything and he didn't want her to have anything. Cassandra didn't want anything out of the divorce and planned to put her portion of the house in the children's name. She just wanted to be free from him, and each interaction with Peter reminded her that she was doing the right thing.

"I don't understand, Peter, do you want me to stay, because it seems like you're putting up a lot of blocks," she said.

"No, at this point I wouldn't even take you back." he said. "Plus you're probably going to get admitted to the psychiatric in-patient unit with all the other crazy people shuffling around half-naked, over medicated, staring off into nothing. Why couldn't you have told me how crazy you were earlier?" He started to blame her for everything wrong in their marriage.

She turned and walked out the door without responding. They had the same thought of each other, that each was throwing everything away. Yet they had different conceptions of what *everything* was – Cassandra valuing the love they once shared which Peter was throwing away, while Peter valued what he considered a normal life, which Cassandra was throwing away.

It was time to meet with the psychiatrist. She got into her car and started to drive, wiping away the tears and steadying her tremulous hands as she drove. The psychiatrist was located within the Princeton University system, which had its own theological seminary.

At the front desk, she signed in, paid in cash, and took her seat in the waiting room. *This is it*, she thought, this was the last opportunity she could give to her family to help them see the truth – this visit was for them.

"Nancy?" The nurse yelled to the waiting room, "Oh, sorry, Cassandra, I mean. Nancy is my name – where is my head!"

"Yes, that's me," Cassandra said.

She was brought back to a generic-looking doctor's office room with white walls, tile floor, an exam table, two chairs, a computer and desk for the doctor. She took a seat on the chair, and a young man walked in with a brown beard, combed-back brown hair and glasses.

"Hi, Mrs. Albright, I'm Dr. Summers, how are you doing?" He said in a warm tone, "What can I do for you today?"

"Well, my family wanted this appointment because, based on some recent events, they think I might be…" she tried to find the right word, "mentally fatigued."

"I see, can you tell me more? And, do you mind if I write some things down?"

"No, of course not. Sure, I can tell you the whole story fairly quickly," she said, and Cassandra began to explain everything – the marriage stress from the past years, the new relationship, the miracles that she saw – Father, the vanishing oil spot, deceased relatives. Dr. Summers listened intently without interruption. He asked her questions to fill in pieces of the story and understand her motivations. When he was satisfied with his understanding of the situation, he turned away from the computer to face her.

"Okay, so it is my job to evaluate you; meaning modern psychiatry gives us the tools to evaluate the health of your emotional and mental state – that's all. It is not my job to evaluate this man, Edwin; your husband; family or these miracles – I do not know them and I was not there, because, y'know the majority of people believe they have seen a UFO or a ghost – those things are not my specialty. Therefore, what I can judge of your mental and emotional state is: you are not psychotic, you're not depressed or manic. You have told your story in a calm, orderly fashion and your story has remained consistent. Now, I will be upfront with you, there may be some hints of delusion or magical thinking which leans towards a schizotypal personality disorder – but you have none of the other symptoms and therefore you do not fulfill criteria – so that's a 'No' there. You mentioned stress, poor sleep, trouble concentrating and recent changes which lean in the direction of an acute stress disorder or adjustment disorder. So, I would recommend a diagnosis of adjustment disorder caused by stress from the marriage ending, a new job, and family issues. This diagnosis might be considered one step up from bereavement and suggests a *somewhat* natural reaction to major changes in life. As such, the first order in treatment would be to monitor, to see which way it goes in the expectation that it will pass. Therefore, I would like to see you back in three to five months. That is all I can recommend as a psychiatrist."

"Oh," she said, surprised. "Okay, so just see you back in three months?"

"Three to five," he said with his back now turned to the computer, wrapping up his medical note and closing out the electronic medical record software. "It was nice to meet you, please see the front desk for the follow-up," he said as he walked out the door to go see the next patient.

Cassandra walked out of the room and up to the receptionist, who scheduled the next appointment and gave her the paperwork. Cassandra looked down at the visit summary. There it was, documented proof in black and white – "diagnosis: adjustment disorder". She couldn't believe it, all of her dread lifted, and she felt almost as happy as when she spoke to Father. She burst out of the clinic doors like a free woman released from prison. She took a picture of the diagnosis and sent it to Marie, jokingly texting, "not crazy!" Then, when the rest of the family heard of the diagnosis they backed off.

## 18 – Reunion

*When all the gold fades*
*I'm just a soul laid*
*Upon the floor of Father's room*

*Nails and screws*
*Would be no use*
*Woven cloth would fall apart*

*Knots would untie*
*Whenever I die*

Edwin had died in a way and was brought back by this intimate companion Ohinx that had willingly shared his death with him as Edwin himself shared in other's diseases. Edwin stayed at sea with the naval vessel for three weeks – the frequency of the ocean waves rocking and lapping against the ship facilitated an accompanying piezoelectric rhythm in his body that helped facilitate the healing currents of his body. During the profound strain of the mission, the neurotransmitters, hormones and electrical discharges had all fired on full bore, saturating and inundating the receptors and receivers damaging the very intracellular machinery attempting to keep pace with the speed at which they received instructions, leaving him injured on the cellular level and concurrently bereft of both the signaling molecules and the receptor complexes, producing significant withdrawal symptoms which left him sleeping for most of the day – shut up in one of the small berthing beds twenty-three hours of the day. He was cold all the time, mental thought itself fatigued him physically and his muscles cramped from just adjusting himself in bed, his body bloated to double its normal size as he continued to bleed for many days afterward. He had numbness and tingling throughout his entire body as the constantly whirring gyro over-paced itself to strengthen the standing magnetic field to speed recovery. This time of year was always difficult for him anyway. He awoke only at night to change the sheets of blood and take in the night ocean air as he ate.

    The mission had coerced him to utilize the most heinous warring and antagonistic principles his mind could conjure – all the pain and anguish he carried around his whole life he unleashed upon that Peruvian mountain range. He wanted to stay separated from everyone on the ship as he did not yet feel human again. Even a kind word spoken to him was not a kind word, but rather evidence that there was no kindness in the world and that it would be better for the universe if the world were not saved. So, he had to take time to heal his own mind from the tendency of those thoughts.

    Back in New Jersey, Cassandra continued to have a difficult time in her house. One night she had become fed up with all the negativity Peter had towards her because he had always wanted this divorce. So, she marched upstairs to demand a turn sleeping on the bed and he should sleep on the couch – yet he would not hear it. He yelled at her to leave, and she went back downstairs.

    After two weeks, Cassandra tried to text and call Edwin, yet he wouldn't answer. Cassandra reached out to Edwin's sister who commiserated with Cassandra that she and Edwin's mother had nearly been driven insane their entire adult life because Edwin would go missing for two to three weeks at a time.

Edwin avoided contacting Cassandra to keep her hidden from the eyes of the government for as long as possible. The government had a largely possessive, obsessive, paternalistic relationship with the agents of the Aether group. On one hand, the members were given everything they could want, but on the other hand, the government also kept a very close eye monitoring their activity and a tight grip on their movement. The very sound of a branch breaking in the yard of their house was monitored, analyzed, documented and stored. When Edwin and Cassandra married, she would be brought into that world, yet he wanted her to enjoy freedom for as long as possible.

Edwin arrived back home one week later when the ship arrived at port. He still didn't feel human and failed to make connections with others. He called Cassandra. Edwin was mostly quiet during their conversation. She told him everything that had happened while he was away, about the forty-day hiatus.

Edwin said, "Why do you have to be so negative? Why do you have to please everyone all the time!" Edwin shouted at her and a cord in him instantly sprang into action, "I'm sorry. I mean if that is what you want, then okay. I've waited my whole life to find you; another few weeks will be okay."

"What was that, Edwin?" Cassandra asked.

"The mission did not go well, but that is no reason to take it out on you. I'm sorry again. You are the last person I want to hurt," Edwin said.

Cassandra accepted the apology. Edwin could feel Cassandra wanted to reconnect with him, yet he did not want her to connect with who he was right now for fear that it might "spread" to her in a way. He encouraged her to talk, but he continued to stay silent. They agreed to finish the last sixteen days of the forty-day hiatus and then ended the call.

The next day, Cassandra told Marie that she was worried about Edwin. He was different now. Marie thought this would be a good opportunity to meet Edwin and come to her own conclusions about him. So, she met with him the following week to get to know him and check on him for Cassandra.

Marie parked in the dirt parking lot of Edwin's apartment building and walked into the building purposely. Everyone in the house said "Hi" to her as if she were Cassandra – and Marie never lied or acted duplicitously, yet she also did not correct them. She carried a bible with her to let everyone know she was there on good intentions, should anyone come to realize that she was not Cassandra. This would be the first time that Marie had a conversation with Edwin. Despite the psychiatric clearance, the family still looked to Marie to convince Cassandra to stop seeing him, so she took this meeting seriously as it would shape her actions during this very critical time.

As Marie opened the door, Edwin knew immediately she was not Cassandra.

"Hello, Marie," Edwin said. Marie had brought coffee and scones and they ate together. Edwin, still recovering, was not as gregarious as usual, and he often kept his words to a minimum. During Marie's visit, he would have periodic fits of muscle spasms that caused him pain. Yet, he became his most talkative when he tried to apologize to Cassandra through a song he had written. He pulled up on his phone a video of background music, and the ambient atmospheric cinematic drone of the song began to play as he spoke the words in the cadence of a poem:

> *Father is God of both chaos and order*
> *malaise and rigor*
> *righteous and sinner*
>
> *And amid that horror and danger*
> *I became a stranger*
> *And a little quicker to anger*
>
> *I had to focus on healing*
> *And work through those feelings*
>
> *Now my music's come back to me!*
> *But you're not coming back to me*
> *I know it's the way things have to be*
> *Ten more days to wait and see*
> *But YOU just mean so much to me*

After that, Edwin relaxed as he seemed to get something off his chest that was weighing him down and they picked up their conversation. He encouraged Marie to go into social work to help children as he saw her in some past life wearing a Greek-style toga walking along a dirt path, surrounded by a crowd of excited children keeping up with her, showing her little rocks and flowers as she walked.

Marie had been there for an hour as she felt it was time to leave Edwin alone to rest. Yet, she was holding on to the expectation that some miracle was supposed to occur. Perhaps she would meet Father as Cassandra did. Or, maybe she would meet Jesus. She relinquished that expectation as she stood up to leave. She felt comfortable with the opinion she formed of Edwin from the time they spent together. As she said goodbye and turned to leave, taking up the bible in her hand, and moving toward the door, Edwin said to her, "There are more chapters to be written."

Marie turned and said, "Oh, okay, well I will be excited to read those when they are," and they once again said goodbye, and she walked out the door.

As Marie got into her car, she instantly called Cassandra and told her about the song Edwin sang to her apologizing for his behavior, and Cassandra's heart was once again soaring in the clouds.

***

The forty days passed uneventfully for Cassandra. The family wanted her to realize the error of her decisions during this time, but the only thing she felt was loneliness for Edwin. It was Easter when the forty-day hiatus ended. At 5 a.m. Cassandra excitedly drove over to Edwin's apartment. She pulled her car into the dirt parking lot, still in the darkness of the new morning. Her headlights caught Edwin waiting for her on the porch of the large house. He held up his hand to wave to her the exact same way in her vision of the Roman centurion atop the garrison. She got out of the car and ran to him. They kissed and embraced as if they had been apart for all those thousands of years.

They were going to spend the day down the beach and visit the Navesink lighthouses. Then, after that, she would drop him off back at his apartment and bring her children over to Marie and Emmett's house for the Easter celebration.

As Cassandra and Edwin started their drive down the shore, the sunrise was beginning. Edwin was sitting in the passenger seat and began to look perplexed. He leaned forward and reached over to a cross dangling from the rearview mirror. He put his hand behind it to let it sit on his open palm.

As he studied it, he said, "that was not the plan – pain, suffering, and the treasures man squanders."

"What did you say, Edwin?" Cassandra said.

Edwin, still leaning forward in his seat, turned his head to look at her. She quickly glanced over at him as she drove. His eye color had changed from blue to a deep green/emerald, and Cassandra saw a different demeanor – a different presence.

"Father?" she said, waiting for a reply. Yet there was no answer.

"Jesus?" she asked.

"Yes," he said, and tears started streaming down her face just like when she met Father. She couldn't explain the feeling of knowing Jesus was sitting right next to her – pure elation. He radiated all purity, reserved, all humility, all love. As Cassandra drove Jesus through New Brunswick; whoever they passed, Jesus would say, "my brother" or "my sister," and he would know their problems and their names. He cried for the homeless, as if sharing in their dejected and despondent states.

When they drove out of the city onto the highway toward the shore, Jesus reached back and took a piece of palm frond from the backseat that was left after Palm Sunday. He wove it into the shape of a person rather than the shape of a cross, as was the convention. He held it up to the rising sun so that the light passed through it.

"The humanity for which I stood," Jesus said, "Not the cross."

A review of this book on the website where you purchased it would be greatly appreciated.

For more information or for news about upcoming books please contact uplink@spiritmachines.tech

Made in United States
North Haven, CT
09 March 2026